RICK P LOW

DROP TROOP BOOK FIVE

HOME FRONT

www.aethonbooks.com

HOME FRONT

www.aethonbooks.com

Print and eBook formatting, and cover design by Steve Beaulieu.

Published by Aethon Books LLC.

WHAT'S NEXT IN THE SERIES?

CONTACT FRONT
KINETIC STRIKE
DANGER CLOSE
DIRECT FIRE
HOME FRONT
FIRE BASE

[1]

"Storm's coming."

I pulled my head out of the guts of the torn-down auto-harvester and wiped sweat away from my eyes.

"What?" The question was a reflex. I'd heard what Vicky said, but I'd been so absorbed with the attempted repairs that it hadn't processed through my overheated brain.

"Out there," she expounded, nodding at the western horizon.

I looked at her for a second before I checked out the westward sky. The sunsets here were beautiful, but nothing was more beautiful than Vicky Sandoval; not to me. Her work coveralls were stained with soot, her dark hair matted with sweat and tied back into a messy ponytail, and she still took my breath away.

She noticed me checking her out and the corner of her mouth turned up.

"I was talking about the weather, Cam."

"Oh, yeah." I grabbed at an insulated bottle sitting beside my toolbox and sucked down a swig of cold water. The summer heat turned it into wine more effectively than any divine miracle and I sighed with relief.

The horizons were always distant here on the Danuvian Plateau, the mountains a rumor, a shimmer on the edge of existence that might have been an optical illusion. Even the shimmer was invisible now, lost in curtains of rain kilometers away. The advancing front was a dark line across the sky, lit up here and there with lightning, the thunder still too far away to hear.

"Might not make it this far," I mused, turning back to the open maintenance panel. "And this piece of shit isn't making it another centimeter until we replace the secondary power coupling."

"Jesus, that's the third coupling we've had to swap out in the year we've owned the damned thing." She dabbed at her forehead with a rag, then tossed it down onto the maintenance catwalk of the harvester, hands on her hips. "I think we need to consider biting the bullet and just buying a whole new machine."

I winced, leaning against the metal, making sure my bare skin didn't touch it. It wasn't thermoplastic or Duralloy or BiPhase Carbide or any of the sophisticated materials I'd grown used to in the Marines, and it could leave—had left—a nasty burn on any unprotected flesh you were foolish enough to expose to it after a long day in the fields.

Still, I wasn't sure which hurt worst, the memory of the burns, or the idea of spending that much money.

"We'd have to dip into our separation bonuses. The Commonwealth Colonization Authority gave us the initial equipment investment at no charge, but until someone gets a production facility up and running in town, anything new is going to have to be imported from out-system, and you know how much that's going to cost."

"It's either that or keep running back to the fabricator shop every month." She was winding up for an argument so I counted to ten and concentrated on deep breaths. "We have enough left."

"It's a lot of money," I agreed. "But it's only been a year, and it has to last us until we get this farm profitable." *Whenever that might be.*

"It's not like we have anything else to spend the money on," she pointed out. "The land was free, the seed was free, they sold us the livestock at cost, and if it all goes completely to shit, we can grow enough to live off and still save enough to plant for next season."

She was right, but I was stubbornly reluctant. It was a *lot* of money, enough to buy us both a ticket off this world. But not if we spent half of it on new equipment.

A flicker of movement caught my eye, something undulating in and out of the fields of corn with flashes of multicolored scales, and my teeth bared instinctively.

"Goddammit," I muttered. "It's a rock dragon." I looked longingly at the squatting, utilitarian ugliness of the rover, but I remembered I'd left my rifle back at the house.

"*Another* one?" Vicky spat, shading her eyes with a bladed hand, trying to spot the thing. "That's gotta mean the sonic fences are down *again*." She speared me with a glare. "Which is something else we need to replace before the dragons kill all of our goats."

I sighed, knowing she'd eventually come around to trying to repair everything ourselves one more time. This wasn't the first time we'd had this conversation and I knew it wouldn't be the last.

Something rumbled off to the west and I thought for a moment Vicky might have been right, that the storm was heading this way after all, but then I realized it wasn't thunder, it was an internal combustion engine. This colony was so remote and primitive, we didn't even rate a dedicated fusion reactor, which meant the vehicles ran off grain alcohol, like the cars in Tijuana when I was a kid.

The rover was identical to ours, built on local fabricators from plans over a century old, like everything we owned that hadn't come off the colony ship with us. It could have been from any of dozens of farms on the plateau, but I knew it wasn't. There was only one man who'd be coming out here this late in the day.

The slope-backed rover skidded to a halt beside the harvesters, throwing up rooster-tails of dirt, and a broad-shouldered, thick-waisted figure squeezed out from behind the wheel, his mop of blond hair compacted under a wide-brimmed hat. He didn't wear coveralls, opting instead for the loudest and most garish shirts his personal fabricator could manage, matched with cargo shorts and knee-high socks.

"Hey Cam, Vicky," he called, clambering up the access ladder on the side of the harvester without asking leave. "Did you see that fucking rock dragon? I got my rifle in the cab. Wanna go hunt the son of a bitch down?"

"Too far away now," I lamented. "Anyway, I'm wiped out. Been up on this piece of junk all afternoon."

"Oh, yeah?" He leaned over and peered into the maintenance hatch. "You need any help with it?"

"Sure, Dave," Vicky said, arms crossed, regarding him with strained patience he would have had to be blind not to notice. "You got a secondary power coupling in your truck next to the rifle?" Vicky didn't dislike Dave Clines, but his personality was like chili powder, best served in measured doses and on special occasions.

"'Fraid you're going to have to hit the industrial fabbers in town for that, darlin'," he told her, ignoring her mood, which he could get away with because he didn't live with her.

"Don't call me darling, Dave," she reminded him for what had to be the hundredth time.

Clines grinned at her, not at all apologetic.

"I don't blame you for being pissed off, Vick," he said, using an appellation she found only slightly less objectionable than 'darling.' He spit off the side of the harvester. "This equipment the government gave us is a bunch of obsolete junk. They don't give a shit about any of us, that's why they stuck us here in the Forbidden Zone."

Vicky sighed.

"No one actually calls it that, you know."

"What would *you* call it then, Vick?" He spread his hands, motioning above us at the sky, beginning to turn a darker blue as the sun sank lower. "All these systems with habitable worlds on the other side of the Tahni Imperium and the damned klepto aliens never even tried to settle here? You know how fanatical they were about putting colonies on every single living world between Tahn-Skyyiah and the Commonwealth, but they just didn't get around to places like this? They just left a dozen systems with habitable worlds for us to find and settle after we beat them in the war? Come on."

I shut the maintenance hatch, tossed my tools back in the chest and closed it before I looked back up to regard Clines with long-suffering amusement.

"So why, then, Dave?" I asked, humoring him. If one of us didn't ask, he'd just keep belaboring the point until we did. "Why didn't the Tahni settle here?"

Honestly, it *was* a good question, though not one I'd bothered to ask when we'd been offered the chance to settle here. All we'd needed to know was that the climate was temperate, the land was fertile, and the scenery was pleasant. And that there'd be no Tahni trying to kill us.

"I'm glad you asked," Clines said, grinning. "It just so happens I was attached to an Intelligence unit when I was working Fleet Security back during the war...."

"A *top-secret* Intelligence unit," Vicky murmured, just loud enough for me to make it out.

"Yes, it *was* top-secret, Vick," Clines said, shooting her a dirty look. "And after we'd invaded the Tahni home planet, they stumbled upon this group of systems in the captured records, and I got a look at their report."

"They just left it laying around for you to read, huh?"

"Well, it was an *enemy* file, darlin'! Who would they be keeping it secret from?"

I had to give him that one. I grabbed the toolbox and my water bottle and started climbing down the access ladder. I'd have this pointless conversation, but I'd be damned if I had it on this metal baking tray.

"So, what did the report say?" I prodded, the turned dirt crunching under my work boots at the bottom of the ladder. "What was the big secret?"

Vicky rolled her eyes, but she knew as well as I did that Clines would tell this story with or without my encouragement, and our best hope was to get it as quickly and concisely as possible.

"Well, that's just it, compadre, they didn't *know*. The Tahni didn't even know." He followed me down the ladder, hopping off about a meter up and wincing as he landed. "Damn knee. Need to lose some weight." He rubbed at the offending joint before straightening and proceeding with his war story. "Anyway, the Tahni didn't settle on these worlds because their religious traditions say they're unclean, for some reason. They didn't get any more specific and the best guess any of the xenoethnographers had...."

"The *what*?" Vicky demanded, face screwing up at the term.

"Well, fuck if *I* know," Clines admitted, "but that's what the report said. The xenoethnographers said they thought it might have something to do with the Tahni equivalent of astrology that developed before they found out that the stars were all just big balls of gas."

"We know all about big balls of gas."

"Do you wanna hear this story or not?" Clines asked her, but then waved the question away, perhaps sensing he wouldn't like the answer. "Never mind. Anyway, *they*...."

"The xenoethnographers," I clarified, carefully maintaining a straight face.

"Yeah, them. They thought these systems were off-limits because they were in the wrong constellation and it would have been bad juju to put colonies here. But I think that's just the easy explanation. The Tahni are superstitious, but they ain't superstitious like we are. For them, everything was wrapped up in the Emperor, right?"

It seemed like a question, and not a rhetorical one, so I answered it.

"As far as we know. But I'm not a xeno...."

"Oh, shut up. I just don't see them writing off all these systems just because they were in the wrong part of the sky. For them, controlling living worlds was *everything*."

"Then what do *you* think it was, Dave?" Vicky asked, giving up on both the harvester repairs and her resistance to the conversation. She dropped down with more grace than me, a hell of a lot more than Clines, and pulled open the back of the rover, motioning for me to stow the toolbox.

"I ain't got no idea. I just know there's something funky out here and I think the government believes it, too. That's why they stuck all us rejects out here."

"What do you mean rejects?" I asked, frowning.

"Vets who they got an obligation to settle on a colony," he clarified. "But there ain't enough room on the established colonies for us because they ain't been rebuilt yet from all the damage the Tahni did during the war. So, they talked us into settling here because no one else would come here. No one else was stupid enough."

"There's the civilians," Vicky pointed out. That was what we called them, dividing the colonists into two camps, the vets, and the civilians. It wasn't just our differing backgrounds that separated us, though. The civilian colonists had been settled here months before any of us vets had arrived, for the simple reason that all of us had been held in the military for a few months after the end of the war.

"The civilians," Clines scoffed. He reached into a cooler in the front seat of his car and pulled out an insulated bottle of the local beer, twisting open the top and taking a swig before he went on. "They're refugees. Their worlds were too torn up by the Tahni for them to be able to rebuild, so they got stuck here whether they wanted it or not. That's why all of the assholes are such...well, assholes. Like that motherfucker Hellnick who lives against my eastern property line. Sour-faced dick won't so much as come to his gate and say hi when I drive by."

"Maybe he just doesn't have all day to bullshit because he has a farm to run," Vicky suggested.

"Either of you guys want a beer?" Clines asked, gesturing between us with the bottle.

"Thanks, anyway," I said, shaking my head. "I'm already halfway dehydrated and it's hot as shit out here."

I was exaggerating. Compared to Inferno, this place was fairly close to heaven, but I guess I'd been spoiled.

"But you mark my words," Clines went on, using the beer bottle as a pointer, "the Commonwealth put all us losers no one would miss out here like Judas goats, to make sure if there's some weird alien threat out here, we get hit by it first before anyone else finds out."

"Oh, Jesus, Dave," I sighed, pushing open the driver's door of our rover and falling into the front seat, letting my legs hang out the side. "They did not just stick us here as fodder for space monsters. You sound like a bad movie."

"Do I?" He barked a laugh and pointed off through the fields in the direction the rock dragon had run. "I talked to one of the pilots on the lander that dropped me here over a year ago, and he told me that the plants and animals here are different than the ones on Tahni colonies, the ones they brought there from their homeworld. Totally different, evolved independently of them. But they're also the *same* plants and animals that you'd find on any of the inhabitable worlds in the Forbidden Zone, even ones with different gravity. That means *someone* seeded the same sort of life on all those planets." He nodded, his brows going up like a lecturer coming to a conclusion. "And all that life, here, the Tahni worlds, Earth, all the colonies we've settled on...it's all based on DNA. Which shouldn't be possible."

"Panspermia," I suggested, though I only had a vague idea what it meant. I'd gone through an accelerated and abbreviated series of general education classes for Officer's Candidate School, and I remembered reading something about panspermia as an explanation for why DNA-based life forms had developed on different worlds.

Clines shot me a skeptical scowl.

"Panspermia? You really think that's the explanation for all this? RNA on comets got all the way not just out to the Tahni but to these worlds too? Over two, three *hundred* light years?

Naw, man, there's only one way this could have happened, and that's the Predecessors."

"Not *that* again," Vicky said, slapping her palm against the hood of the rover. "I'll sit through your conspiracy theories about Tahni superstition and hidden alien threats, but I will *not* listen to you go through this Predecessor bullshit again."

"We can't do anything else with the harvester until we go into town tomorrow and get a new power coupling fabbed," I declared. I looked up at Vicky. "Wanna make a day of it, grab some lunch, hit the zocalo?"

"That sounds good!" Clines enthused. "I'll meet you guys at the hopper pickup in the morning."

Vicky tried to look upset with Clines, but she couldn't keep up the façade and finally just started laughing.

"Sure," she acceded.

"And until then," Clines said, jogging back to his rover and pulling out the rifle, cocking an eyebrow toward me. "Wanna go see if we can find that dragon?"

I looked a question at Vicky.

"Fine," she said. "But you'd better be home before dinner."

Clines laughed and slapped me on the shoulder.

"You take the gun, compadre," he said, sliding behind the wheel of his vehicle. "I don't want to drink and shoot."

"But drinking and driving is fine," Vicky whispered to me.

I gave her a kiss, tasting the salt of her sweat, then picked up the rifle. Its weight was welcoming, comforting, somehow. I slid in beside Clines and pulled the door shut.

"Let's go kill something."

[2]

"Get everyone out of here!" I yelled at Vicky, and I hit my jets.

The mecha was leaning forward, its weight on its front foot, slightly off-balance because it had never been built for agility, just enough brute force to carry around an antiproton reactor and a shitload of weapons. I rammed my shoulder into the thing's trailing leg, my teeth clacking together with the impact, and ran the jets so far into the red I could almost hear them screaming for mercy.

It didn't knock him over. I hadn't thought it would. I just wanted to buy time, and that I did. He lost balance and had to slam his trailing foot to the ground, which, unfortunately, took me to the ground with it. The armor was tough. It could take a huge beating and keep working, but unfortunately, us humans had to be inside it.

Every time we got a new guy in the platoon, they would always wind up asking why we had to be in the suits, why the Marines didn't just put an AI program in the suit computers and let it do the fighting, and someone would have to repeat the same explanation that Captain Covington had given to the platoon leader who had given it to everyone else. It was the old story about how automated weapons had been tried during the Sino-Russian War and had turned against their own side. It might have just been because the computer systems weren't sophisticated enough back then, but no one with the power to change things had ever trusted them again, so us poor, vulnerable humans still had to pull the triggers.

When my back hit the concrete foundation of the building, I could really have come up with some great arguments for automated weaponry. I'd had cracked ribs before, and I was fairly sure I had them again. The pain sucked the breath right out of my chest, replacing it with white fire, and I wanted more than anything else to just lie there on the ground and rest, to let someone else do the rest of the fighting.

That wasn't an option for a few reasons, the main one being that if I stayed on the ground, the mecha was going to squish me flat. The massive oval of its foot pad hovered above me and I punched the jets again, sliding through oceans of debris but getting out of the way of the stomp. The mecha's foot pad cracked the floor beneath it, shaking me right through the BiPhase Carbide of my armor. I had to get up, and even though the Vigilante would do the work, the only way it could react was by me using the muscles that I would have needed if I'd been just trying to move my own body and not the three-meter suit of armor. And moving fucking hurt.

I rolled to my feet, screaming into the privacy of my helmet, knowing no one would hear, and turned to face oncoming death. Instinct screamed at me to get distance, but experience yelled just as loud that I should stay close. The mecha was an artillery piece, and its heavy weapons were designed for distance fire. Neither the proton cannon nor the coil gun turret could depress far enough to reach me, but the damned KE guns could.

Tantalum needles cracked off my armor, no single one of them able to penetrate, but the combined effect of hundreds of the things enough to wear my protection down and kill me, given time. Thankfully, even though my plasma gun wouldn't penetrate the mecha's armor over anything vital, there was one target I was fairly confident about servicing.

I blasted the thing's right-hand KE gun with a plasmoid, the ionized gas melting the infantry-defense weapon to slag. The Tahni pilot must have really liked that gun, because he seemed to take its loss personally. His leg was the size of a tree trunk, and when it impacted the left shoulder of my suit, it threw me four meters, straight through the back wall of the building...

...and I woke up screaming.

"Cam!" Vicky said, her hands warm against the clammy skin of my arm, her voice soothing. "It's a dream, Cam. It's just a dream."

I was panting, dripping sweat and I forced my eyes open wide, trying to reassure myself that I was back in our bedroom on Hausos, not fighting for my life on Tahn-Skyyiah. The room was dark but not pitch-black, moonlight filtering in through the open window along with a cool, night breeze...and an ear-splitting roar that shook the walls.

"What the hell?" I gasped, swinging my legs off the bed and lunging for the window.

We left it open at night in the summer, counting on the sonic screens to keep out the insects, though given how poor a job they did against the rock dragons, maybe we shouldn't have been so confident. I pushed aside the filmy veil of the shade and searched the night sky, holding up a hand to block the light of the Asvins, the twin moons of Hausos, sailing their nightly course from one horizon to the other.

A few degrees below the gibbous moons, another pair of glowing circles pierced the darkness, much closer together and lower to the ground. It could have been thunder rolling over the plains from the storm that had never passed over us, but it wasn't. It was a sound almost more familiar to me than thunder. It was a shuttle. There were a couple of small transport jets on-planet, kept mostly for the use of the Corporate Council, but they were a quarter the size of a shuttle, their turbofans almost silent by comparison with the atmospheric drives of an aerospacecraft.

"Where the hell are they going?" Vicky wondered. I hadn't noticed her get out of bed, but she was beside me in the window, the oversized T-shirt she wore to bed fluttering slightly in the breeze. I wore only shorts, and was beginning to notice the chill creeping up my back from dried sweat.

Her question was a good one. The spaceport, a grand name for what was basically a field of fusion-form pavement a kilometer long, was outside the town, a hundred kilometers west of here.

"They're damned low," I observed. "They're coming in for a landing. But the only thing over that way is Dave's farm...and his neighbor, that Hellnick guy."

"Klaus Hellnick," she filled in the details. "We met him once in town."

"Yeah," I said, nodding as I recalled the man. "Weird, shifty-looking bastard. Lives out there all alone, not even any hired hands."

"His wife and kids died in the war," she chided me, smacking me lightly on the bicep.

"Sorry." I frowned, peering at her in the moonlight. "How do you know that?"

"Jed and Riley told me. You know, the couple who run the fabricator shop on Main Street."

"Sucks about his family," I allowed. "But he's still shifty. And I still wonder why there's a damned shuttle landing on his property in the middle of the night."

"He probably had something delivered from out-system,"

she reasoned. "Maybe even a new harvester." She put an acerbic edge into the words and I flinched. "Space crews don't give a shit if it's the middle of the night local time. The workday on a ship is whenever they need to work."

I didn't want to be quite as reasonable as her, but I shrugged.

"We're ignoring the elephant in the room, though, aren't we?" she asked, putting an arm around my shoulder, pressing me into a hug. "You're still having the nightmares. What was it this time?"

I thought about telling her I didn't remember, but there was no reason to lie. Not to Vicky.

"Deltaville again. The mecha."

She sighed, resting her head on my shoulder.

"At least it wasn't Delp this time."

There was nothing to say to that. I'd seen poor Vince Delp's face in my nightmares more times than I could count.

"Sorry I woke you up," I told her, turning, putting my arms around her.

"It's okay," she said. "The shuttle would have done it if you hadn't first."

I kissed her, suddenly very conscious of how good she looked in the light of the dual moons, in just a white T-shirt, very aware of the warmth of her body against mine.

"No use letting the opportunity go to waste," I said, arching an eyebrow, pulling her back towards the bed.

"Cam," she giggled, pushing against my chest, "we have to be up in like three hours!"

"Who cares?" I insisted, falling backwards onto the mattress, and bringing her down with me. "We're taking the day off tomorrow, having some fun. Might as well start now."

She offered a token scowl of disapproval, but it quickly turned into something more lascivious, and we both tactfully ignored the real truth of the matter. I didn't want to go back to sleep.

"I don't remember Gamma Junction ever being this crowded before," Clines grumbled, shaking his head as he stared around.

I couldn't disagree. Gamma Junction wasn't a city, was barely a town. Originating as a pair of buildfoam storage domes hurriedly thrown up by the Corporate Council to stow the supplies they'd been commissioned by the Commonwealth government to drop down for the colonists, it had grown like a crystal in a growth matrix as some of the newer settlers had decided they didn't want to be farmers. Instead, they'd built shops and bars and restaurants, all clustered around the warehouses, hugging the landing zone, turning it into what we laughingly referred to now as a spaceport. There was even a hotel now, if you can call a buildfoam half-shell with a dozen rooms a hotel. It catered to spacer crews who wanted to sleep somewhere besides their ships for the night, and we almost never had more than one ship in orbit at a time, no more than one shuttle load of strangers at a time.

Until today. I'd noticed the crowd first from the air, flying in on the hopper taxi. The ducted-fan hovercraft ran a regular run three times daily from two different pickups at the junctions of the dirt roads running out to the farmsteads, and the three of us had caught the first flight into town. Looking down from the window seat, I'd just assumed it had to be some Settlers' Association meeting I hadn't seen on the schedule, but now, walking through the open-air shops and kiosks, I counted at least two dozen people I'd never seen before, men and women who sure as hell weren't farmers or shop-keepers. They might have been spacers, but if they were, they weren't from any Corporate crew, not the way they were dressed. Corporate Council freighter crews didn't generally wear vat-grown leathers and fragments of old military fatigues, nor did they allow the sort of holographic facial tattoos and bare cybernetics many of these people sported.

And that's not even mentioning the guns.

Guns were common on the frontier, of course. We hunted the rock dragons with them and there being no law enforcement to speak of on Hausos, everyone kept a rifle loaded and ready in their rover when they were out in the fields. But I hadn't seen anyone openly carrying a sidearm on their hip since I'd left the military. It wasn't something anyone thought to do, maybe because there just weren't that many of us and we hadn't been on the world long enough for crime to become a problem.

"Independent spacer crews usually carry guns out on frontier worlds like this one," Vicky told me when I brought it up. "They don't know there's no crime. For all they know, we could have gangs of people who hijack shuttles every time they touch down."

I eyed her doubtfully.

"And how would you know any more about independent spacer crews than I would?" I wondered.

"I follow the news." She sniffed as if the question was insulting.

"You saw it in a movie, didn't you?" Clines said, grinning.

"Maybe," she admitted. "Come on, let's get to the fabricator shop before we wind up waiting in a line."

The strangers barely spared us a look, except the occasional leer and snicker as they paused at one kiosk or another, pawing through the locally-produced tools and hand-sewn clothes with snorts of disdain. They couldn't have been more obvious about sneering at us local rubes if they'd hung a sign around their necks, but I suppose I didn't hold that against them. Gamma Junction made Tijuana look cosmopolitan.

And I was staring at them like one of the rubes they thought we were as we passed, heading through the street markets towards the rows of squared-off, single-story businesses built as cheaply as possible from local wood and stone.

"I wonder if these are the same guys who flew that shuttle over to Hellnick's land last night?" I nudged Clines. "You must have heard it, right?"

"Yeah, I heard it," he said. His mouth clamped shut as if he wanted to say more but was reticent, which was so totally unlike him it worried me.

"What?" I prompted.

"It wasn't the first one I heard," he said. His mouth pressed into a tight line and I thought he might say nothing more on the subject, but he snarled his way out of the expression. "I started hearing them a few weeks ago, coming in pretty regular."

"And you never said anything?" Vicky seemed astonished, and I was sure it was not at the idea that Hellnick was having regular, clandestine shuttle flights out to his property but at the concept that Clines wouldn't have been clucking about it every single day like a constipated hen.

"I went over there once," he admitted. "Over to the property line near where the shuttles were coming down. I just wanted to see what was going on, you know? And I saw those guys." He nodded back toward the strangers. "I mean, I don't know if it was those guys right there, but it was guys like that. Dressed like them, carrying guns. Rifles, carbines, pistols, loaded up like it was back in the war, you know?"

"Why didn't you tell us?" I asked him. I mean, not that there was much we could have done about it, but news was news, especially here.

"Because they saw me. They saw me and one of them, this

big motherfucker with a big, honking gun came up to the fence-line and he told me if I didn't get the hell out of there and not come back, no one would ever find my body."

"Shit, Dave! We could have helped you...," I trailed off, wondering just what the hell we would have done if he'd come to us. Charge in, guns blazing?

"There was nothing you could have done," he said, waving it away. "And I didn't want you getting caught in that. Whatever that shitheel Hellnick is mixed up with, it's nothing good. I wouldn't be surprised if these guys are pirates."

"Pirates?" I repeated. "Come on, there're no real pirates anymore, not since the Pirate Wars."

"Maybe they don't raid Commonwealth colonies anymore," Clines insisted, "but there are still criminal cartels in the Pirate Worlds. And that's not just bullshit from action movies."

We turned onto a side street, stepping out of the way of a chugging cargo truck hauling a load of ore from the warehouse down to a fabrication shop. And then I stopped in the middle of the road, frozen in place like a statue, unable to breathe, my eyes fixed on the group of strangers walking down the road in a tight cluster. No leathers and tattoos for these. They wore odd clothing fashioned from multicolored strips crisscrossed in tunics long enough to be called dusters, trousers extending down from them into knee-length boots. They were males, all of them, broad-shouldered and thick-necked, their hair shaven into a mohawk running down to a long queue that would have hung to the center of their back if it hadn't been wrapped around their neck.

"It's okay, Cam," Vicky whispered to me urgently. "You're okay."

"Oh, yeah," Clines said as if he hadn't noticed my reaction. "Those fuckers are all over the place in the colonies now, I hear. Got all fucked up in the head because their Emperor turned out to be a false god and a bunch of the veterans who'd fought in the war just dropped out of their society and volunteered for work on cargo ships or whatever, just to get off planet."

I heard the words, but they didn't register. Both of them might as well have been speaking a different language, the same sing-song gabble barely audible over the engine of the truck. All I could see were the faces, so close to human, yet so obviously not, the ridged brows, the black, piggish eyes, the pancake ears and flattened noses, the steam-shovel jaws.

"Cam," Vicky said, her hand grabbing at my arm. It wasn't until I tugged against it that I realized I was surging forward, heading towards them, hands balled into fists. "Stop. It's okay, you're safe here."

But I wasn't safe. None of us were safe.

They were Tahni.

[3]

My hand shook as I poured, splashing droplets of amber liquid around the rim of the shot glass, tequila beading on the polished wood surface of the bar like raindrops, glinting in the glow of the small lamp. I set the bottle down before I dropped it, then grabbed a rag and wiped up the mess with sharp, angry swipes. Grabbing the glass, I downed the shot, barely tasting it as it burned its way along my esophagus.

The burning spread to my chest and then my head, a crackling haze over my thoughts, like static electricity hanging in the air before a spring thunderstorm. I smacked the shot glass against the bar, annoyed it wasn't wiping away the images. The Tahni faces were old and young, staring at us with a stoic acceptance of their own, inevitable death, and we'd thought it was because they believed we'd kill them. But it was really because they'd already decided to give up their lives, their children's lives, to kill us. They'd ignited the truck bomb close enough to wipe out a whole squad of Drop Troopers—not mine, but still Marines.

I hadn't been so close to the Tahni before, not outside their armor. Inside their battlesuits or even just their normal combat armor, it was easy to just pretend they were faceless automatons, or even just other humans. We'd always done pretty well fighting other humans. It wasn't until I had to look them in the face that the differences became clear. I tried to remember the faces I'd seen in Gamma Junction, but all I could picture were those fathers and sons who'd blown themselves up in a cargo truck filled with explosives just to kill us.

"That's not the answer."

Vicky's words were soft, gently spoken, and yet they were a scourge across my back. I winced, not turning but withdrawing my fingers from the shot glass as if it was red-hot.

"I know that. But it's what I've got." I closed my eyes, leaning against the bar. "Sorry. I didn't mean to wake you up again."

"You're eligible for veteran's benefits," she reminded me, moving into the living room without switching on the lights. She didn't touch me, maybe because she was upset or maybe because she sensed how prickly and intense I was feeling. "That includes psychological counseling."

Now I did turn and face her, though her eyes were swallowed up in shadow.

"That would mean leaving here long-term," I said. "The closest veterans' health facilities are back at Tahn-Skyyiah, and they aren't going to let us stay there long-term, not unless we re-up in the military. We'd have to go all the way to Aphrodite, use our separation bonuses to live on while I'm being treated."

"All that's true," she admitted. "But I'd do it if you want to. You're more important to me than this place." She shrugged. "If we had to, we could go back to Brigantia, stay with your friend, Dak."

"I thought we were coming here because Brigantia had too many bad memories," I murmured. I stared at the bottle. I wanted another drink. I *needed* another drink. The numbness had worn off quick, as if the effect was lessening with time. "But the memories are in my head, no matter where we go."

Dak would help us if I asked, but stubborn resistance dragged at my heels. I'd turned down his offer to settle on Brigantia, and coming back to him now with my tail between my legs would chafe at my soul.

"Why do they let them come here?" I asked, spinning around to throw the question at her like an accusation, trying to drown out the despair in anger. "We just fought a war with the bastards. They're violent fanatics, from the old women right down to the teenagers. Why are they letting them leave their own God-forsaken planet at all?"

"Because the war's over and no one wants to go on fighting it. Because keeping their disaffected warrior class penned up on their homeworld is just asking for someone to build it back up into an army fighting for some other cause, a secular leader."

Which sounded very reasonable, and the logic of it pissed me off even more than the presence of the Tahni here.

"How do you know these things?" I shook my head, impressed despite my frustration. "I mean, we live in the same house. I always thought I kept up on things, but every question I ask, you already know the answer."

"When you can't sleep," she said, picking up the bottle and pouring a shot, "you drink." She downed the tequila with barely a wince. "When I can't sleep, I read."

I blinked, understanding the implication of the words.

"How often?"

"Not as often as you," she allowed. She set the glass down gently, as thoughtful and careful about the motion as she was about everything else. "But then, I didn't see as much as you. I didn't *lose* as much as you." Her fingers brushed my arm. "I don't know how you've kept it together as well as you have as long as you have."

"I started early." As if somehow, that made it better. She didn't argue the point though.

"I'm from the Underground, too," she said, and since I knew that and she knew I knew it, I didn't respond, assuming she was trying to make a point. "I didn't have it as bad as you. I had a mother and my two brothers and they tried to take care of me when they could. They were in a gang, and they had pull, and used it to keep me out. They all supported me when I decided to join the Marines. They knew there was no other way out of the Underground for any of us. I miss them, but I can send them messages and get theirs, and I know they're okay."

I nodded. I'd seen the messages her mother recorded, though they'd come fewer and farther between since the end of the war. Mostly, I'd been impressed that her mother hadn't been begging for a share of her separation bonus. That was an old story, and one that Clines complained about constantly. Of course, his family was on one of the colonies, with just enough upward mobility to realize what the money could do for them. Maybe people stuck in the Underground knew that a few tens of thousands in government scrip still wouldn't be enough to get them to the Surface.

"And as much as I miss them, I have never regretted what I did. I know I'm a better person for it, in a better situation. And I never would have met you if I hadn't left." She grabbed my hand in hers and squeezed it.

"You know I feel the same way," I insisted. "If I hadn't gone into the Corps, I would have wound up dead in a year. Or in the Freezer, which is pretty much the same thing."

I know theoretically, long-term punitive hibernation wasn't *supposed* to be a death sentence, but everyone knew better. After a hundred years in the Freezer, anything could happen. Governments could change, laws could change, records could be misplaced on purpose. No one I ever talked to who was facing a long-term sentence in the Freezer ever expected to come out of it.

"I think the difference between us is, I always had an eye on after the war, on getting out and coming someplace like this, on using the Marines as a steppingstone to a better life. For you, the Marines *was* your better life. The only reason you ever thought about after the war, after the military was because of me."

"That's not true." The denial was reflexive and I didn't know if I meant it or not. I hadn't thought about it. "I mean, the lawyer program that made me the offer even talked about getting out with a separation bonus and a spot on a colony of my choice."

"But the Corps made you a better person. Don't try to deny it. You were important. People respected you, and you respected yourself. You went from a private to a 1st Lieutenant, a company commander, and you would have been a captain by now if you'd stayed in." Her gaze flickered downward, unwilling to meet mine. "You'd be happier if you hadn't left."

"I'm happier with you," I told her, taking her by her upper arms and pulling her close to me, looking her in the eye. "Even if I would have been a captain, even if I was heading for general, it wouldn't mean anything without you. I swear to God, I can be happy doing anything as long as you're with me." I shrugged. "And as far as the...other stuff...well, I'll deal with it. I'll see if I can order some medication from Veterans' Assistance, something to help me sleep."

"Until it gets here," she told me, "you have to promise me you're going to cut back on the booze."

"All right," I said. Then I chuckled softly. "But maybe I'd better start after tomorrow night. Remember, we invited Dave over for dinner?"

"Oh, God," she moaned, resting her forehead against my

chest. "Dave's not a bad guy," she admitted, "but that man can drink. And you know what he talks about when he drinks."

I did. It never failed. It was always....

"...the fucking Predecessors!"

Dave Clines tossed the empty bottle with incredible accuracy for the sheer number of beers he'd downed, landing it in the recycling bin at the edge of the porch, where it clinked and clanked amidst the others. Glass—real glass—was almost unheard of on Earth, where everything was plastic. But the plants to manufacture those plastics and the equipment to drill for the oil to make them were expensive and not considered worth shipping out to small colonies like this. But all it took was a small shop and some sand to make all the glass you needed.

"Wait now," I said, holding up one hand, the other holding onto a glass of vodka that I was nursing very carefully because of my promise to Vicky. "You're saying that the Predecessors made the Tahni? Like, on purpose?"

"I'm saying that they did *all* of this, dude!" he said, waving around us, above us with a wayward hand as he reached down into the cooler he'd brought with him and grabbed yet another beer. "All our colonies, all the Tahni worlds, *this* world. It's pretty fucking obvious. I mean, those rock dragon steaks we had for dinner—which, by the way, great job grilling those things, my dude. But those steaks! There's no way we should be able to eat those damned things! Even if that panspermia shit was real, it's just not possible. There's shit on Earth we can't eat and it evolved on the same planet as us!"

Vicky had her chair leaned back against the wall, one heel propped on the porch railing, and she tilted her head toward me.

"He's kind of got you there, Cam," she admitted.

I didn't want to admit it. I stared out at the western sky burned red by the setting primary star and tried to find an argument out there in the fiery clouds. I picked one out, though it was less from the clouds than from my ass.

"But how would we know that?" I pointed out. "After all, we don't have an example of a planet where the life *isn't* based on DNA to compare it to. Maybe this is just how things are and we were wrong with our theories before. I mean, that's how science works, right? We have to look at the actual evidence and change our theories, right?"

"Yeah," Clines said, "except that we *know* how life evolved on Earth, because we've been digging up fossils there for like, hundreds of years. We haven't been able to do that yet on the Tahni homeworld, so we ain't got no idea if the whole ecosystem was dumped there as-is. But everything we've found on Earth says that all this shit is impossible. Life evolved the way it did on Earth because of a whole shitload of unpredictable things. I mean, we've had what? Five mass extinctions?"

"I don't know," I admitted. "I mean, I might have read something about it, but it's not something I keep current on."

"Well, there's five, take my word for it. And in one of them, like ninety-five percent of all life on Earth died. So how the hell you gonna tell me that on Tahn-Skyyiah, just because they started out with RNA from a comet, they wound up with humanoid sentient life so close to us you could mistake one of them for human if you ran into them on the street on a dark night?"

"So, you think what? That the Predecessors, whoever they were, took...well, hell, they'd have had to grab like anthropoids at least, right? To get the Tahni that close to us."

"Maybe." He took a long, thoughtful swig of the beer. "I mean, it doesn't *have* to be that way. I mean, these Predecessors were pretty fucking smart. They could have just engineered the whole business from scratch, just using DNA. They terraformed all these worlds anyway. Everything except Earth and maybe a couple others."

"What?" I sat up straight, nearly spilling my drink. "Now you're just talking crazy!"

"Actually...," Vicky trailed off, seeming reluctant to agree with Clines again but too honest not to.

"Not you, too?" I pleaded with her.

"Oh, come on, Cam, you have to have seen reports about the algae stuff."

"The algae?" I repeated, drawing a blank. Vicky rolled her eyes.

"The bacterial mats in the oceans and lakes of every colony world, ours and the Tahni's. They're basically the same organism on every world, but adjusted just slightly to the ecosystem and they're incredibly efficient at producing oxygen. They were the *only* life form on a couple of the worlds we found, and they're the oldest on *every* habitable world. And yes," she said, rolling her eyes, "the people who believe it's all panspermia say that it's the first life that rises up on every world, the one that evolves first when the building blocks of life arrive off the comet or whatever. They say what you're saying, that we just didn't know because it was too long ago, but the problem with the idea is that the algae is still around on all those other worlds, but it's not on Earth."

"Maybe it died off in one of those catastrophes Dave was talking about." I was grasping at straws now, but unwilling to give in on this. "Maybe that's why things are so different on Earth."

Clines rubbed a hand over his face like he was the one getting frustrated.

"Cam, Cam, Cam...," he sighed. "Just look at the evidence

here. We *know* there was a race of advanced aliens who either lived in or visited our part of the galaxy at least once ten thousand years ago. You'll give me that much, right?"

"Well, of course," I granted. "I mean, someone left the wormhole map on Hermes. We only found the first jumpgate in the asteroid belt by accident. If it wasn't for the map, we'd never have found all the others. And without finding the wormholes, we wouldn't have ever figured out Transition Space and wouldn't have invented the Transition drive. So, here's to the Predecessors," I said, trying to make a joke of it, raising my glass and taking a drink. "Without them, we wouldn't be here on this porch, getting drunk and arguing about bullshit."

"Well, I'll drink to that," Clines agreed, taking a swig of beer, "mostly 'cause I'll drink to anything. But think about it. We know the Predecessors existed. They left the map. We know the algae is on every world except Earth, and we know it was responsible for terraforming all of them." I started to open my mouth and he raised a palm to stop me. "Either by design or by accident, that's what they did. They made all these worlds habitable to *us*. Not to methane-breathing gasbags or giant ice worms, but to *us*, oxygen-breathing mammals. And the Predecessors had to have been like us or they wouldn't have put that wormhole map in the side of a mountain on a world like Hermes. So, you've got one world where we know everything evolved over a period of billions of years, where there were so many cosmic coincidences that you could never repeat the whole thing, and that resulted in us." He clarified who "us" meant with a hand on his chest, as if I might not understand, and I wondered if he was already drunk or just thought I was.

"And then," he went on, "you got all these other worlds where we know this algae stuff made them habitable. To *us*. And you got the Tahni, who are way too much like us for coincidence. It's pretty obvious what happened if you ask me. The Predecessors set this whole thing up for *us*."

"This whole thing?" I shook my head, uncomprehending.

"The Cluster. All the stars we can reach with the Transition Drive, which, by the way, ain't that many compared to the whole galaxy. But all the stars that have terrestrial planets in the whole Cluster have habitables, have life. And the wormhole map was left on Hermes, around Proxima Centauri, the closest star to *us*. Not the closest one to the Tahni. And the Tahni already knew about the wormholes, though they ain't ever said how they found out."

"Okay, let's just say for a second that I agree with you that the Predecessors left us the map and made all these habitable worlds just for us because they're like, I don't know, galactic philanthropists or something. Why the hell would they make the Tahni? Their whole biology is totally fucked when it comes to making a technological civilization. I mean, the males can barely control themselves around females and have to live separate from each other! I don't know how the hell they even developed space travel."

"Maybe they didn't," Vicky mused.

She had a glass of wine, which she'd taken up drinking since we'd moved here. Red this time, because it apparently went with rock dragon steaks. She swirled it around in her glass, staring at it in silent contemplation for a moment.

"Think about it this way," she said, finally. "You're some powerful, ancient alien with a long-term mindset, with the technology to terraform planets for kicks. You come to this Cluster of systems where there's only one living planet, so you start terraforming a bunch of worlds. And you see us, maybe ten or twenty thousand years ago, sitting in our mud huts, hunting antelope or whatever, and since you're thinking long-term, you say 'hey, what if we design our own version? Maybe we can make it better.' And then, every once in a while, you kick the Tahni some technological advantage under the table, because you really want your boys to come out on top."

I gaped at her and she grinned at my expression of utter disbelief.

"This could all be like a giant science experiment to them. We're the control group, they're the experimental group."

"Just what kind of shit are you reading when you can't sleep?" I wondered, shaking my head. "Do you really believe that shit, Vicky?"

She laughed, sipping at her wine.

"Believe? No," she admitted. "But would I be surprised to find out it was true? Also, no."

"Who are you," I asked her, "and what have you done with my wife?"

I was so absorbed with the bizarre turn the conversation had taken that I almost missed the distant roar of jets.

"Goddammit," Clines spat, tossing another bottle toward the recycling bin, missing this time, sending a small puddle of beer trickling out of the open mouth like blood. "That's two of the fucking things this week. Damn Hellnick and those smuggler assholes."

I was about to point out that he didn't know they were smugglers, though I couldn't think of anything else they'd be doing that would require that kind of secrecy and isolation, but I was interrupted. By an explosion.

"What the fuck!"

I don't know who said it first, since all three of us were combat veterans and while profanity may be a crutch for inarticulate motherfuckers, it was also a mainstay of the Marine vocabulary. But we were all three of us on our feet, scanning the sky, trying to find the shuttle.

We found the smoke first, a black line of it staining the sky, streaming out of the starboard jet engine of the shuttle. The lines of the aerospacecraft were plain in the red glow of sunset, bulbous and ungainly, a fat lifting body shape built for utility rather than looks. The silver gleam of its hull was broken by dull squares here and there where the fuselage had been repaired with patches.

Gonna need a couple more, I judged.

"It's going down," Vicky noted. "And it's not going to make Hellnick's place."

She was right about that. The thing was already tottering in mid-air, the remaining jet not enough to keep its bulk in the air, and they weren't using their belly jets, which perhaps meant those thrusters weren't working or perhaps meant they didn't *know* if they were damaged and didn't want to find out until they were somewhere they could set down. And they were losing altitude fast, coming down not over Hellnick's land, but over Clines' farm.

It hit. We were kilometers away, but the *whump* of the impact rolled across the fields, filtered through the groves of trees separating one property from the other before reaching us distorted and broken. A cloud of dust and smoke rose above the crash site and we all looked at each other.

"Let's go," I said, grabbing my jacket off the back of my rocking chair. "We'll take our rover."

Vicky and Clines followed. Whether these guys were smugglers or just independent spacers, one thing was for certain, they needed help.

[4]

The rutted dirt road battered the rover's suspension and us along with it, the shadows falling deeper with the dusk, hiding chuck-holes and rocks until we hit them. It wasn't hard to plot a course—I just followed the smudge of black smoke still billowing into the night sky. Flames were licking above the tree line by the time we reached it, and I hit the brakes when I felt the heat, not daring to park the vehicle any closer.

The aerospacecraft itself wasn't on fire, though the whole starboard side was charred, smoking, and partially melted. The reactor must have scrammed, venting plasma during its emergency shutdown, and although there was nothing on the shuttle that could burn, the same couldn't be said for the tall grass surrounding it. The flames had spread to the nearby trees, but I wasn't worried about the fire surrounding us, since there was a swathe of cleared land between us and the crash, but even from a hundred meters away from the shuttle wreck, the heat was already almost unbearable.

"Well," Clines said, slipping out the rear passenger's side door, hand resting on the frame of the vehicle as if the solidity of it comforted him, "I don't think we're gonna be pulling anybody out of that thing."

I nodded, slowly opening my own door, not in nearly as much of a hurry now. The cargo bird had shattered on impact, the fuselage split from belly to spine at the cockpit and the end of the cargo hold, and as bad as the damage to the aerospacecraft seemed, the damage to the people who'd been flying it would be even worse.

Images superimposed themselves over the crashed ship, memories swimming across my vision unbidden of drop ships falling out of the sky, trailing fire, Marines in battlesuits leaping from the burning craft in desperation. Too high, much too high to survive the fall, but jumping anyway because you didn't just give up and ride the bird down, you kept fighting until the very last second.

I snapped back to the moment, shaking away the flashback and forcing the present to cohere back to clarity.

"We should check for survivors anyway," I said, though the words sounded as if they were coming from someone else, from somewhere over my head. "Just in case."

I reached back into the cab and grabbed a pair of work gloves, thick enough to protect my hands from the heat. The jacket was heavy, insulated. I needed something to cover my face and I went to the back, ignoring Clines' disbelieving glare as I fished in our emergency survival kit for a spare T-shirt. I wrapped it around my face experimentally and decided it would have to do, then added goggles to the mix.

Vicky was next to me, equipping herself with similar gear without saying a word. She didn't try to argue me out of doing it, so I returned the favor, just nodding to her.

"You guys are nuts," Clines insisted, gaping at us. "Ain't nobody lived through that!"

"Then don't come," I told him.

He sighed and started digging through our equipment, cursing under his breath.

"Goddamn officers," he murmured. "Always dragging my ass into the fire."

I didn't recall dragging his ass anywhere, but he came along for all the grumbling. Even though the ship hadn't caught fire, it was still insanely hot. The plasma vent had been enough to melt the starboard jet engine to slag and the heat radiated off it in waves, bad enough that the few centimeters of exposed skin I'd left stung as if I'd stuck my flesh over a campfire. I paused and adjusted my clothes, covering up what hurt and hoping it wouldn't blister, particularly the small section at the bridge of my nose.

It was amazing just how huge the cargo bird was this close up to it. I'd been on dozens of drop ships during the war, but I'd been in my suit, and the bulk and mass of the Vigilante had given me a distorted perspective of the size of the boats. This one was a good two hundred meters long from stem to stern and a bit less than that half that distance at the widest point of its wingspan. Walking beside it was like being an ant wandering around the corpse of an elephant.

They hadn't even tried to lower the landing gear, which I suppose was smart. They'd been hoping, no doubt, that they could slide across the grass to bleed off some momentum, but their angle had been too steep. The nose had been crushed by the impact, obliterating the cockpit, and looking very much like Clines had been right and we were wasting our time. But the gap in the hull just behind the command section offered access to the cargo hold, and it was possible there had been a loading crew strapped in back there.

I approached the rent in the hull cautiously, one hand extended in front of me in case the heat became bad enough to ignite my fire-retardant clothing, but it actually seemed to be cooler the closer I got to the front of the ship, and I thought maybe the shielding between the cargo hold and the reactor had actually done its job, even if nothing else on the ship had. I touched the jagged metal at the edge of the gap with a tentative, outstretched finger and found it not too far above ambient temperature, cool enough to use as a handhold and pull myself up into the shuttle.

Not so much as a chemical strip light illuminated the interior of the cargo hold, shutting out even the red glow of twilight and plunging the whole compartment into darkness. I'd brought a small flashlight along from the rover and I scanned its beam back and forth from the cockpit back to the cargo, searching for survivors. I'd been worried that the interior would be filled with smoke, making both breathing and vision difficult, but it wasn't. The smoke was outside and the crash had dug its own firebreak between the ship and the tall grass.

The particulate debris and dust inside the craft danced in the rays of light, but I could see well enough to know there'd be no survivors among the flight crew. The cockpit had accordioned in on itself, and if there was anything left of the command stations, it was crushed flat between layers of BiPhase Carbide, and I wasn't going to reach it with anything less than an industrial plasma cutter.

The stairs leading down from the cockpit to the passenger compartment, the small section fore of the cargo hold where freight workers could strap in, were twisted and torn, splintered plastic and jagged metal, and the deck beneath the acceleration couches wasn't in much better shape. The couches themselves had been thrown across the compartment in the crash, though the safety restraints had held. The circle of light danced across one of the seats, and I gritted my teeth at what was left of the man who'd been strapped into it.

Some of the cargo had broken loose from its magnetic

anchors and the poor son of a bitch had either slammed into one of the loose crates or it had slammed into him. Whichever had happened, it hadn't ended well. His chest had been caved in and while that might have been survivable if someone could have popped him straight into an auto-doc, but there had been no treatment, no rescue. He'd bled out in minutes and died in a puddle of frothy crimson.

"This one's dead," Vicky announced, kneeling over a pudgy, bald man whose shoulders might have strained against the confines of the chair once, when his chest had been filled with air, his body filled with life. Now, illuminated in the glare of her flashlight, his head was tilted at an unnatural angle, his eyes staring without seeing, his mouth agape.

There were two other occupied seats. The waifish, short-haired woman in the acceleration couch against the far bulkhead was still, her right temple caved in from a loose cargo crate, her face covered in blood. Her shoulders jerked with a pair of gasping breaths, then sagged again. She might not be dead yet, but she would be before we could get her unstrapped from her seat.

It had been so damned long since I'd seen a dead body. Nearly two years. Vince Delp. He'd been younger than this woman, and when he'd died, his face had been clean and unmarked. I could have believed he'd been sleeping. Yet I still saw his visage imposed over hers for the space of a heartbeat.

"We got a live one," Vicky announced.

I shook away the memory, pulled off my goggles and picked a few cautious steps across the passenger compartment, searching for the few centimeters of the deck plating that hadn't fractured into sharpened splinters and wasn't littered with debris or cargo crates. I heard the moans before I reached the man, saw his foot kicking in the glow of Vicky's flashlight.

I don't know how this guy had lived through the crash, but I knew he wasn't enjoying the experience. He was wearing a sleeveless, leather vest, unfortunately, which meant I had a very clear view of the splintered ends of his radius and ulna sticking through the skin of his left arm. I clamped my jaws shut against the bile rising in my throat and forced myself to evaluate the man for any other injuries. He had them, of course.

His eyes were open but unfocused, and when Vicky flashed the beam of her light into them, he didn't blink and the pupils didn't respond. That was bad. He had a severe concussion, which was probably the only reason he wasn't screaming from the pain of his broken arm. A pressure cut was open over one eye, blood streaming out to obscure his face. God knew what else was wrong with him, but he was breathing and, despite the gruesome arm wound, he hadn't bled out. Yet.

"We should do something about his arm while he's still woozy," I said. I didn't *want* to say it. I wanted very much to back out of the shuttle and pretend I'd never seen any of it.

I pulled off the shirt I'd wrapped around my head and sliced it down the middle with my belt knife. I wore it everywhere because it was what you did out here on the frontier. A knife was a constant companion, an ever-ready tool. I didn't even notice its weight on my belt anymore.

"You got anything stiff we can use for a splint?" I asked Vicky. She began searching around on the deck and I turned back to Clines, catching him staring down the beam of his own flashlight into the cargo hold. "Dave, can you find something about twenty-five or thirty centimeters long to use as a splint?" He didn't respond, and I kept myself from yelling the words in a command only by an act of will. I wasn't an officer anymore, or even a sergeant, and Clines was a friend, not a subordinate. "*Dave*," I repeated, with just a touch more volume and emphasis. "We need a splint."

"Take a look at this, you two."

Clines' voice was soft, thoughtful, so unlike him that I followed his gaze and his light with my own. The cargo bay looked as if a toddler had come across a neat stack of building blocks and kicked it over out of spite, then grabbed the largest bits and smashed them into each other for the hell of it. The cargo crates were a bit more durable than the humans who had been in charge of them, and most of them had held together, battered but still sealed and secure.

Except for one. It was huge, much larger than the rest of the containers, ten meters long and three or four across, cylindrical, and it had split under the weight of what was within, spilling the thing out on top of the rest of the freight. It was finished in a utilitarian matte grey, inlaid with circuitry, and fitted with power couplings that were large and durable enough that they had to be military.

"That's...," I trailed off, tugging at the frayed edge of a memory, something I'd seen on one of the Fleet ships I'd called home during the war. A tech crew had pulled apart the nose of an assault shuttle and I'd seen that laying on the deck, huge and yawning and menacing. "Is that a...."

"It's a proton cannon," Clines told me, his voice grim. "Military-grade, highly restricted. You put one of those on a ship and you can penetrate the shielding of anything you'd run into, up to and including Fleet cutters and assault shuttles."

The implications of the thing were obvious, but I shunted them to the side, focusing on the task at hand.

"Hand me those two bits of shelving, Dave," I told him, motioning at a spot two meters ahead of him with my flashlight. He eyed me doubtfully. "Now, please."

"Should we take him out of the seat?" Vicky asked as I took the twenty-centimeter strips of metal storage shelf supports over to her and the victim.

"No," I said. "He might have spinal fractures. We should wait until Emergency Services gets here."

I gritted my teeth as I grabbed his arm, but I didn't have any other choice. It was either this or watch him bleed to death in front of us. I straightened his arm and pushed the bones back into position. The sound, the feeling was unspeakable, horrifyingly close to the experience of twisting the head off a chicken, something I'd seen my mother do often. It hadn't given me nightmares then, but it might now.

"Okay, hold the splints in place," I told Vicky, "while I wrap the dressing."

I tied it tight. Not tourniquet-tight, but tight enough. I sat back, sucking in a breath, smelling blood and shit. Someone, maybe more than one someone, had voided themselves when they died.

"You hear that?" Vicky asked, her head popping up, eyes going to the overhead but searching for something beyond the hull of the shuttle. And I did hear it, an insistent buzzing, like a mosquito making passes at the back of my head.

"Hoppers," I said. Ducted-fan hovercraft, the cheapest aircraft out here, easy to build from fabricated parts if you had the money and the need.

"It could be the Emergency Services Patrol," Vicky said.

And she was right, it could be. We'd called them before we'd let the house. The ESP was small, a volunteer outfit paid for by the townspeople and the settlements, someone you could call if you had a medical emergency you couldn't handle with what you had on the farm, or a fire, or some other major problem. And a crashed shuttle qualified as a major problem.

But Gamma Junction was a half-hour flight away, and that wasn't counting how long it would take to get the people together, which always seemed to take longer than it should. There hadn't been time.

"Let's get outside," I told them, making my way to the hole in the fuselage, not looking back to see if they'd listened because I knew they would. "Fast."

I stifled a cough from the smoke drifting up off the burning grass, squeezing my eyes shut against the acrid sting. When I opened them, I realized it was dark, that the sun had gone below the horizon while we'd been inside the corpse of the shuttle. The darkness made the running lights of the two hoppers stand out in the night sky, outshining the rising moons. I'd had a vague idea that we could get to the rover and get out before they saw us, but it was already too late for that. They were circling the clearing, the wind from their twin fans twisting the clouds of smoke into artistic whorls, glowing a preternatural white in their landing lights.

"Oh, shit," Clines said. "What now?" He glanced furtively at the rover. "There a rifle in the truck?"

"Be chill," I said, my voice so much calmer than I should have felt. "You saw nothing, you *say* nothing. Let me do all the talking."

I should have been panicking, should have been running, even though it wouldn't have done any good, should have been curled up on the ground screaming, given the way I'd been reacting lately to anything that reminded me of the war. I did none of those, though I couldn't have said why. I just stood there and watched the hoppers land, hands at my side, concentrating on being as innocent as possible, on letting innocence and ignorance waft off me like a perfume.

The hoppers touched down within a few meters of each other, their canopies swinging open before the landing struts settled into the rich, turned earth. The men and women who clambered out of the aircraft were familiar. I'd seen their like in Gamma Junction, as well as inside the shuttle. They were off-worlders, spacers, rough-edged and wild-eyed, every one of them visibly armed, some with just holstered handguns, others with carbines slung over their shoulder.

Vicky didn't come to my side to meet them, instead separating herself by ten meters, off at an angle to my position. She was, as always, using her head, thinking tactically. Clines on the other hand....

"Dave," I said softly, reminding him of something he should have learned in basic training, "ten meters separation."

He grunted as if I'd hit him, but stepped away, almost staggering, his eyes glued on the spacers heading our way.

Smugglers, I corrected myself. *Gun runners*.

"What are you doing on our shuttle?"

It was hard to pinpoint who had said it at first, the way they were all bunched up and veiled by flickering shadows from the fitful remnants of the grassfires. But then one of them stepped forward, aiming himself at me, though why he figured I was in charge, I wasn't sure. He was a tall man, rangy and long-limbed, lacking any of the showy facial tattooing or flashy jewelry of his fellows, his clothes utilitarian work fatigues except for the crimson-tinted leather jacket he wore almost like it was a badge of office. The gun holstered at his right hip looked just as pragmatic and utilitarian as his clothes, the grip worn and wrapped in rigging tape. His gloved right hand rested on it and the snarl on his scarred, bearded face told me he *wanted* to use it.

"We're not currently *on* your shuttle," I pointed out. "We went to check for survivors. There is one, by the way, but he's in bad shape. Bad concussion, compound fracture of his left arm, maybe stuff we couldn't see. I splinted his arm and put on a pressure bandage, but he needs a real medical center or an autodoc, if you have one."

He said nothing for a moment, his ice blue eyes locked on mine, scanning me like a lidar projector, as if he was searching me for signs of deception.

"Gregor," he said, inclining his head to the right, speaking to one of his people. "Take Sasha and the medical kit and check it out."

Two of their number separated from the rest and jogged toward the downed aerospacecraft without hesitation. This guy, I knew, was the leader, and not one who any of them questioned. Good leadership for them was possibly bad for us.

"Who are you?" he asked.

"This is my farm," Clines said and I bit down on a curse. I'd *told* him to keep his mouth shut, but I suppose that had been too much to hope for. Instead, he sounded outraged, full of righteous indignation, fists planted on his hips. "I don't begrudge that your ship had engine problems and had no choice in the matter, but you ain't got no call to be landing your hoppers here without my leave and waving guns around."

"You're that guy Clines," the bearded man judged, the corner of his mouth curling up. "I heard about you."

"You heard *what* about me?" Clines demanded, taking a step forward. "Who said it? That asshole Hellnick?"

One of the spacers raised the muzzle of their carbine. It looked, I thought, like a slug shooter, not a pulse gun. No surprise there. Pulse guns weren't incredibly complicated, but they were expensive and almost impossible to fabricate out in the sticks. It wasn't a Gauss rifle, either. Too light and compact. It was something older, easier to make. Probably a Gyroc carbine. Simple, easy to use, easy to make. Fired spin-stabilized, unguided rockets most of the time. You could get guided ones, but then your weapon would have to be linked to a Heads-Up Display in a helmet visor or a set of goggles, and none of these goons were wearing either one. Still accurate enough to blow a fist-sized hole through Clines chest at this range, guidance or no.

"Dave," I said, the word softly spoken and yet still packed

full of all the frustration the man was engendering in my gut. "Shut up."

"Better listen to the man, farmer," the bearded one advised. "He's clearly the smarter of the two of you." He eyed Vicky sidelong. "Though she may be the smartest. She hasn't said a word."

"There's always that possibility," I agreed. "What's your name, mister?"

Not that I really cared, but keeping the man talking seemed the better alternative than encouraging a situation where the only response left was shooting us.

"Mister, huh?" The bearded man snorted a laugh. "Not too many calling me 'mister' anything in quite a while. You can just call me Captain Eld."

"Well, Captain, we only came here because we thought someone might need help. If your people have that taken care of, we can just leave the rest to you. I'm sure you'll have a lot of work to do transporting your shuttle out of here."

"I told you my name," Eld said, cocking an eyebrow toward me. "Seems like it would only be good manners to return the favor."

"I'm Cameron Alvarez." I motioned towards Vicky. "This is my wife, Victoria Sandoval. We own the farm next door." I motioned behind us.

"Well, it's our pleasure to make your acquaintance, *Mister* Alvarez," he managed to turn the sneer into something almost friendly. "Suppose you tell us what you saw on board our shuttle?"

"Just the dead and the dying."

"Nothing else, huh?"

He didn't sound convinced and I wasn't much of a liar. If I'd been a better liar, I probably would've been able to make a living on the streets of the Trans-Angeles Underground as a con man instead of a thief. Of course, then I would probably have wound up dead in some pointless beef with a bunch of criminals.

God must have a very ironic sense of humor.

"We weren't looking for anything else," Vicky said.

"Captain Eld!" It was one of the two he'd sent into the wreckage, the man he'd called Gregor. "We got Jared in here, hurt pretty bad. The rest are dead."

"Get him loaded in the hopper," Eld directed. "We'll fly him back to Hellnick's farm, treat him there. The rest can wait for the trucks."

"Trucks?" Clines repeated like a big, stupid parrot.

What part of 'shut up' does this guy not understand?

"Yes, Mr. Clines, trucks to take our property off your property. That's what you were bitching about just two minutes ago, wasn't it?" Eld took a step toward Clines, just one, long stride, yet it seemed to carry him well over a meter, bringing him almost within arm's reach of our neighbor. "Or would you rather try something different? Maybe we should think about making your property our property?"

"Is there a problem?"

The voice was nothing I'd ever heard before, nothing that had evolved to speak English or any other human language. I frowned, squinting against the light from the hoppers' landing lights, trying to make out the tall, broad-bodied figure walking up from behind the aircraft.

"No, no problem, Zan-Thint," Eld said, his tone shifting subtly, nothing most people would have noticed, but I'd heard the like before. It was the way a high-ranking subordinate spoke to someone who scared even him. "Just ironing some things out with the locals."

Zan-Thint? What kind of name is...

The tall shape blocked the glare from the hoppers, visible

just barely in the light from the fires, the features oh, so close to human but not quite.

"If there is a problem," Zan-Thint said, his accent sing-song, "then maybe we should, as you humans say, sort things out."

He was a Tahni.

[5]

I hadn't panicked before, hadn't felt the fear I'd expected, but it hit me now, smashing into me like a wave. Criminals, I could deal with. I'd spent my formative years talking down people who wanted nothing more than to kill me, or at least beat me to a pulp. Tahni, I only knew one way to deal with, and that was to blow the shit out of them with a plasma gun while I was encased in a BiPhase Carbide battlesuit. As my current suit was nothing more formidable than an insulated, synthetic fiber and my hand held nothing deadlier than a flashlight, that option didn't seem open to me.

"Who are these...people?" Zan-Thint asked, staring at me with black, piggish eyes. "And why do we tolerate their interference?"

"Your kind tolerated quite a bit of our interference during the war," Vicky said, finding her voice where I could not. I stared at her, shocked, but her back was straight, her chin stuck out in defiance. "In fact, between the two of us, I'm pretty sure my husband and I interfered our way through every major battle, including the invasion of Tahn-Skyyiah." She sniffed.

"Though I gotta admit, I've never heard one of you try to speak English before."

"Things change, do they not?" the Tahni said, coming even with Eld, even more visible now.

There was something different about this one from the ones I'd seen during the war, even from the ones I'd just seen in town. He wore human-style clothes. Oh, tailored to his form, surely, but he eschewed the tightly-wound strips of his people, going instead with loose, grey trousers and a heavy jacket of the sort I might have worn back on the frozen wastes of Hachiman. Of course, to him, a temperate night on Hausos might have felt just as cold.

"There is a human saying I have learned in my pursuit of your language," Zan-Thint told her. "To the victors go the spoils. And so, I must learn to speak as you in order to forge a new way in life, as so many of us have had to do. Just as you have learned a new way. For none of you are warriors anymore, no longer Marines, but simply farmers now."

"Another saying we humans have," I interjected, finding my voice somewhere in Vicky's courage. "There is no such thing as an *ex*-Marine." I arched an eyebrow, noting the queue of braided hair wrapped around his neck, the sign of a Tahni soldier who has killed in battle. "Is it the same for a warrior of your people?"

"Sadly, no," he replied. His command of our language was masterful enough to even include the emotional inflection I would have expected from a human. He even cocked his head toward us. "Once you humans proved quite conclusively that our Emperor was not a god and that we were not undefeatable in battle because of his existence, many of us had to seek out other vocations."

I nodded toward the weapon strapped in a rig across his chest that was half tactical sling and half holster. It was the

Tahni equivalent of a handgun, and the only ones I'd ever seen carrying one were senior officers.

"Doesn't seem like it's too far afield from your old vocation. Captain? Major?"

The terms didn't translate exactly, since the Tahni military organizational structure wasn't the same as ours. They had something close to the equivalent of our squads, but their next largest element was about the size of a company and from there it just went all to hell. But I knew if he'd gone to all the trouble of learning our language right down to the inflections, he'd understand the reference.

"A direct translation," he told me, nodding, "would be 'Ten-Lenon-Zan-Karan-Thint, the Emperor's Own Hand Over the Souls of 128 Octuples,' but Colonel Zan-Thint is close enough."

"Colonel." I nodded. "Let me guess, Shock Troopers? Combined Infantry?"

"Just so. And you have the sockets in your temples...you were both Drop Troopers, no? Though your mate has grown her hair to try to hide them, you still keep yours cut short as if you were ready to step back into the suit." He offered an expression that might have been an attempt at a smile, though it failed spectacularly. "It is a funny thing how in the Tahni military, the High Guard who wore our version of your battlesuits were the most elite and respected soldiers, yet in yours, the Drop Troopers were the rejects, the criminals, the ones fit for nothing better. Perhaps that is why our High Guard killed so many of your Drop Troopers for every one you killed of us. You won simply because you had more cannon fodder than we did. Your dregs outbred our elite."

Anger smoldered behind my eyes and I endeavored to contain it there, knowing he was trying very deliberately to anger me, either to shake me up and get me to reveal something or simply because he found it amusing.

"Of course," I responded, "expectation and reality aren't always the same thing. I am definitely one of those dregs." I kept talking, buying time. The more time we talked, the less time they spent shooting us. My gaze darted from the Tahni to the others and I noticed they were slowly but surely spreading out, penning us in. "I was born in the ruins of a city that hasn't existed for a century. My parents were killed by the criminal gangs that controlled the place and I wandered across a desert for the privilege of living on the streets of the poorest sections of our largest city. I was too poor, too much of a reject to even join the gangs there, so I stole from them instead. I was arrested and given the choice of punishment or being a Drop Trooper."

Zan-Thint attempted a smile again and this time, achieved the cruel satisfaction he was trying for.

"Typical. What I would have expected."

"Yeah," I agreed. "And by the end of the war, I was directly responsible for the deaths of over three *hundred* of your High Guard soldiers. That's not even counting the dozens upon dozens of your Shock Troopers and regular infantry I killed without bothering to count them."

The Tahni said nothing for a moment, staring at me with an undecipherable gaze, his eyes seeming to retreat further beneath his ridged brows.

"You," he growled, "are a liar, human."

"I dropped on Brigantia," I told him. "I destroyed the deflector shields there personally." His mouth opened, as if he were about to object, but I pressed on. "I was part of the initial infiltration team on Ambergris. I was with the platoon that destroyed the ambush force in the bunkers on Silvanus. Port Harcourt. Point Barber. Tahn-Skyyiah. I dropped on every one of them. I wiped out the last-ditch covering force you tried to secure the Imperial Palace with, and the only reason I wasn't with the Force Recon Marines who killed your Emperor was that our suits wouldn't fit in the tunnels."

I realized, suddenly, that I'd made a tactical error. I'd been concentrating so hard on not letting the Tahni make me angry that I'd done the exact inverse. Zan-Thint's left hand was crawling toward his gun as if it had a life of its own and was no longer being directed by his brain.

I shared a look with Vicky and her eyes darted toward the right, to the shuttle, and I got the message. If the shit went down, we'd take cover inside, as best we could. In truth, we'd probably wind up dead, all three of us, but a plan was a plan.

Light burst on us like a summer thunderstorm, showering from the sky, accompanied by the harsh, insistent buzzing of propellers. Maybe the reason we hadn't heard the hoppers approaching was our little dick-measuring contest, or maybe they'd been flying nap-of-the-earth, but the landing lights announced their entrance only seconds before they landed. Four ducted-fan helicopters came in, only a few dozen meters separation between them, flying just over the stand of burning trees, close enough to send sparks raining down around us, and if none of the spacers pulled the trigger, it was only because they weren't sure where to shoot.

The hoppers were unmarked, generic grey, but I knew who they were because I'd called them. Emergency Services had finally showed up.

The canopies popped open and men and women hopped out, some of them seeming confused by the armed strangers, but none panicking. Three or four reached back into the hoppers and pulled out hunting rifles, holding them at the low ready as if they were the Gauss service weapons the former Marines had trained with since Boot Camp.

The spacers began to exchange nervous glances, some

looking to Captain Eld for guidance, others to Colonel Zan-Thint.

"Easy," Eld said, his voice firm, but something in his eyes, perhaps disappointment, though it might have been relief. "Nobody do a Goddamned thing unless I say."

"Hey Cam, Vicky, what the hell's going on here?" The voice was measured and steady, not showing the slightest bit of fear, and I wasn't surprised. Brad Torrey had been a captain in Force Recon in the war and was as close to unflappable as a man could be. He glanced over at Clines and the corner of his mouth turned down slightly. "Dave."

"Brad," Clines returned, managing to pack as much disrespect as possible in the word, as if reminding him that he didn't have to call him sir anymore.

If Torrey minded, he didn't show it. The man's face was as bland and white-bread as it ever was, like a doctor or an AI-subroutine legal counsel, and those grey eyes didn't even blink when he saw the Tahni.

"Grandy, Vingh," he snapped. "Get a couple of extinguishers and put out those damned brushfires."

The two Emergency Service Patrol volunteers didn't question him, just slipped into the shoulder straps of the extinguishers, and began spraying fire-retardant foam over the burning trees and patches of grass. Smoke billowed up and the darkness closed in just a bit more on the edges of the clearing, though the lights of the extra hoppers kept the circle of friends and enemies illuminated.

"I didn't think I'd see you out here," I told Torrey. "I mean, it's a good hour's drive from your place just to the hopper landing field, much less town."

"I happened to be staying in town with friends for the night," he explained. "Negotiations with Browner's Fab Shop for a new water pump ran long and I didn't feel like driving five hours back well into the morning. Ned offered me a cot. Junie over there...." He nodded toward a woman beside the next hopper over, red hair, crazy eyes, and a big-assed rifle painting a picture of someone you didn't want to screw with. "...came and ran over from the ESP staging area and told me about your call."

"There's been a crash, Brad," I said, not because I didn't think he was smart enough to figure that out on his own, but in an attempt to defuse the situation. "These ladies and gentlemen came to check the shuttle for survivors. I believe they were about to evacuate one of the wounded to Klaus Hellnick's place for treatment." I speared Eld with a glare. "Weren't you, Captain?"

Eld nodded slowly, then motioned to the rest of his people. The muzzles of their guns lowered.

"Yes, I think we were." He shot me a grin. "We'll wait here until the trucks arrive to...clean up the mess." The grin turned sardonic when he turned to Clines. "If that's all right with you, Mr. Clines."

"Yeah, I'm good," Clines said, finally showing some intelligence. "Take as long as you like."

"You sure there's nothing we can do to help?" Torrey asked, eyes still locked on the Tahni. "Maybe keep an eye on things to make sure there are no other accidents?"

"Naw," I said. "I think the three of us are going to get in our rover and head back home, and we can all just stay out of trouble." I waved to Vicky and Clines. "Let's get out of these people's hair, shall we?"

"It looks as if the fires are out here," Torrey said. "Come on, everyone, let's pack it in and get back to town before the people we left behind start to panic." He smiled at Zan-Thint. "Wouldn't want anyone to panic."

I was already walking, praying silently to a God I hadn't bothered much since the end of the war that He would get us out of the clearing without one of the dumbass smugglers or one of my dumbass neighbors taking a shot at someone. Vicky was beside me, while Clines was stepping backwards so he could watch the spacers. I half-hoped he'd trip and bust his ass just as a payback for totally failing to keep his mouth shut.

"Mr. Alvarez." The Tahni gave an odd, otherworldly lilt to my last name. He was watching me back by the hopper he'd emerged from, arms folded in front of him.

"Lieutenant Alvarez," I corrected him, though I don't know why. It wasn't as if I had ever asked anyone to call me by my rank since I'd mustered out. Must have been sheer bloody-mindedness.

"*Lieutenant* Alvarez," Zan-Thint said, inclining his head toward me. "It has been instructional meeting you. I'm sure I'll see you again."

"Not," I assured him, slipping into the driver's seat of our vehicle, "if I see you first."

[6]

"No, Goddammit, I don't care!" Clines raged, throwing up his hand and stalking across our living room, heading for the door. Again. "I'm going back to my house, gonna grab my rifle and I'm gonna go up in the hills behind Hellnick's house and pick off those fuckers one by one, I swear to God!"

"Dave, sit your ass down," Brad Torrey insisted, this time not even bothering to get up from our dining room table, nor deigning to look up from the glass of vodka I'd poured for him. "It's too damn late in the day for your hysterical bullshit."

"Hysterical bullshit?" Clines rounded on him; face flushed. "Those are fucking Pirate-World cartel heavy hitters, *Brad*! They had a proton cannon in that shuttle! I'll bet you anything they're paying Hellnick to let them store weapons out on his property!"

I rubbed at my temples.

"Jesus, Dave, stop yelling. Just have a seat. Brad is here, we're here, let's sit down and talk about what to do."

"Easy for you to say to stop yelling," Clines grumbled, falling into one of the carved wooden chairs we'd bought for an absurdly low price here on-planet. Back on Earth, harvesting wood was illegal as shit and buying pre-ban wood furniture cost more than most people made in a year. "You didn't have those assholes sticking guns in your face and threatening to take *your* property."

"And if you'd listened to me and kept quiet," I reminded him, "no one would have been threatening anything."

"What are we gonna do about this?" Vicky asked, coming back from the kitchen with a glass of milk. She was, I noted, as cool as the first snowfall. Her hand didn't shake and the surface of the milk stayed level and unbroken as she sat down beside me. "Seriously," she added, glaring at Clines. "No more talk about sniping people. For one thing, they have hoppers and they'd just hose your position down from overhead and kill you. For another, you were Fleet Security and you've never sniped a Goddamned thing in your whole life. You can barely hit a rock dragon at a hundred meters."

"Hey, now...," he began to protest, but I interrupted him.

"Dave's right, though, Hellnick is in on this. They're either threatening him or paying him. We need to contact the Corporate Council, get the CSF down here."

Clines snorted a laugh, slapping a palm on the tabletop and making Vicky's milk splash a few droplets onto its polished surface. She shot him a glare but he wasn't paying attention.

"The Corporate Security Force is a joke. They're only interested in making sure the Council's interests are looked after. They couldn't care less about us shit-kickers."

"If we try to handle this ourselves and don't call them," I pointed out, "and everything goes to shit, Hellnick is going to be the one reporting us. And we aren't going to have much of a defense, legally."

"Legally?" Clines repeated, staring at me wide-eyed. "What makes you think any of this will ever see the inside of a court?"

"We can't call the CSF yet," Torrey said. "Not until we talk to Hellnick. We need to know what he knows."

"You really think that stuck-up asshole is going to tell us anything?"

"I think we're going to give him the chance before we call the CSF *or* grab our guns and charge in shooting." Torrey pulled out his 'link and began typing a message on the screen. "I'm calling an emergency meeting of the Hausos Settlers' Board for tomorrow afternoon, and I'm sending Hellnick an invitation he damned well better not refuse." He looked up from the 'link, his smile thin and rueful. "And the only reason I didn't make it for tomorrow morning is because it already *is* tomorrow morning."

"You're welcome to sleep here, Brad," I offered. "Or I can give you a ride back to your place." We hadn't discussed how he was going to get back home when the ESP hopper had dropped him off at our house. He lived a good hour's drive from here, so I was hoping he'd agree to sleep over.

"Tell you what," he said, "why don't I sack out at Dave's place? Then I can make sure he gets to that meeting tomorrow instead of doing something stupid like going after a bunch of weapons smugglers with a damned hunting rifle?" He tilted his head toward Clines. "Is that okay with you, Dave?"

Clines looked as if he was going to debate the point, but then he checked our faces and when it became clear that neither Vicky nor I were going to support him on this, his shoulders sagged in defeat.

"Hell," he sighed, "you might as well drive. I'm so worked up, I'd probably steer us into a damned tree."

"You two be there on time tomorrow," Torrey told us, emphasizing the point with a knife-hand directed at each of us in turn. "And just like the Corps, on time means fifteen minutes early. Remember, you were both officers. Don't let this civilian farmer shit turn you into slovenly former NCO's like Dave here."

"Fuck you, Brad," Clines said, shooting him a bird as he headed out the door. "I don't know why the hell we put an officer in charge of the Settlers' Board. All you ever want to do is order people around."

"Which is why they put me in charge."

And then they were out the door. I should, if I'd been worried about being a good host, have walked them out to the porch and watched them go, but I felt drained, exhausted, as if I'd just fought a battle. I wasn't sure if it was the hour or the comedown from the adrenaline high, but I could barely move and I didn't want to think. Thinking would make me actually consider what had happened.

"You don't agree," Vicky said. It wasn't a question, but I answered it anyway.

"No, I don't."

"What do you want to do about it?"

"What I want to do," I told her, honest with her because I always was, "is pack everything up and buy tickets on the first ship out of here."

She smiled, her dark eyes piercing through me.

"And what are you *going* to do?"

"We should get to sleep," I told her. "We're going to need to get an early start."

The comms building wasn't hard to find. It was wooden shack sitting at the foot of a transmission antennae a hundred meters tall. It had seemed like a waste of resources to me the first time I'd seen it. After all, on Earth and the core colonies, there were strings of satellites to handle off-world transmissions, but this wasn't Earth, and it wasn't even one of the Periphery colonies, much less the core. Hausos was in the ass-end of nowhere and we didn't rate comm satellite strings. Instead, we got this one transmission tower in the center of our one poor excuse for a town, and if it was facing the wrong direction, well then, you waited until it was facing the *right* direction before you transmitted.

And God forbid you wanted to send a message out-system. This system didn't have a wormhole, which meant that the only way to get a message out was to store it in the communications log of an outgoing starship and pay them to transmit it in the first system they came to with an InStell ComSat.

Lucky for me, the message I was sending didn't have that far to go.

The clerk behind the front desk looked up from a scansheet as Vicky and I came through the door, clearly not happy at the interruption.

"You folks need something?" He was, I thought, not ex-military. I don't know how I could tell, but I could. He was Corporate, about as low on the ladder as it got, stuck on this backwater world, hating his life, and probably blaming us for it personally.

I shut the door behind us before I answered, pausing to take one last look behind to make sure no one was watching. A light rain fell on the street outside, barely enough to justify the jackets Vicky and I wore, but you never knew when it would cut loose.

"I want to send a message to the Corporate Council station at Eos," I told him. "To the Corporate Security Force."

The clerk gave us both the sort of look reserved for idiots who didn't know enough to come in out of the rain.

"You know you could have just sent the message to the automated systems here with your 'link, right?" He gestured at a bank of servers sitting in the corner of the shack. He'd left an insulated drink cup sitting precariously balanced on the edge of one of them. "I mean, I don't even come in here half the time. No one ever comes in this place."

"I don't *want* to send it over my 'link," I told him. I dug in my pocket and fished out a Tradenote, tossing it down on the counter. The clerk's eyes widened slightly and he covered the plastic chit with his hand, sliding it off the surface of the desk and into his pocket. I fought back a wince. Tradenotes weren't easy to come by out here. "I don't want there to be a record of this in your outgoing logs. *Comprenes*?"

"Yeah, sure," he said. He reached back onto the server stack and slid a folding tablet out from beneath a pile of what looked like dirty T-shirts, tossing it onto the countertop in front of me. "You can write the message yourself if you want. I'll just go back here and finish my breakfast."

If Vicky's glare was a laser, the clerk would have been a pile of ash on the floor, but I didn't care if he was lazy. Lazy was good at the moment. It took me ten minutes to figure out the menu system in the tablet, then another ten to reach the address for the Corporate Security Force message system and by the end, I was beginning to side with Vicky's assessment of the man.

Once I actually had the message form on the screen, I paused, thinking one last time about what I should say. I'd considered it all the way into town, from the morning hopper flight right up till the walk downtown. Would Torrey and Clines miss us at the noon flight? We'd already cooked up a story about wanting to do some shopping, but the problem was, I was a shitty liar.

I shook the worry away, coming back to the message.

To: Corporate Security Force local director

From: Lt. Cameron Alvarez and Lt. Victoria Sandoval, Commonwealth Marine Corps (retired)

Subject: Criminal activity on the Hausos settlement

Message Body: Illegal weapons smugglers have taken up residence at the Hellnick farm. Have seen at least one proton cannon and know they have much more cached at the property. They have multiple cargo shuttles and an unknown number of starships in orbit. We need enforcement support immediately. Known parties are a Captain Eld and a Tahni former infantry colonel named Zan-Thint. Recommend you contact Commonwealth law enforcement.

It was short and to the point, and the part of me that had been trained as an officer who loved nothing more than to add one report on top of another wondered if I should have added another four paragraphs of detail, including descriptions of everyone I could remember, but I was dealing with Corporate Council types here, people who could ignore memos from unimportant schmucks like a farmer colonist. Better to keep it short and make sure someone read it from beginning to end.

I touched the send button, then closed the tab and folded the tablet. I shrugged at the questioning look from Vicky.

"I don't know," I admitted. "Dave could be right. They might not even bother to read it, and even if they believe it, they might not give a shit."

"But you're right, too," she told me, pulling me along out the door, back into the petulant, nagging sprinkle of rain, spitting just infrequently enough that I couldn't justify raising the hood on my rain jacket.

I walked quickly, trying to get away from the transmission shack before anyone we knew spotted us there. The streets weren't quite deserted, but there was no one coming our way, much less paying attention to us. I knew I was being paranoid, but it was the only mindset my life experience had prepared me for, so I thought I might as well go with it.

"Brad thinks we can handle this internally," she went on, her voice low enough no one else could have heard it without stepping between us, "but that's just because he's in charge of the Board and doesn't want to admit it's too big for him. This isn't the military, no matter what Brad says, and we don't have air or orbital support. Hell, I doubt anyone on the Board even owns a handgun, much less any heavy weapons."

There were, I noticed, none of the strangers on the street this morning. Every face I saw was, if not familiar, then at least not out of place. The workers, the shop owners, the cargo truck drivers for hire waiting on the farmers to come to town and arrange a pickup, they all belonged in Gamma Junction. I hadn't seen any shuttles on the landing field during the flight in, and I wondered if that meant Eld and his people had relocated them to Hellnick's property or if they'd just vacated the planet altogether. I assumed they had a ship in orbit, so maybe they'd taken it back to wherever they were buying or stealing their weapons.

"They're not around," I mentioned to Vicky. "Maybe what happened last night spooked them. Maybe they'll pull in their horns and lay low for a while and hope we forget about them."

"You dealt with gangs just as much as I did when you were a kid," Vicky said, shaking her head. "Does that sound like the way they'd react to a bunch of self-important locals challenging their authority?"

"No, it doesn't," I admitted. "But it'd be real nice to be wrong one of these times, wouldn't it?"

"We did what we could. Let's grab breakfast at Torrentinto's Place. I could go for one of her Southwest omelets."

"Sure." I offered her my arm and she slipped hers through it. "Then we get to watch the show."

[7]

"Where the hell have you guys been?" Dave Clines demanded; arms spread like we'd stood him up for a date.

The acoustics of the meeting hall were well engineered, designed so that the board meetings could be held without the use of sophisticated electronics, which we could have afforded to buy anywhere else but couldn't afford to have shipped out here to the middle of nowhere. So Clines' booming voice wasn't just his normal slightly-too-loud-to-be-polite, it was enough to echo throughout the hollow building and make several heads turn from the tables arrayed in a semicircle around the central podium.

Vicky's face had homicide written all over it, so I quickly stepped in.

"We left early to get breakfast at Ms. Torrentinto's. We didn't know how long this was going to take and we wanted to start out on a full stomach." Which had the advantage of being partly true in case anyone checked on it.

"Dave Clines," the woman sitting next to Brad Torrey said, eyeing the bluff, loud farmer with the eye of a disapproving mother, "you need to find yourself a wife. You've been living on that farm alone for a year and it's turned you into a braying jackass."

"He didn't have far to go," Vicky said, then shot the woman a smile. "Good afternoon, Kayla. Brad."

Kayla Gruhl was an odd match for Brad Torrey, homey and domestic and seemingly made for farm life. From what we knew of her, which wasn't much, she'd grown up on Hermes, and had been happy to leave at the end of the war because the place was "getting too damned crowded," in her words. She had a plain, open face suited for this world, and her only prepossessing feature was flaming red hair, though I didn't know if it was natural, affected or genetically selected by her parents.

"Howdy you two," she said, smiling as she shook our hands, her grip dry and firm as always. "I don't blame you for getting some grub first. God knows I'm not looking forward to this, whether or not Hellnick decides to show up."

"How the hell am I gonna find a wife way out here?" Clines asked plaintively, sitting at the other end of the table from Torrey and his wife. "It ain't like this place has a booming nightlife or anything. I got that one girl I been exchanging videos with over in the Elektra system, but she's got her own farm and she ain't gonna give it up to come here."

"You could always move there," Torrey suggested, with more than a little malice aforethought, I judged. "I hear Corona has a very nice climate and a settling bonus for anyone who emigrates."

"Gee, thanks, Captain Torrey," Clines sneered. "I tell you what, if this shit keeps up with Hellnick, I will give it some fucking thought."

"Language, Mr. Clines," Kayla said archly. "This is an official meeting."

"And it's almost time to start," Torrey added, checking his 'link, then scanning the crowd.

They were a thorough shuffling of the colonist population here, with most of us farmers in work clothes, while the shopkeepers and tradespeople had worn fancier garb since they were closer to home. This wasn't an economy large or diverse enough to warrant bankers or retail sales, so there were no business suits in evidence, though Torrey had broken out a dress shirt to go with his blue jeans and work boots. I recognized them all, of course, not only because I'd done business with them on a monthly basis over the last year, but also because Torrey liked to have these Board meetings way too often.

"Damn," Clines murmured, resting his chin on his fist, his elbow on the table. "Guess Hellnick didn't show up. Who coulda guessed that? Oh yeah, *me*."

"I suppose I'll have to convene things anyway," Torrey said with a sigh. "I'd give the man more time, but everyone's got work to do with the harvest and there isn't time to wait all day for him."

He strode purposefully toward the central podium and picked up the gavel he'd had fabricated specifically for this purpose.

"I bet he sleeps with it," Vicky whispered close to my ear and it was all I could do to keep from busting out a sharp laugh.

The flat of the gavel's head smacked into the wooden circle mounted on the top of the podium and the general buzz in the chamber died down to a low mumble. Torrey nodded, turning back and forth like a sensor dish to meet everyone's eyes.

"Good afternoon members of the Settlers' Board of the Hausos Colony," he intoned with the gravity of a chaplain at a memorial service. Above, the rain finally cut loose and his voice had to compete for attention with the insistent pattering on the sheet-metal roofing. "Welcome to the sixty-first official meeting of the board."

"Oh, my God, I can't believe he knew that," Clines said, *sotto voce.*

"We are here today to address a problem some of you have already seen first-hand last night. For the rest of you, let me summarize."

And he did, though Torrey's idea of a summary took longer than the actual events, and by the end, I was wondering if I had time for a bathroom break. Those who hadn't actually lived through the incident seemed appropriately worried, though, given the undertone of murmuring in the room, a rainstorm rising from below to rival the one attacking the roof.

"Where's Hellnick?" I couldn't see who'd yelled the question, but it sounded as if it had come from the table where the Kim family sat, the owners of one of the two industrial fabricators in Gamma Junction. "Why isn't he here to answer for this?"

Yeah, it was Grace Kim. She was short and couldn't have topped fifty kilos soaking wet, but she'd been a Force Recon Marine and you didn't want to fuck with her. Her husband was a good twenty centimeters taller than her and forty kilos heavier and yet rarely said a word in the company of his wife. The pair had two children, both born since the war, and they were remarkably well-behaved for a toddler and an infant, as if they, too, were scared of Grace Kim.

Someone wasn't scared of her, though.

"Who the hell are you to demand Klaus Hellnick appear?" The woman was skinny and drawn out, her skin the color and consistency of old leather. Melina Pappas was one of the civilians, the refugees, washed up on this place after the war, not choosing the voluntary exile as we veterans had, but being dropped here because their homes were too badly damaged in the war to make them worth rebuilding. "You think you're our commander, Brad Torrey, but you only hold the authority we give you!"

"Do you have a motion you'd like to make, Ms. Pappas?" Torrey asked her, strained patience dripping off the words. She responded by shooting him a bird and he grunted a humorless laugh. "In that case...." He turned his attention back to Grace Kim. "I sent a notice to Mr. Hellnick. If he hasn't shown up, I have to assume he either has chosen to ignore the authority of the Board, or perhaps he's under duress and this Captain Eld and the Tahni involved have him captive. If that's the case...."

The double doors slammed open with a sudden spray of cold rain and Klaus Hellnick stepped through.

If a weasel and a lizard jumped into a gene sequencer while a Corporate Council executive was having their offspring designed, Klaus Hellnick is what would have come out of the artificial womb. The man had a face so narrow, I wasn't sure how there was room for a full set of teeth in those jaws unless they were narrow, lizard teeth, and the fact the man incessantly licked his lips only helped with the image. He wasn't a tall man, nor overly broad, but he wasn't a weakling. You didn't make a living out here on Hausos if you were a weakling, even with the autoharvesters

He didn't bring any family with him because he didn't have any. He'd lost his wife and children to the Tahni on Demeter, or so Vicky had heard. Even though the colony there was being rebuilt, he'd felt like he couldn't stay behind with the memories, so he'd come here at the end of the war, before the Tahni Emperor's corpse was even cold, becoming one of the first settlers. And yet, his farm didn't even produce as much as ours and unlike Clines, he didn't hire workers from town to supplement his own efforts, just sat on his farm all alone. Until now.

He didn't enter the meeting hall with his family, but neither did he enter alone. Filing in behind him were Captain Eld and a half a dozen of his people, every one of them visibly armed. The fact their handguns were holstered didn't do anything to make them look less threatening, and I scooted my chair back from the table, ready to leap either in escape or attack, whichever seemed like the better idea.

"You called for me," Klaus Hellnick declared, pitching his voice to carry across the room, "and I came."

"Who are these people?" Grace Kim asked without the slightest hint of fear, shooting to her feet—though, at her height, it wasn't easy to tell the difference. "Why have you brought armed thugs into our meeting?"

"Grace," Harold Kim said softly but firmly, shocking me. He put a hand on her arm. "Be at ease." He nodded toward their children, the toddler sitting on the floor playing with a tablet, the baby still asleep in a portable crib.

She looked as if she wanted to snap back at him, but she looked at her son and daughter and nodded, sitting down.

"I am Iain Eld," the smuggler captain declared, stepping into the center of the tables, his people spreading out around him. Hellnick pulled a chair out at an otherwise empty table and sat, the look on his face insufferably smug. "And I understand the good people here have some concerns about my business interests."

Brad Torrey stayed stock-still at the podium, staring at Eld the way a bull bison might stare at a grizzly bear, challenging, not showing fear but wary all the same.

"This meeting is by invitation only," Torrey said, his voice showing no sign of panic.

"I invited him," Hellnick snapped, waving a hand in a dismissive gesture. "Let him talk. He has an offer for all of you."

Torrey chewed on the decision for a long moment, then backed away from the podium, hands on his hips.

"Go ahead."

Eld nodded to him, the half-smile creasing his dark beard a sign of how amusing he found Torrey's bravado.

"I'm not going to bullshit you," Eld told us, letting his gaze linger on our table, on Clines and Vicky and me. "We're not gathering toys for a Christmas giveaway for wayward children." His people laughed at the joke, but none of us did. "We're smugglers. Criminals, not to put too fine a point on it. But we're not marauders and we're not here to hurt anyone. I'm a businessman, not a pirate." He shrugged, an expressive motion that used his whole body, like a theater actor. "My people go armed not because we mean you any harm but because we engage in activities frowned upon by the government, and thus are unable to call on outside help when threatened. If anyone decides to take what we have, we're on our own."

"We're all on our own out here," I told him, standing from the table slowly, hands at my side, trying not to look threatening to all those armed 'businesspeople.' It went against my instincts to speak up and paint a target on myself, but he already knew me, knew my name, knew where I lived. "Which would be the reason you chose this place, no?"

"It is," he admitted, pointing a finger at me, "Lt. Alvarez, right? The bottom line is, the end of the war has opened up a lot of new markets, and my aim is to be the first to exploit them. That requires us to locate new bases of operation. We're not looking to run the show here or anything. We just made a business arrangement with Mr. Hellnick here to use his property for storage of goods that we will eventually move out to sell elsewhere. We anticipated this might, eventually, draw some attention, but we hadn't counted on the technical issue we had with our cargo shuttle."

"Reactor flush," I guessed. "Probably a bad coolant valve, and then a structural failure from metal fatigue on the vent line."

"Were you a shuttle mechanic as well as a Drop Trooper, Lt. Alvarez?" he asked, eyebrow arching toward me.

"Let's just say, when you're spending a lot of time flying around in a fusion-powered heavy-lift shuttle, you become aware real fast of all the ways they can fall out of the sky."

"I bet you do." He smiled thinly. "And yes, our mechanics think it was a bad coolant valve. And it was unfortunate not just because it's going to cost us time and money to fix, but also because of the spectacle it caused. It pushed ahead our timetable of making some sort of arrangement with the town and the other settlers the same way we have with Mr. Hellnick."

"You mean," I interpreted, "you want to pay us to look the other way while you store illegal, probably stolen goods on this planet."

"And you should care about the legality of it why, exactly?" he asked me. "If I remember correctly from last night, didn't you mention that you used to make a living on the wrong side of the law?"

"And look where that wound me up. Last time, I ended up facing punitive hibernation or joining the Marines. No war going on this time. What's to keep all of us from getting our asses slapped by the Man when this all comes out?"

"Who's to say it ever has to come out?"

"Oh, come on, Captain Eld." I snorted my skepticism. "I never went to college, never went to the Military Academy, but even in the abbreviated academic courses I took for OCS, I learned a bunch of really useful, scholarly-sounding quotations from famous people. You might not know who Benjamin Franklin was, but he said a shitload of really pithy, memorably things way back like 500 years ago or something. And one of the truest things he ever said was, 'three can keep a secret if two of them are dead.' There's a lot more than three of us here, and eventually, someone's going to talk."

"You're a lot smarter than you look, Alvarez." He shook his head, shaking his finger in my direction. "It's easy to forget, to think of all of you as dumbass Marines, but you're not. And you're right, someone is going to talk. But there's a difference between *saying* something and *proving* something. None of you are going to see what we're storing at Mr. Hellnick's except Mr. Hellnick, and he has a vested interest in keeping his damn mouth shut. And by the time any authorities might catch wind of this and decide they care enough to send an investigator out here, which, trust me, will take months at a minimum, everything we've brought here will be moved out and headed for a buyer."

"How much?"

It was Pappas again, no surprise. The woman had frequently been the loudest voice at the meetings, though not the most influential. The civilians outnumbered the vets here, but Torrey and the rest of us had usually been able to sway enough of them to our side of most issues. Never her, though.

"You keep talking about the stick," she said, rising from her seat, arms folded across her chest. "What about the carrot? You want us to be your shills, what's the pay?"

There were a lot of objections, some of them shouted, but Eld waved them down and his people took a couple steps forward to reinforce the order.

"A thousand a month for every member of the board," he told her. "Paid in Tradenotes. Physical, untraceable."

I shaped a silent whistle. It wasn't enough to make any of us rich, of course, but Tradenotes had the advantage of being accepted everywhere and for the same exchange rate, while Corporate scrip or Commonwealth dollars were slaves to the vagaries of an interstellar economy I didn't pretend to understand and were only accepted in these parts by the Corporate Council Marketplace. And like most company stores in the history I'd studied, the Marketplace was overpriced and understocked and mostly designed to peel away as much of a vet's separation bonus as they could. If we had a thousand Tradenotes, we could have ordered a new autoharvester from an independent shipper for half the price of getting one through the Marketplace.

And unlike money we made from selling our output on the open market, the Tradenotes weren't taxable.

"If you agree to this," Eld stressed, "you would all be bound by it. There'd be no backing out."

"This is ridiculous!" Clines exploded. He'd looked like he was about to pop a cork the whole time Eld had been speaking and I guess he couldn't keep it in anymore. He popped up from the table suddenly enough to make two of Eld's armed escort reach for their guns. "There's no fucking way we're going to take money from weapons smugglers! God alone knows what they're going to do with those guns! They could kill innocent people and the blood would be on our hands!"

Eld's eyes narrowed and I wanted to curse Dave Clines for his inability to keep from mouthing off, but I shrugged the concern away. Torrey had announced what we'd seen to the gathered meeting, and if Eld hadn't found out from Clines, he would have found out from one of Hellnick's civilian allies. Still, I gave him a dirty look on general principles.

"That ain't up to you!" Pappas yelled. "We gotta vote on it! You veterans don't tell us what to do!"

"This has nothing to do with us being veterans or not," Torrey said, taking Clines' side for once. "This has to do with putting ourselves in danger of being prosecuted, of involving ourselves with criminals. Do you seriously expect us to vote to do this?"

"What I expect, Mr. Torrey," Eld said, all of his hail-fellow-well-met gone as he took a step toward the man, somehow towering over him despite the fact he was only a couple centimeters taller, "is that you'll all do the *smart* thing. Because the alternative is not going to be pleasant."

A crack as loud as a gunshot echoed from the other side of the room and I ducked instinctively, my head snapping around, but it had been Klaus Hellnick smacking his palm flat on the table.

"Enough bullshit! I call for a vote!"

"This isn't right," Torrey declared, shoulders tensing as if he were about to do something stupid. I shared a look with Vicky, wondering if we were the only sane people in the room, or at least the only ones who realized the damage seven bad guys with guns could do to a roomful of unarmed farmers and shopkeepers, even if at least a third of them were combat veterans.

"Brad," I said and his gaze flickered my way for just half a second, as if he was afraid to look away from Eld. "Let them vote. Use your head, man. What do you hope to accomplish here?"

He glared at me, but Kayla touched his hand and drew his attention down to her. She shook her head and the wind went out of Torrey, deflating him like a popped balloon.

"Fine." He pulled out a chair and fell into it, as if he refused to be part of counting the vote even if he was going to allow it to happen.

"I'll take the damned vote myself," Hellnick said, walking up to the podium, shooting Eld a smile rife with satisfaction, as if this was exactly what he'd told the captain would happen. "All right, break out your 'links...," he began, pulling his own off his belt. But then he paused, his smile growing broader. "Oh, the hell with that. We'll do it the old-fashioned way. Show of hands. All in favor of taking Captain Eld's generous deal, getting a nice payday, which is a huge fucking change from the shit money the Corporate Council gives us the chance to earn with all their tariffs for trading off-planet, and all we gotta do is keep our mouths shut, raise your hand."

He stuck his own arm up as if to show everyone what he meant, just in case we were all too stupid to remember which body parts were which. And unfortunately, but predictably, the civilians voted with him, even the ones whose votes Torrey was usually able to swing. So did a large percentage of the veterans, which depressed me but didn't surprise me. There were families here and not a one of them considered upholding the law a more important thing than protecting their kids and their livelihood. And all the mean-looking criminals with weapons were a bit more convincing than appeals to civic duty.

"I don't think we need to count those opposed," Hellnick said, aiming a sneer at Torrey. "Motion carried. You can all thank me later, when you actually have the money to make these stinking shithole farms profitable."

Eld motioned to his people and they moved toward the exit, eyeing us all carefully, as if they thought we'd jump them on the way out.

"Good afternoon, ladies and gentlemen," Eld said, tossing us a mock salute on his way out the door back into the rain. "It was a pleasure doing business with you."

[8]

"None of this makes a damn bit of sense," Dave Clines said, but I shushed him with a gesture and motioned for the others to follow me.

Most of the board was still engaged in a heated argument, those vets who had opposed the vote screaming in the faces of the ones who had supported it, and I was afraid things were going to get ugly. I decided I'd rather get wet than get in the middle of a three-way fistfight.

The rain, as it turned out, had died down in the aftermath of the vote and I threw back my hood, breathing in the fresh, ozone tang of the storm, blinking as an errant drop of rain hit my eye. A peal of thunder rolled across the plains outside Gamma Junction, the vibration rattling the walls of the meeting hall behind us. The streets outside the meeting hall were empty, the storm having chased everyone inside, which gave us a great opportunity to get the hell away.

Vicky said nothing, watching behind us while I scanned the front, making sure Eld and his people hadn't stuck around. Clines seemed to take the hint and fell into a wedge formation with us, Brad Torrey, and Kayla Gruhl, which would have been more impressive and effective if any of us had been armed with anything deadlier than a belt knife. I led the group around the corner past a storage building and then into an alley between the warehouse and a fabrication center, stopping behind the cover of a few discarded plastic cargo totes waiting to be recycled into something useful.

"You were about to tell us all," I reminded Clines, "how none of this shit made any sense. And I was about to agree with you."

"Well, it doesn't!" he said, throwing up his hands, and I made a quelling gesture to get him to tone it down. "What Eld said in there is bullshit, man!"

"Why?" Torrey demanded, sounding as upset as Clines, though more confused. "It sounded pretty straightforward to me."

"Because look where we *are*, Brad!" Clines made an expansive gesture. "Eld is peddling this idea that he and his people are storing weapons here because of new markets that have opened up since the war. But markets *where?* There's nothing out here except the Forbidden Zone, and who the hell needs proton cannons when there's no one in the system but a few farmers and some Corporate Council gas miners?"

"The Tahni," Vicky suggested. She'd planted her back against the fabrication shop wall and her fingers were clenching and unclenching as if she expected someone to come after us here. "Maybe that's what that Zan-Thint guy is really doing here. Maybe he's trying to start some terrorist group to try to attack the occupation and Eld is getting him the guns."

"Maybe," I said, already shaking my head, "but something about that just doesn't feel right. There are still Tahni colonies out there. Hell, there's still a Tahni settlement on Brigantia, even after we took it back, they still live there. If they're going to set up some sort of resistance, wouldn't they store the weapons somewhere with a Tahni population? What's the point in storing everything out here? The Transition Lines outward only lead to Forbidden Zone systems and the only route inward goes through the Tahni home system. Just getting the weapons here is taking a huge risk."

"Then what do you think their plan is, Cameron?" Kayla asked, remarkably unfazed by all this.

"I don't know that. I just know they're lying to us."

"We can't just let them keep doing this shit," Clines said. "Whatever they mean to do, I don't believe for one second they intend to just pay us to look the other way and then get out and leave us alone in a couple months."

"What do you think we should do?" Torrey asked me.

I frowned. Him asking me for advice was about as rare as a First Sergeant who didn't like PMCS. I searched his grey eyes, wondering if he was only asking so he could shoot down whatever idea I came up with, but he seemed honestly concerned. I looked to Vicky for advice and she nodded.

"Before the meeting," I confided, "I went ahead and sent a message to the Corporate Security Force out at Eos. I told them what was going on and advised them to contact the Commonwealth." I shrugged. "Whether that means the Patrol or the military is up to them."

"I suppose," Torrey said, one eyebrow going up, "that I should be angry with you for ignoring my decision about that, but given what's happened, I suppose you were right and I was wrong."

"I know one thing," I told him, "sure as shit, the first place Eld went after the meeting was probably the comm shack to lock down any messages going out of here." I shrugged. "We just have to hope our call went out before he did."

"You really think the Corporates are going to do a damned thing?" Clines demanded, still way too loud. "Hellnick was right about one thing, man, the Corporates don't give a shit about us. They stuck us here to do their dirty work and the only thing they care about is skimming their tariffs."

"Give it some time, Dave," Vicky urged him. "Maybe you're right, maybe they won't help, but we have to give it a chance. It could save lives."

"Don't do anything foolish, David," Kayla said, touching a finger to his shoulder as if the motion would restrain him.

"Yeah, yeah, I'm the idiot," Clines waved off our caution, scowling. "I'm the drunk, the loudmouth. I know what you guys think. But you listen to what I'm saying, we do *not* have the time to wait for the Corporates or anyone else to save our asses. Do you think this guy Eld and his Tahni buddy are gonna hang around and see if everyone just plays along and behaves?"

"No," I admitted. "But what's the alternative?"

"I'll tell you the fucking alternative." Clines stepped so close to me that I could smell the must off his old raincoat, still damp from the earlier storm. "You and me, Vicky and Brad sneak over the property line and record some hard evidence against these guys, find out what they're *really* up to. Then we show it to the vets on the board and convince the stupid bastards to get off their asses, and do something while we still can."

"We don't have any real weapons," Torrey reminded him.

"We can *make* them! If we do it now, before Eld and his people clamp down on everything and take control of the fabricators. We can make just as good as they have, at least what we saw last night."

"He's right about that," I admitted. "We can even fab the ammo."

"You're getting behind this, Alvarez?" Torrey asked me, squaring off as if he was getting ready to challenge me in the hand-to-hand ring. "That's crazy! We have no idea how many of them there are!"

"No, we don't." I met his defiant grey stare unblinking. "Which is why we should probably do exactly what Dave suggested and recon the enemy forces." He opened his mouth to object and I raised a hand to forestall it. "Yeah, I know, we don't have the guns made yet and organizing everyone without alerting the...," I trailed off, scowling. "Well, the *pirates*, or smugglers, or whatever they are is going to be tricky. But we're not going to accomplish anything sitting in our houses and hoping they leave us alone, either. If the CSF comes and helps us out, then maybe we don't have to take care of this ourselves, but we can't assume that's gonna happen."

I saw the doubt in Kayla's face and I knew without even asking that Torrey wouldn't be coming along. I wanted to argue with him, wanted to try to talk him into it, because he'd been Force Recon and I had about two days' worth of experience fighting outside my battlesuit. But for all that Kayla Gruhl hadn't been in the military and had never been more than a farmer, she was Torrey's commanding officer as sure as if she'd worn stars.

"Okay, I'll tell you what," I suggested, "Dave, Vicky, and I will go scout out their operation tonight. It's supposed to rain, which should cover our approach. We'll just try to get close enough to see what their operation looks like, how many people they have, whether or not they have any heavy weapons. Get some video on our 'links. While we do that, you stay here and talk to Jed and Riley Martinez, see if you can get them to start turning out Gyroc carbines."

"If they don't have the pattern," Clines offered, "I got it saved on my 'link."

"You do?" Vicky asked him, eyes growing wider.

"Doesn't everybody?"

"All right," Torrey said, sounding relieved. "You guys be careful. In and out, don't look for trouble."

"Us, look for trouble?" Vicky said, putting a hand on my shoulder. "Never."

"You know," Vicky told me, running a finger down the stock of the hunting rifle, "I promised myself after we got out that I'd never fire a weapon again."

I turned from stuffing supplies into my backpack and gaped at her.

"You did? You never told me that."

"I didn't think it would come up," she admitted. "I mean, look where we are."

We were in our bedroom, but I knew what she meant. This world wasn't just isolated, wasn't just sparsely-populated, it had been empty. Not a single sentient being had ever lived here before the end of the war, so far as we knew.

"I'm sorry."

"Wasn't your doing, Cam." She smiled wanly. "Maybe it's just fate." She jerked back the bolt of the weapon, locking it open, then inserted the five-round magazine and hit the release to let the action strip off the first round and load it into the chamber. The sound reminded me of the chest plastron of a Vigilante battlesuit swinging closed. "Or maybe it's the only damned thing either of us has ever really been good at."

"You guys ready?" Clines called from the living room.

I fastened the backpack's main compartment, stuffed with water, food, spare clothes, and ammunition, then slung it over my shoulder and grabbed my own rifle.

"Coming."

Clines was decked out like a cut-rate commando, wearing dark utility fatigues, a balaclava, and a tactical vest. He'd also come up with a big, primitive-looking stamped metal handgun from somewhere and carried it holstered at his right hip, his hunting rifle held in the crook of his right arm.

The two of us were just in regular, grey work coveralls, though I'd found a knit cap somewhere in my leftover snivel gear from Hachiman that I'd bought on my own tab and not turned in at the end of my term of service.

"You look ridiculous," Vicky told Clines. "This is supposed to be a recon, not a commando raid. Part of our plausible deniability is that we're just farmers hunting down some livestock that got taken by rock dragons. They take one look at you and they'll know exactly what we're up to."

"They'd know anyway," he insisted.

"He's probably right," I acknowledged. "Our best bet is to not get caught." Vicky looked as if she wanted to disagree, but she didn't say anything, so I went on. "What's the plan?"

It felt as if I was back in the Drop Troops, quizzing my platoon before a mission, but it was just as important now as it had been then, and for the same reasons.

"We're taking the northern boundary path up the edge of my property to that canyon that stretches out over Hellnick's land," Clines said, repeating the details we'd gone over twice already. "We drop the rover at the mouth of the canyon and go the rest of the way in on foot."

"Eight klicks," Vicky added, not sounding happy about it. Well, neither was I, but it was either that or risk taking the rover on one of the broader dirt roads and hoping Eld and his crew didn't have security sensors looking for approaching vehicles. The three of us might escape notice, since they'd have to adjust the settings to keep from springing alarms every time a rock dragon crossed onto Hellnick's property.

"And?" I prompted.

"We take the canyon in past his property line," he went on, peeling off his balaclava and tilting his head to the side to show

how ridiculous he thought it was that I was making him recite this like a kid in class. "We come out in that draw about two klicks from his house and high-crawl up until the cover ends and see what we can see from there. If we need to go closer, we low-crawl slow and quiet. And we record everything with our 'links."

"And the most important part?" Vicky asked him. Clines glowered at her, but still answered obediently.

"The most important part is that we don't get spotted and don't engage. We need intelligence and we need evidence, and that's the only reason we're there."

"You're goddamn right it is, Dave. I don't want you thinking you're some kind of spec ops hero and trying to take someone out with a knife in the night. None of us were trained in how to do that shit."

"I got it, Vick." He stuffed the balaclava in a hip pocket. "Can we get going now? It's already gonna be tricky enough making it back to the canyon before sunup."

"He's right about that," I said, heading for the door. "Let's get this over with."

"I wish Brad would have come," Vicky murmured, her voice almost lost against the patter of the steady rain against the porch roof. I pulled up my hood before I stepped off into the centimeter-deep puddle at the bottom of our steps. "Maybe we should have tried recruiting another of the Force Recon guys. Henrietta Taggert might have been up for it."

I shook my head then realized she couldn't see it under my hood.

"No," I told her. "The more people who know, the more people who could flap their gums about it." I hesitated to say the next bit, opening the driver's door of our rover, and sliding inside to put it off. "I kind of wish we hadn't even told Brad and Kayla."

"Why?" she asked, blinking either at what I'd said or maybe the raindrops dripping down into her face as she threw back the hood of her rain jacket. "Don't you trust them?"

"Brad, sure. But Kayla was never military and she probably has never even heard the term 'op-sec.' If they go talking to the fabricator shop about making the guns, she might let slip what we're doing."

The back door slammed shut as Clines got in, shaking off the excess rain like a dog.

"Damned civilians," he added. "You can't count on any of them. I can't believe they voted to take Eld's money. I'd just as soon trust a rock dragon to guard my goat herd."

"They're mostly people who lost their homes in the war," I reminded him. "Most of them lost their families, their friends... you can't expect them to turn into some kind of militia and fight a hardened group of criminals."

"Why not?" he demanded, his voice breaking in the middle as I pulled away from the house, throwing him back against the seat. "That's what the people did on Brigantia. You were there, right? You saw what the militia there did against the Tahni."

"I did." I didn't look back at him, eyes fixed on the dark road ahead, lit only by the rover's headlamps and the occasional flash of lightning. "And a lot of them wound up dead."

He didn't reply to that, and I was glad of it. We drove in silence into the night.

[9]

"This is it."

I let off the accelerator and the rover drifted to a stop, its tires squelching softly in the thin coating of mud over the sandstone. I switched off the headlights and the glow outside the windscreen faded to nothing. I felt a pang of longing in my gut for the higher-end models I could have bought with night vision filters built into the Heads-Up Display. Vicky and I had decided they weren't worth the extra money, since we were only using the things for farming and wouldn't be skulking around in the dark,

Ha.

"How can you tell where the hell we are?" Vicky wondered, squinting into the sameness of the night. "This bit of black looks exactly like every other bit of black to me."

I had to agree. I couldn't see the canyon, could barely make out the line of slightly-darker blackness on the horizon that was the mountains. The rain had died down to a sprinkle and the lower clouds had passed on, but there was still a layer of grey in the sky between us and the moons.

"It's my property," Clines said, popping open his door and

stepping out, switching on his flashlight. "I know my property."

I couldn't argue with that.

"I hope they don't see the flashlights," I worried, flicking on my own with more than a bit of trepidation.

"They won't from here," he assured me. "Not unless they have spy drones up. But if they do, we're fucked anyway, so we may as well assume they don't."

In the glow of the flashlights, I could finally see the mouth of the canyon. Half of it anyway. It was wide at this end, though I knew it narrowed drastically just a few hundred meters in. From where we stood, it was a sloping cliff of sandstone on the left, rivulets of run-off water trickling down the center, carrying with them debris from farther up. You had to watch canyons like this, because if there was rain farther up in the mountains, you could get a flash flood that would run you down.

We had fairly good weather data and it said that the rain was localized, but I still felt a hint of anxiety as I stepped into the flattest part of the canyon floor. Clines and I held the lights while Vicky kept her rifle at the ready, though Clines did draw that big hogleg of a pistol.

"Where the hell did you get that thing, anyway?" I asked him, glancing aside at the gun as the glow of the flashlights glinted off of its flat, metal side.

"Won it in a card game with an independent freighter jock six months ago," he said, shrugging. "It ain't much, just an old internal propellant slug shooter, 10mm I think it is. He only had about fifty rounds of ammo for it, and I never got around to having any more fabricated."

"Have you ever shot it?" Vicky wondered.

"One time. Knocked a couple watermelons off a fencepost at ten meters."

"Great."

We fell silent, not because they would have heard us out

here but more from a sense of claustrophobia as the walls quite literally closed in around us. The layers of the canyon were a textbook on local geology, but I lacked the training to read it. I couldn't have told you whether the canyon had been formed by water, by the freeze-and-thaw cycle of winter and summer, or a freaking laser boring machine. All I knew was that the sides were getting closer, going from nearly sixty meters apart when we entered down to less than five.

Every shadow seemed to hide a rock dragon, or a barb-cat, or a Tahni and I found myself jerking the beam from my flashlight left and right in furtive, haunted motions until I put a concerted effort into controlling my breath and my paranoia. This wasn't my element, not the terrain nor the tactics. It could have been. If a traumatic childhood experience and a life lived in the roofed-over confines of the Underground hadn't left me with a monstrous case of agoraphobia, I could have been a Force Recon Marine instead of a Drop Trooper.

And then I wouldn't have met Vicky, wouldn't have served under Captain Covington, wouldn't have lived through Brigantia. Just one little quirk of my tortured psyche, but it had changed my whole life. For the better. Because despite everything, despite the people I'd lost—Maria and Scotty, Henckel and Captain Covington, and Delp—the version of me that had come out the other side of that was still a better one than I'd had any right to hope for.

The reverie had calmed me down and while there still might have been lingering threats in the dark recesses of the canyon, I at least wasn't inventing them from whole cloth. The rain began again, not as hard as it had been earlier in the day, but steady and relentless, spattering against the fabric of my hood, soaking the lower legs of my coveralls. I didn't mind it, despite the discomfort. The sound of it covered our own footsteps, gave me the illusion of invisibility.

And the regular rhythm hypnotized me, making the interminable hike seem to pass by in-between one blink of an eye and the next, six kilometers and well over two hours fading into some trackless niche of my memory. And before I realized how far we'd come, Clines was putting a hand on my arm, leaning in to whisper to me.

"We're on Hellnick's property now," he said, the words barely audible. "The draw's up ahead on the right. I think it's where a stream from the mountains fed into the river that cut this canyon."

I would have been embarrassed that Clines knew more about the geology of the place than I did, but then again, it was his land, not mine. I motioned to Vicky that we were going to be exiting the canyon to the right, then followed Clines.

The fork in the path was so sharp that it could have been cut by the notional laser boring machine I'd posited in my scientific ignorance, leaving a ridge of granite and sandstone I might have cut myself on had I run into it. The ground changed consistency beneath us, going from hardened sandstone to softer sand, sodden with the rain and slick beneath the soles of my boots. It headed upward, gradually at first but then at a steeper angle until I had to dig the toe of my boot into the side of the path and my quadriceps burned with the strain of climbing the hill.

It seemed we were getting close to the crest of the rise when Clines waved at me to get my attention and made a show of switching off his flashlight. I took the hint and shut mine off as well, tucking it into a pocket of my jacket. Utter blackness descended over all three of us for the space of a few seconds until my eyes began to adjust to the darkness. I would have killed for some night-vision gear, even as much as the cheap, fragile civilian goggles not much thicker than sunglasses, but that was just another one of the things we'd decided not to spend money on.

But I could see. Not well, not clearly, yet, but as my eyes grew accustomed to the night, I realized there was a background glow coming from over the rise, giving some definition to the shadows around me. It had to be coming from Hellnick's place, or maybe the landing field where the shuttles came in. We were close. And we hadn't been found out yet, which was more than we'd had a right to hope for. Sure, it wasn't outlandish to think this route might not be watched. After all, even if the smugglers had spy drones, there was a *lot* or property to watch, and they'd direct most of their attention to the roads. But we'd all come to suspect they weren't just gunrunners, which meant we shouldn't be assuming anything.

At the crest of the rise, the draw narrowed further and I followed Clines mostly by touch, hands running along the sand and rock along what had once been a riverbank and was now a wadi. Clines scrambled up the side of it and I followed him, coming down the loose dirt and sand on the other side and falling into a crouch, swinging my rifle off my back and into my hands. I waited for Vicky to climb up beside us, then went down on elbows and knees, high-crawling forward toward the light.

I hadn't high-crawled anywhere for any reason since Boot Camp and I didn't remember it hurting this bad, but then, I wasn't wearing any sort of body armor to pad my knees and elbows and I seemed to be finding every single rock that existed on this planet. And what wasn't rock was mud, and while the rain jacket protected my upper body, my pants were quickly soaked through.

It's just another hundred meters. I kept telling myself that even after two hundred meters, but finally, I was right and we topped the crest and all dropped to our bellies as the diffuse glow cohered into a cluster of floodlights in a loose oval perimeter about a kilometer long.

It was the landing field. We'd intuited it existed, but had no idea how large it was. It was nearly the size of the field outside Gamma Junction, though the surface wasn't paved over with fusion-form concrete. It was scraped flat, probably by an attachment to Hellnick's autoharvester, and I suppose if that made the walk from the shuttles a little muddy, it was a sacrifice Eld and the others were willing to make. The tractors didn't seem to be having any trouble with the mud.

They must have come with the cargo landers, I figured, because there was nowhere around here for Hellnick to have gotten hold of them. They weren't quite as efficient as the power loaders we'd used in the military, but I imagine they were easier to fabricate out in the Pirate Worlds or wherever these guys came from. They were old designs, running on knobbed tires, their loader arms running on gimbals, able to slide on all sides of a standard cargo container or slip underneath a larger load on a freight pallet.

I didn't know what they were hauling out of the hold of the cargo shuttle, but it was large enough to rival the proton cannon we'd seen the night before. *Where* they were taking the load was even more interesting than the cargo itself. I'd never seen Hellnick's house or his barn, though I assumed they were average for the settlement, the same prefab structures the colony ships had thrown up for the rest of us. I still couldn't see them, even though I knew approximately where they were, just a half a kilometer away.

I couldn't see them because someone had built a warehouse on the other side of the landing field. A hundred meters long, maybe half that distance wide and about twenty meters high, it wasn't anything fancy or elaborate, just bare sheet metal slapped together and welded in place around a frame of plain steel girders, something a dedicated crew could have thrown up in a couple days with the right equipment. What was troubling was the fact they thought they could bring enough cargo in to fill it.

Clines already had his 'link out, capturing video of the place, though he'd been smart enough, I noted, to turn his display screen down until I could barely see it in the glow from the floodlights.

"Does that look like something they're going to clear out of here in a couple months?" he hissed next to my ear.

I didn't bother to answer. It was obvious this wasn't something they intended to evacuate once they'd made their sale and cleared out their inventory...and it was just as obvious they weren't through yet. It was hard to see in the shadow of the warehouse, but they were building something else off to the side, something low-slung and spread out, something that looked more like a bunkhouse than another storage facility.

Tiny figures wandered around in the light filtering through the open doors of the storage building, too far away to make out too many details, but I could tell they were carrying rifles or carbines. Something else about them nagged at the back of my mind, something about the way they stood, the way they carried themselves, an unnatural stiffness to their gait. And then I knew. They were Tahni, and I could see at least a couple dozen of them just guarding the warehouse.

"We need to get a look around the other side of the warehouse," Clines said.

"Are you out of your mind?" Vicky whispered and I resisted an urge to try to explain to her that talking in a normal, low voice would carry less of a distance than a whisper. I should have mentioned it before we left and it was too damned late for lessons now. "Look at all those guards!"

"This won't be enough," he insisted, motioning with his 'link. "There's nothing that proves they were lying."

He was right about that. It was obvious to us, but we'd already had suspicions. We had to convince people who were afraid and didn't *want* to be convinced. Still, there was no reason to put us all in danger, and the more people moving, the more likely someone would see.

"I'll go," I told them. Vicky looked at me like I'd just told her I wanted to replace my limbs with bionics and become a Skinganger, but I went on before she could ask if I was just as crazy as Clines. Which I probably was. "How much experience have either of you had creeping around on foot behind enemy lines?"

"You did it *once*!" she reminded me, voice getting a little shrill and rising to a dangerous volume. She realized it without me telling her and visibly fought to control herself. "It's not going to do us any good for you to get captured and executed by these assholes. We can get what we need from here."

She was probably right. I *wanted* her to be right, wanted to agree, because I really didn't want to be the one to make the crawl alone. I wanted Torrey to be here, to be the one to volunteer and use all that Force Recon stealthiness. But that wasn't going to happen and for all that I'd only done it once, it was still more than Vicky or Clines.

"Stay here," I said. "If I get cut off and can't make it back to you, I'll signal on my 'link and you guys can fire off a couple shots to draw their attention this way, then haul ass and I'll meet you back in the canyon." I paused, slipping out of my rifle's sling, and handing the weapon to Vicky. "I'll move quicker without it."

She grabbed me by the shoulder when I tried to move away, her dark eyes burning coals in the night.

"You get yourself killed, Alvarez," she warned me, her voice almost a growl, "and so help me God, I'll cash in your separation bonus, blow this backwater and find some restruct-surgery model to help me spend it. You hear me?"

I pulled her hand off my shoulder, kissed it, then let it go.

"I'll be back."

[10]

If high-crawling a few hundred meters had seemed painful and awkward, low-crawling the same distance was pure torture, something even my Boot Camp drill instructors wouldn't have inflicted on us in a fit of sadism. Technically, I wasn't doing a textbook low-crawl because I wasn't wearing a helmet to dig into the dirt, but it was close enough. I kept my eyes down, glancing up now and again to stay on course, not wanting to let the floodlights reflecting off my skin or eyes give my position away. Not that there was any exposed skin left to reflect once I rubbed my face in the mud a few times.

Scotty, I thought, would have been laughing his ass off at this, at the thought of me crawling in the dirt like a Force Recon straight-leg. I don't know why I thought of him, why the memory of the man came back so strong at a moment when I should have been concentrating on not getting spotted and killed, but it did. The last time I'd seen him, I hadn't seen his face. He'd been just another grey golem, a faceless statue of a Vigilante heading down into the Tahni bunker with a demolition charge I should have been carrying. He'd died instead of me.

It felt like there'd been so many people who'd died instead of me. Scotty Hayes, Joyce Ackley, my brother Anton, all the way back to my mother, killed by a stray bullet less than a meter away from me. And of course, Vince Delp. It had happened during the battle at Tahn-Skyyiah, when I'd called in an airstrike on our position to keep a last-ditch force of Tahni battlesuits from overrunning us. I'd been injured, my suit damaged and there was no way I was going to get clear, but Vicky and Private Delp had come back for me. Delp had been killed and Vicky had been damn near to it, burned badly, so severely injured they'd barely saved her.

Maybe that was the real reason I'd wanted to go on the scouting run alone, so I wouldn't drag Vicky down with me. Maybe this time the right person would die.

At least then I'd get some real sleep.

One more glance off to the side and I realized I'd passed beyond the landing field, behind the cover of an earthen berm left over at the perimeter from when the harvester had flattened the soil. It wasn't much, just a meter of loose-packed dirt, but it was enough to let me go from my belly to hands and knees without being seen, and it felt like pure heaven. I patted clumps and clods of mud and dirt off my chest and stomach and mostly managed to build up more mud and dirt on my hands rather than clean off my torso.

The dirt berm ended but I didn't go back to my belly. The corner of the warehouse was just twenty meters from the edge of the landing field and I decided to take the chance to make a run for it, partly because I thought the glare of the floodlights would keep the Tahni guards from spotting me but mostly because I was so damned tired of crawling through the mud.

I didn't look at the guards, just hunched my shoulders and sprinted, or as close to a sprint as I could come wearing four or five kilos of mud caked on my body. No gunshots or shouts of alarm followed me, though, and within a few seconds, I was tumbling to a halt against the side wall of the building, crouched in the shadows, holding my breath, and waiting.

Nothing.

I swallowed the lump in my throat and edged toward the corner, peeking out just far enough to get a glimpse back at the Tahni. They weren't being very vigilant for troops presumably brought in to guard the place. I couldn't understand what they were saying to each other in their sing-song language, but they were deep in some sort of conversation, gesticulating toward the shuttles or perhaps the tractors unloading them. They weren't dressed in the civilian garb I'd seen back in Gamma Junction, nor had they gone the way of their commander, Zan-Thint and adapted human style clothing. Instead, they were in the same sort of light body armor I'd seen their regular infantry wear during the war, minus the helmets.

I recognized the guns they carried from the war, as well. They were KE rifles, standard issue for Tahni infantry, electromagnetic weapons that shot high-velocity tantalum needles at a high rate of fire from a snail drum arrangement behind the grip. They were distinctive and unmistakable and also a hell of a lot more powerful and hard to acquire than the Gyrocs Eld and his smuggler crew had brandished...or anything we could fabricate out here on the ass-end of nowhere.

Damn.

I ducked back around the corner and crept as stealthily as an ex-Drop Trooper could manage around the other end of the warehouse. I'd become a hunter since I'd moved to Hausos, but not the sort of woods-wise stalker Dak Shephard was. Rock dragons weren't exactly masters of camouflage since they were the top of the evolutionary heap on this planet, masters of their domain and the apex predator. They failed to see a need to hide until the rifle bullet taught them the lesson they'd never get to use.

So, it was a damned good thing the warehouse had been thrown up with speed in mind rather than ergonomics and there were no windows and doors on the side of the building, and no danger of some ill-timed busybody sticking their head out and catching me red-handed. I still had to worry about the workers and the Tahni guards. All it would take was one of them wandering away from the warehouse entrance and looking the wrong way at the wrong time. I could almost feel them coming and fought an urge to keep looking back over my shoulder.

I chose speed as the quickest route to safety and got to the next corner and the safety of the deep shadows there. The other side of the warehouse was what I'd come to see, and I pulled my 'link off my belt, prepared to record whatever I found there.

What I found was a hole.

I thought at first that what I was looking at was a construction site, perhaps roots and rocks dug up in order for Hellnick and his new masters to pour a foundation for a more permanent structure than the sheet-metal storage building. But it wasn't. As I approached nearer to the edge of the thing, though, I realized how deep it went. The only illumination was what leaked past the warehouse from the floodlights and a dim glow from the exterior lights of Hellnick's farmhouse in the distance and the barracks style building on the other side, but it was enough to let me see that the hole went down at least twenty or thirty meters.

It considered the idea that they were digging some sort of emergency shelter, a bunker or something, but the excavation was wrong for any sort of construction. There was an absence in the center of the hole, a sense that something had been dug up, though I had no clue what of any significance would be buried thirty meters down on this world.

Maybe weapons? Maybe the Tahni had left a weapons

cache here and that was what Eld and Zan-Thint wanted. Maybe that was where his guards had got ahold of their KE rifles. I rejected the idea almost as quickly as I'd thought of it. There'd been no sign of Tahni habitation on this world or any of the others in what Clines insisted on calling the Forbidden Zone. They hadn't built homes here, hadn't built a military base, hadn't so much as left any satellites in orbit, or tried to mine the gas giants. Whatever their reason, these systems had been off-limits, and if they hadn't left behind any other trace on Hausos, the concept that they would have buried weapons here made no sense at all.

I dutifully recorded the dig site, getting as close as I could without tumbling into the hole myself. The excavation had happened a while ago, I judged, from the lack of visible tread marks around the hole. The rain had washed them away, which would have taken days, at least, maybe weeks. Parts of the dig had collapsed, other bits filled with water, centimeters deep, where the ground beneath had been saturated by the rain. Again, a sign of the passage of at least a couple weeks.

Had this been the reason they'd come? The reason they'd bothered to land all these weapons and troops on a nowhere planet with nothing else of value?

I needed to see what was inside that damned warehouse.

The rear of the building was shrouded in darkness, the bulk of the sheet metal wall blocking off most of the light from the front...but there was one narrow sliver of white maybe a meter long, creeping out from the lower edge of the wall. It was a rear exit. Small, a door for people rather than cargo, just something they'd thrown in during the building, most likely so they could get to the barracks and Hellnick's house without walking all the way around the building.

There would be people inside. The tractors were at work, unloading cargo, the Tahni were out there guarding it all. This was an operation carried out under cover of darkness, on a world where there was no round-the-clock satellite surveillance by any government or law enforcement agency. Their only worry was us, the colonists, stumbling across it all by accident, maybe a hopper overflight catching them with something sensitive out in the open.

And they were still bothering to work at night even after we'd seen the proton cannon, even after Eld had made his pitch to the meeting. Was it just habit, a schedule they'd already set and couldn't alter this late, or was it another clue he'd been lying to us?

I edged up to the door, feeling around in the shadows until I found the handle, just a bent piece of wire wrapped with tape, as jury-rigged as the door itself, which was little more than a rectangular section of sheet metal cut out of the wall and hung on fabricated hinges. I pulled on the handle, expecting there to be some sort of catch or bar on the inside, but it opened a few centimeters, the hinges squeaking in protest, and light flooded out in a wedge like a slice of cake projected on the muddy ground.

Sound washed out along with the light, voices, both human and Tahni, and the grinding of metal and plastic. I waited for a three count, straining my ears for a warning of the door being open or a call of "who's there?" but nothing came, or at least nothing I could make out. It was hard to hear over the sound of moving cargo and the even louder drumbeat of my pulse in my ears. Now that I had a second to consider it, the light through the door seemed muted, as if I wasn't seeing the bare glow of a bulb or a light panel, but instead the suppressed and filtered illumination from a barrier partially blocking it.

This isn't going to get any safer for waiting.

I pushed the door halfway open and slid inside in one, smooth motion, not skulking or sneaking, moving as if I belonged there, something I'd learned long before the Marines, when my home had been the streets and survival had meant avoiding the notice of the gangs and the cops. If you acted like you were trespassing, people would notice, would single you out from the crowd. If you pretended you owned the place, no one gave you a second look.

As it turned out, I needn't have bothered. The back door opened into a small alcove, arranged not by design but by a haphazard stacking of storage containers, two crates deep and ten high, stretching in a line to a point about three meters from the far wall, just enough of a gap for a cargo jack to get through carrying a container, reaching nearly to the ceiling and held in place by magnetic anchors. Light from the other side, from panels lining the ceiling, filtered through the gaps in the crates, creating the shaded glow I'd noticed from the door.

I pushed the door shut behind me and backed up against the cargo containers, sliding sideways along the length of them, scanning back and forth from the door to the end of the stack as I moved. I kept my 'link down by my side, the camera facing forward, still recording. The more I saw, the greater the doubt I felt about whether the board or even the whole group of us vets *could* do anything about this even if we managed to convince them, but I was here and this was the mission. And if I got cornered and couldn't get out, at least I could send a burst transmission to Vicky and let her know what I'd seen.

The voices became clearer the closer I came to the edge of the stack, until I was able to judge that some of the humans talking were very close, maybe ten or fifteen meters away. There were three of them talking, two men and a woman, and one of the men had a grating, whiny voice that made me want to smash my fist in his face without even seeing him first.

"...all right, I suppose," he said, already in a conversation I hadn't been able to catch from the beginning. "But look, there just ain't enough women on this world. I mean, there're the farmer types, but they're all settled down and probably wouldn't be that much fun even if they were willing to give it a go. And I ain't gonna force anybody, I don't go for that shit."

"So, you're saying you're still a virgin, Lang?" the woman asked, then brayed a laugh. "Because I can't think of any woman who'd sleep with you willingly, unless you were paying."

"Fuck you, Rosa," Lang shot back, more petulance in his whine than before. "Some of us want a sex partner that don't run on batteries."

"Hey, at least if my sex partner whines, I know the motor's going bad and I can get a mechanic to fix it. There ain't nobody out here who can stop *you* from whining."

"She's got you there, Lang!" the second male said, his tone ingratiating, as if he was trying to take the place of the battery-operated device.

I tuned them all out, keeping a tiny section of my consciousness listening in case any of them said something that wasn't inane and meaningless, and tried to hear past their voices, worried someone might barge around the corner without warning, their approach drowned out by the chatter. I finally reached the end of the aisle and eeled around the squared-off caps of the cargo crates, keeping one shoulder against them, watching the opposite wall for shadows.

On the other side of the stacks of cargo creates, the warehouse opened up abruptly, leaving me standing pretty much in the open and I nearly shit my pants. The three humans were only ten meters away, thankfully turned the other direction, and they looked about how I'd imagined them. Lang was a scrawny, horse-faced, beak-nosed little man, just as ugly and unlikely to score with the opposite sex as Rosa had intimated. She was older but not by much, and the years were probably come by honestly, since most people out in the Pirate Worlds didn't have access to the anti-aging treatments people on Earth and the core colonies received as a matter of course. The last guy was even older, with honest-to-God grey hair, something I hadn't seen since I was a kid in Tijuana.

All three were strapped, carrying sidearms, and I wondered if it was a requirement, the only uniform the smugglers shared. Even the operator of the cargo tractor coming through the freight doors of the warehouse wore a shoulder holster. He was concentrating on maneuvering a pallet loaded with four cargo containers into a spot against the far wall and wouldn't have noticed me anyway, but I made an effort to cross my arms and lean casually against the row of crates beside me just in case.

Five more of the Tahni guards were clustered just inside the doorway, talking to each other, and totally ignoring the humans around them, probably in an intentional snub. Every Tahni I'd had the displeasure of meeting in the wake of their defeat had done their best to not acknowledge the presence or even the existence of any of us, unless someone shoved a gun in their face and forced them to.

I ignored them, not because they weren't a danger, but because the center of the warehouse commanded all my attention. Stretched across an area probably ten meters across and twenty meters long was a huge, grey tarp, hung from hooks in the ceiling to form a tent right in the middle of the warehouse. This was it, the thing they'd dug up. I don't know how I knew, but I did, as sure of it as I was of my mother's love or the sun rising in the east. Nothing else would be important enough for them to build a warehouse to hide it and then block off that big a chunk of the structure's interior just to keep it out of sight of even their own people.

Cargo crates surrounded it on three sides, almost as if they were blocking it off, making sure no one could sneak under the tarp and...do what? I wasn't sure, but the thing seemed to draw my eye toward it, even hidden behind the tarp. There was a vibration in the air, something deeper than the rumble of the tractor motors or the tires on the concrete flooring, something subsonic, just below the edges of my perception. I was certain it was coming from inside the tent, but I couldn't be sure if I was imagining it, if it was just a symptom of the flashbacks and paranoia the psych counselors had so accurately predicted I might experience.

The 'link. The solution was the 'link. If whatever was beneath the tarp was indeed producing the vibration, the recording would reveal it.

I wanted to get inside, wanted almost more than life itself to see what was concealed there, and I found myself actually taking a step toward it before I gained control of the impulse. I wrenched my eyes away from the tarp, sweeping them over the interior of the place one last time, just to make sure I hadn't missed anything important.

And there was something else, against the far wall, tiny compared to the tented center of the room, but not insubstantial. A row of eight containers stood side by side, over three meters tall and two meters wide, and most significantly, they weren't the standard shipping crates stacked elsewhere in the warehouse. They were Tahni. I'd seen their like before, and there was no mistaking the oblong polygons for anything else. The number eight was notable as well. It was the Tahni holy number, the basis for all their military, religious, and government organizational tables.

I made sure I recorded the containers, panning the camera back and forth in a 180-degree arc around the place before I began backing out of the open area, back toward the narrow gap between the stacks and the side wall. No eyes followed me, no heads turned, no hands reached for guns. This had gone better than I could have hoped for, and if I hadn't been able to penetrate the mystery of what Eld and Zan-Thint were doing here, at least I'd determined there *was* a mystery and where the epicenter of it was.

And maybe it would even be enough to convince the others that we needed to do something about it. If we couldn't manage an armed resistance, at least we might be able to band together to send a unified message to the Corporate Council, to make them believe there was a problem and that they needed to come sort it out.

I tucked my 'link into its pouch on my belt. Getting in had been the hard point, I told myself. Getting out would just be a matter of reversing my steps, and I knew where to go, knew which route would take me back safely. As I turned the corner and jogged back to the rear exit, was convinced nothing could go wrong now.

My fingers had barely touched the cold metal of the door before it was yanked open from outside.

Zan-Thint stepped through it.

[11]

Tahni all look alike to me. I probably wouldn't have known it was Zan-Thint if it hadn't been for his clothes—none of the other Tahni affected human dress. In the moment between the door opening and him emerging into the muted light of the entryway, I seized on the notion that the reverse was probably also true. He wouldn't be likely to recognize me, particularly not in this setting.

I sucked in a deep breath, pulled up the collar of my rain jacket and tried to step past him out the door without speaking, hoping he'd be just as taciturn as the rest of his kind, ignoring us nasty, brutish humans. It almost worked. I was a half-step through the doorway when I felt his large, inhuman hand on my shoulder, gripping tightly.

"You are not one of Eld's." The voice scraped metal against metal inside my head, coming from vocal cords never evolved to speak any human language. "Who are you? Why are you in this place?"

"I work for Mr. Hellnick," I said, hoping the Tahni commander wouldn't know enough about Klaus Hellnick to realize the man kept no hired hands on his farm. "He wanted me to...," I hesitated for a second, not having come up with a good reason why one of Hellnick's nonexistent hired hands would be out here in Eld's warehouse. I grabbed desperately at the first thing to trickle from the gibbering recesses of my thoughts and went with it. "His pleasure 'bot is missing and he thinks some of Captain Eld's people might have stolen it. He wanted me to ask around."

I couldn't decipher the expression on Zan-Thint's face, and I wondered if it was closer to amusement, disgust, or puerile fascination.

"And did you ask?"

"No," I told him, shaking my head. "I was gonna, but I got scared."

"How typical." The expression didn't change and now I pegged it for disgust. "You confirm every opinion I have ever had about your species. The galaxy would have been a better place had we won the war and wiped your so-called civilization clean and allowed you to start again."

"Yes, sir," I agreed, trying to give the impression that I would have agreed with him no matter what he said. "Can I go now, sir?"

I don't know if he bought it. And I never would.

Gunshots rang out in the distance, echoing through the building, making it impossible to determine their source, and yet I knew exactly where they'd originated. Zan-Thint's hand came off my shoulder as he spun toward the front of the warehouse, and I ran.

I didn't look back, didn't check to see if anyone was targeting me or pointing at me, ignored the yells and alarmed cries seemingly coming from every direction, I just ran. Mud and dirt sprayed backwards from my boots, some of it splattering against the back of my pants, beams of flaring yellow from portable spotlights cut through the night, searching for threats, and brakes squealed on the tractors as the operators stopped them in place, scrambling for cover, and still I ran. The sputtering hiss of discharging Gyroc pistols was undercut by the crackling whine of KE rifles and I didn't duck or even pause to see if they were targeting me, I just let the fear and desperation kick me in the ass like an afterburner.

Vicky was out there, just her and Clines and a couple hunting rifles, and me being with them might not do much to even the odds, but I'd die to reach her before I'd let her die alone.

Amazingly, I *didn't* die. It could have been the darkness, could have been the fact that the lights were searching for threats coming in instead of ones running out, could have been that they thought I was one of their own going to try to join the fight. Or it could have been God looking out for me, though if that was the case, we needed to have a talk about His priorities. Whatever the reason, I reached the crest of the hill without getting shot.

Vicky and Clines weren't there. But the body of one of Eld's crew was, lying on his back, arms wide as if he were embracing death as she came for him. His jacket had fallen open, revealing the ragged hole in his multi-colored shirt, dark blood drowning out the showy flash of the clothes fabricated locally off of cheap patterns. His eyes were wide as well, staring past me when I leaned over him, his face already gone pale from draining blood.

I didn't care about what those eyes saw, didn't care what twisted path had led him to this end. All I cared about was the Gyroc pistol half-buried in the mud beside his right hand. I snatched it up and wiped mud away, patting at his belt for spare magazines. There was a pouch with two of them and I stripped them out and stuck them in my jacket pocket before I left him to the night. I didn't know how he'd stumbled across Vicky and

Clines, didn't know if there were already more on their trail, but I knew where they'd be heading.

I'd barely taken a step toward the canyon when another volley of Gyroc fire rolled across the rolling hills, their discharge like the fireworks rockets launching during the Founders' Day celebration I'd witnessed on Silvanus after we'd liberated them from the Tahni. There were no multicolored bursts at the detonation of the warheads to guide me to their position, but I knew the shots had to be coming from up ahead, near the entrance to the canyon.

I paused to pull out my flashlight, then sped up once it illuminated my path. It was a huge risk, putting a target around my neck by using the light, but urgency burned in my chest, a conviction that if I didn't reach the canyon before the smugglers did, they'd follow Vicky and Clines and force them into taking cover before they could make it to the car. If that happened, they were dead, because Eld's people had hoppers. If they saw us driving away, if they could follow the vehicle, we wouldn't be able to get clear. I had to get there first.

I knew it couldn't be much farther, that it hadn't seemed this far on the way in and I was moving faster now than we had then. Either my personal sense of time was being stretched on a rack to torture me or I'd wandered wide of the direct route Clines had led us on. Either one was just as possible and just as maddening, but neither had an obvious solution...until another gunshot rolled like thunder over the sandstone, coming from dead ahead, and I knew I was on the right path.

At least they were still alive and still fighting back, though the return fire also meant they hadn't reached the vehicle yet. Now I just needed to know where the bad guys were. I had a thought, a wild, reckless thought, one that would have gotten me killed if I'd been facing the Tahni or an organized and trained human military force. But these guys were smugglers, pirates, thugs, probably with not much tactical training.

"Hey!" I yelled at the top of my lungs. "We've got reinforcements coming! Where are the motherfuckers?"

A pause, and I wondered if I should yell it again.

"Over here, man!" A light shone out, waving up and down. "We're over here! Head over to the right of us and outflank 'em!"

"On my way!" I promised, then I switched off my flashlight and followed his.

They were closer than I'd thought, off to my left maybe fifty meters, through a clump of the sort of tanglefoot brush local to this world and the others in the Forbidden Zone and *yes, damnit,* I was starting to use Dave Clines' stupid term for the sector. There were only four of them and they'd taken cover behind a pile of rocks caved off the side of the canyon wall. I could barely make them out in the glow of the flashlight, their figures blinking in and out of existence as it waved back and forth in the one man's hand.

I paused, feeling on the side of the Gyroc pistol with my thumb, then my forefinger, searching for a safety and not finding one. I shrugged, raised it to shoulder level, the aiming reticle of the pop-up optical sight bouncing up and down over the chest of the guy with the light. He hadn't been looking my way, instead keeping an eye on the canyon. It was a tactically sound move, watching the perceived threat and not staring at the light to kill his own night vision.

The thought that I had never killed a human being before had time to bounce from one side of my brain to the other before I pulled the trigger. I'd never fired a Gyroc before, never shot any pistol other than familiarization fire with the issue Marine sidearm during the war, the ZWH-24, and I clenched it in a death-grip, unsure what to expect. But the kick was nothing, barely a push as the inertially-guided mini-rocket pushed free of the barrel with a sibilant hiss of its thruster and a tiny, red, firefly glow.

The man with the flashlight grunted as if he'd been punched in the side, and the light stopped its up-and-down signaling motion, wavering in one spot for just a moment before it slipped from his strengthless fingers. It hit the ground a second before he did, but I wasn't watching him. I had a general idea of where the others were, the remnants of the light on them, the persistence of vision I think it was called technically.

I used it to fire off the rest of the rounds in the pistol's magazine, touching the trigger over and over, grateful that the weapon was a simple fab job instead of something custom made for law enforcement. I'd never seen one, but I'd heard that the Patrol and local colonial cops on the core worlds had biometric security built into their guns so no one could use them except the one they were issued to. This one was a whore, happy to put out for whoever picked it up, and it was empty in less than three seconds.

I had no idea how many of them I'd hit and I knew I didn't want to try to stand there and find out. I threw myself to the side, rolling behind a rock outcropping for cover and fished in my jacket pocket for a spare magazine with one hand while the other searched frantically for the release to pop out the empty.

I hadn't killed them all. A man was screaming, shrill and incoherent, the sort of scream a man gave when he was in too much shock and agony to form words or string together a solid thought. A woman was cursing, loud enough I could make out her invective behind the screams.

"Shit! They got Martino! Felix? Lee? Are you hit? Where's the shooter?"

She was yelling the questions, but no one was answering,

though I wasn't sure if it was because they were unable or just unwilling to draw fire by speaking up.

I found the release and the empty mag dropped free of the gun, surprising me and making an obscenely loud clatter against the rocks when it fell.

"There!"

There was *here*, and the first clue I had that however many of them who were still capable were shooting at me was the bang of an exploding Gyroc round against the opposite side of the rock I was using for cover. I flinched at the daisy-chain of miniature warheads and nearly dropped the loaded magazine I'd been trying to insert into the grip of my appropriated weapon. It was hard enough finding the mag well in the dark on a pistol with which I wasn't familiar—well, hell, I wasn't familiar with *any* pistol if I was being honest—but being shot at added a degree of difficulty to anything.

And somehow, it was different being shot at outside the suit. Not that the electron beamer from a Tahni High Guard battle-suit couldn't do even nastier things to a drop trooper than the warhead from a Gyroc could do to an unarmored man, but there was a psychological factor to it. The suit was a separation from the reality on the ground, the damp earth soaking through my clothes, the wind slapping me in the face with the night chill, the sand and grit blowing into my eyes. This was too real, too distracting. I took back every bad thing I'd ever thought about Force Recon. Anyone who could handle this on a regular basis deserved respect.

I clenched my teeth to keep them from chattering and slapped the fresh magazine home, the metallic click as it seated a satisfying, visceral sound. But now that I had ammo again, what was I going to do with it? One of them was shining a flash-light at me again, trying to pin down my location, which gave me something to aim at but also made sure if I leaned out on either side of this rock to return fire, they'd have a clear shot at me.

And yet I had to move. If I stayed, they'd send someone to flank me. I pulled the pistol up into a high ready, my back against the rock, readying myself for a lunge forward. I was going to get some distance, then cut to my right, swing around them, I hoped. I was probably going to get shot, but maybe I'd last long enough to take out the two or three of them who were left.

My plans were cut short by the distinctive crack of a hunting rifle, a sound I'd heard many times since we'd settled here, and right on its heels the scream of a woman. Not Vicky, someone closer, probably the same one I'd heard shouting a few seconds ago. The light shifted and I knew by instinct that the one holding it was pointing it back down the canyon, trying to spot the shooter.

I rolled out from behind the rock and took up a prone position, the pistol extended out ahead of me, gripped in both hands. The sideways glow of the flashlight showed me two of the smuggler crew left, crouching at either side of the cluster of small boulders, pumping rounds downrange, the dull-red glow of the miniature rockets a swarm of fireflies in the night.

The aiming reticle bounced with the rhythm of my breath, but I was close enough it didn't matter. I put four rounds into the farthest out of the two, waiting for the impact of the first two shots to spin him around before I added the last. Just one left.

The flashlight was spinning back toward me along with the barrel of the man's gun, and we both fired in the same instant, just a fraction of a second too early for him. His rounds passed wide of my head by centimeters, while mine punched through his chest. He convulsed as the warheads detonated inside his torso, and a splash of blood spilled from his lips before he tumbled forward, smothering the light with his body.

"Vicky!" I yelled, scrambling to my feet, trying to keep the barrel of the pistol trained on the fallen smugglers in case one of them still had enough life to try a "fuck-you" shot. "Are you okay?"

"I'm fine." Her words were flat, emotionless in that way she'd gotten during the war after a battle, when she was pushing everything down. "I'm gonna need your help with Dave."

I paused as I passed by the smugglers, taking the time to kick their weapons away. They weren't moving, but it was too dark to tell if any were breathing. Hatred for them smoldered in my chest, though not hatred for their crimes or their bringing their operation to our home, not even for their attack on us personally. Instead, I found, to my surprise, that I hated them for what they'd made me do.

So many years I'd spent living on the street, in almost constant danger, but I'd never killed anyone. I'd killed the hell out of the Tahni during the war, and they were sentient beings, but they weren't human. I'd always been able to comfort my conscience with that little qualifier. I was a killer, but I'd only killed *aliens*. Not anymore. No more qualifiers, no more asterisks. I was a killer. Period.

I wanted to put another round into each of them, not just to be sure, but out of spite, out of resentment for what they'd made me become. I didn't, though not from a sudden attack of conscience. I just didn't have the time.

I pulled out my flashlight and made my way down into the canyon, finding Vicky pulling Dave Clines out from behind the cover of a rock alcove, her hands under his armpits, his body limp.

"He's been shot," she told me, as if the spreading red stain across his chest wasn't clue enough.

I knelt down over him and touched my fingers to his neck,

searching for a pulse. There was none. I held my hand over his nose but no breath tickled my skin.

"He's gone, Vicky."

Her jaw worked as if she wanted to snap at me, wanted to argue, but she clamped down on the words.

"He pushed me out of the way." She ground the admission out of her, chewing it into small bits and spitting it. "He took the bullet that would have hit me, the stupid bastard. Why would he do that?"

"Because he was a good man."

I pulled the handgun out of his hip holster and offered it to her. She sneered at the thing, but took it anyway. I left his rifle there with him because I could only carry mine. Vicky stared at me in obvious disbelief as I straightened from his body.

"We can't leave him here!"

"We have to." I pointed behind us. "They have hoppers, they have Tahni troops with KE rifles. They're going to be on us in a minute. We don't have time to carry him. We may not even have time to get back to the car."

She stared at Clines' body, agony passing across her face, and I wanted to take her in my arms and tell her everything was going to be okay, but I didn't. I couldn't lie to her.

"Damn it," she murmured, the words barely audible, and then she turned and headed down the canyon.

I followed her, leaving our friend behind.

[12]

The rover was right where we'd left it, and I had to resist and urge to just run up and throw myself into it. I put a hand on Vicky's arm and came to a stop about fifty meters away, then signaled for her to follow me as I circled wide of the vehicle, checking for anyone who might be watching. I didn't *think* they could have made it out here that quickly without flying directly over us, but I wasn't going to assume anything. Not after what happened to Clines.

The area around the car seemed clear, and seemed was as sure as I was going to get without night vision and thermal, so we climbed inside. I tossed my rifle into the back seat, setting the Gyroc pistol beside me, easy at hand if I needed it, and pushed the accelerator. The car surged forward and I twisted the wheel hard, spinning us around, heading back for Clines' house.

"Did he have any family?" Vicky asked. She was staring into the darkness ahead and so was I, but for a different reason. I could, just barely, make out the edges of the dirt path without turning the headlights on, but I had to squint and concentrate, and it was already giving me a headache.

"Yeah." I dredged up the memory, nearly going off the road into the rocks and chuckholes when I lost focus. "His parents split up. Mom lives on Aphrodite; dad works in the gas mines on whatever that gas giant is that's in the same system as the Loki colony. I think he said he had a sister who died in the war, but he didn't talk about her too much."

We'd known the man for a year, yet all the details about his life I could remember could have fit in a four-paragraph memo on my 'link.

"He's got three hired hands, right?" she asked.

"They live in town. He only brings them out a couple times a week. Keep a look out behind us, okay?"

Her glare was hard enough to strip paint, but she did it anyway. I knew what she was thinking. I was being cold, callous, for all that she hadn't even liked the man that much. But I wasn't. I was doing what I'd always done, compartmentalizing, sticking the hurt away somewhere safe. Theoretically, putting it somewhere I could dredge it up later and deal with it, though that never seemed to happen. Several sessions with a military psych counselor had confirmed that was the problem, though I still wasn't clear on the solution.

The sky was clearing up. I wasn't sure if that was a good thing or not when it came to the bad guys tracking us down, but at least it was making it easier to drive in the dark. The Asvins were up and their twin light brought the edges of the road into sharper definition, lessened the frequency of the sharp bumps, the suspension bottoming out as one of our wheels slipped into a hole or passed over a root or rock.

"What the hell are you doing, Cam?" she asked. "Where are we going?"

"Dave's place first," I decided, pulling the answer out of my ass because I hadn't honestly thought about it. "We need to see if they know where we came from. If they're at his house, they're probably at ours, too."

"And if they're not? Do we just go home and pretend none of this happened?"

I tried to push down resentment at her anger. I knew it wasn't with me, knew it was mostly a reaction to being scared. Vicky didn't like being scared. She'd never been scared inside her Vigilante. She wasn't used to it.

"We go to Brad," I said. "We show him the footage I took, see if we can get him to send it to the Corporate Council. It might give him the pull he needs to get them involved in this."

"Eld is going to have thought of that already," she insisted, smacking her fist into the door hard enough to rattle it in its frame. "He's got to have taken out the transmission tower already."

"Maybe he has," I admitted. "We'll work on that when it comes up. Right now, I want to get this footage to someone else, so if they take us out, it won't die with us."

The angry scowl collapsed into devastation, and I thought the implications of what was happening here finally fell in on her like an avalanche. Her shoulders sagged for a moment, but she was a combat veteran and she gathered herself back together almost instantly.

"I'm not going to let them kill us," she declared, shifting the rifle in her lap as if taking comfort from it. "I didn't live through Tahn-Skyyiah to die here."

Pride battled with despondency and I went with the more positive of the two.

"It's not the plan," I assured her. "But that's one of the things they taught us in OCS, remember? Expect the best but prepare for the worst."

"Do we really care what Eld does here if we get killed?" she wondered. "I mean, I like this world and some of the vets are good people, and I'll help them if I can, but making sure a bunch of smugglers go to jail isn't the last thing I want to do in this life."

It was a good point, and I struggled to form a reply. I'd been going on a gut feeling and while she might have trusted my instincts, I owed her more than that.

"There's something bigger going on here, Vicky. I don't know what it is, but Eld and Zan-Thint didn't come here just because there wasn't any law enforcement on this world. They came here for something specific, something they'd been looking for, and I think they found it on Hellnick's land." I told her what I'd seen, the dig and the tarp-covered section of the warehouse. "They wouldn't risk bringing this big of an operation, this many people and this much cargo into a place on the other side of the largest military buildup outside Inferno if there wasn't a pot of gold at the end of that rainbow."

"I'm not sure gold would be enough," she mused. I glanced away from the trail, trying to read what she was thinking by her expression, but a rut nearly sending us into a skid snapped my head back forward. "That Tahni colonel isn't here for a profit. You talked to him. You think he's interested in buying himself a yacht and cruising the colonies, maybe settling down in a mansion on Hermes?"

"He's disillusioned," I said, not really disagreeing with her but needing to play the argument out in my head. "He left his world when his god turned out to be a lie, took a bunch of pissed-off soldiers with him, and somehow brought their guns along. And then he and Captain Eld hook up and want the same thing. What would they both want, a guy like Eld and a Tahni colonel with a ready-made little army?"

"You don't think it's money," she said. "That only leaves power. Or maybe revenge."

"Let's hope it's power," I said. At her questioning look, I

elaborated. "People who want power, even the ones who are off their nut, they're usually predictable. People who want revenge...." I shook my head. "They can do anything."

Dave Clines' house squatted in isolated despair, as if it knew he wasn't coming back. A single light glowed on the porch, left burning to guide him back. His rover was still at our place, so it just looked as if he'd driven off for a night in town, drinking with his friends in the one real tavern, trying to convince one of the few unattached females in Gamma Junction that life would be better out at his farm.

He'd have found someone eventually. Clines was a good guy, even if he did get on Vicky's nerves now and then. *Had been* a good guy. He'd been a friend in a place where those weren't easy to come by, where the comradery I'd shared with the other Marines in my company back in the war was hard to find. I hadn't given much thought to the far future, hadn't looked beyond just making the place profitable and getting a few hired hands to help out next season, but when I had envisioned it, in flights of fancy, I'd seen Vicky and me, and our eventual kids hanging out with Clines and whoever he'd roped into settling down with him and *their* kids. And maybe a dog. I wanted a dog.

Now, there was only an empty house.

I let off the accelerator and cruised to a gentle stop about a half a klick from the place, at the edge of his fields, switching off our lights and just watching in silence for a moment.

"At least no one beat us here," Vicky said. She nodded toward the re-trans antenna bolted to the side of his roof. "We could try calling Brad."

It was an annoying weakness of the 'links here that they

wouldn't work just anywhere, the way they would on any other colony. We could use them line-of-sight no problem, or route them through other 'links that were line of sight in a daisy chain, but there were no satellites to relay the signal over the horizon, and no regional transmission towers either. What we had were re-trans antennas on each settlement and arrayed around Gamma Junction, which gave us a connection anytime we were in their transmission area.

We wouldn't have been able to call Brad on the ride back, but she was right, we could now.

"You think it would be secure?" I asked her.

"I don't know. But you were the one worried about them killing us and no one finding out what was really going on."

She had me there. I pulled out my 'link, the display screen lighting up the interior of the cab as it flashed to life. There were twenty messages on the damned thing, most from other members of the board, all of them vets like us, and I scrolled through a couple just to see if something catastrophic had happened while we'd been incommunicado, but they were all just trying to see if we wanted to get together and discuss what we were going to do about things. One was an apology for voting to take the deal with Eld and a half-hearted explanation of why they hadn't wanted to put their lives at risk for what was a government problem.

One was from Brad and Kayla. They were asking if we'd actually gone through with the scouting mission, wondering where we were and if we were okay.

No. Pretty not okay.

I touched the control for an audio hookup with Brad's 'link address and waited for a return signal. It was still an hour or so until dawn and Torrey and Kayla might still be asleep. I didn't know if they would have turned their alerts off, not knowing we might be out at the Hellnick place, but I had no idea if they were sound enough sleepers to keep snoring right through the sound.

"Alvarez?" Torrey sounded groggy. I thought I'd woken him up. And yet he still called me "Alvarez," like we were back in the Marines. "What happened? Did you go? Are you back?"

"We went," I told him. "Vicky and I are okay. We're sitting outside Dave's house, using his re-trans. I took some video I need to send to you. It's important you try to find a way to get it to the CSF, Brad."

"Why? What happened? What did you see? Are you guys all right?"

"Cam." It was Kayla Gruhl, speaking over Torrey's shoulder, her voice slightly muffled, more distant. "Did you get out without being spotted? Is everyone okay?"

I exchanged a bleak look with Vicky.

"Vicky and I are all right. Dave...didn't make it."

"Oh, sweet Vishnu," Kayla moaned, in soft counterpoint to her husband's violent cursing.

"What the fuck happened out there, Alvarez?" Torrey demanded. I felt like he was trying to reach through the 'link and grab me by the front of my jacket, shake me until I broke down and told him.

"It was a patrol," Vicky said, leaning over in the cab so the 'link's microphone would pick up her voice. "Some of Eld's people on foot spotted Dave and me while Cam was inside scouting the warehouse."

"Warehouse? What warehouse?"

"It's in the video I'm sending you," I snapped. "They have a huge setup out at Hellnick's place. A warehouse full of ordnance, Tahni troops with military weapons, barracks, the whole nine yards, Brad."

"Jesus, Alvarez. And Clines? What happened to him?"

"We were pinned down," Vicky went on, her jaw quivering,

though whether with the pain of remembering Clines' death or from frustration at Torrey's interruption, I couldn't be sure. "Trying to get to cover. Dave saw them before I did, pushed me behind cover and took a shot aimed at me. We had to leave him behind...." Her voice broke and I put a hand on her arm.

I had been attaching the video to the stream while she spoke, and now I hit send.

"You should be getting the recording in a second," I told him. "I don't know if the transmission tower in town has been taken over by Eld and his crew, but you have to find a way to get this out. The CSF won't be able to ignore it."

"Of course. I'll see to it immediately."

"What about the guns, Brad?" I wanted to know. "Did you talk to Martinez about the guns?"

"He said he's going to try, Cam," Kayla answered for him. "He doesn't know if he can do it, switch over to mass-producing weapons, without the others noticing, without one of the civilians reporting it to Eld, but he'll try."

I sighed. It wasn't exactly a guarantee, but at least Martinez hadn't said no.

"Where are you...," I started to ask, but Vicky interrupted me, her head cocked to the side.

"Do you hear that?" she asked me, leaning forward, and trying to peer upward out the windshield.

I hit the switch to roll down the driver's side window, the gentle chill of the night breeze whispery against my face, a sibilant whisper through the stalks. And somewhere high above that whisper was a roar, distorted by a Doppler effect, coming downward, coming toward us. Fast.

"Shit!" I blurted, dropping my 'link in my haste to jam down the accelerator and twist the steering wheel.

I took down a row of cornstalks in my abrupt right turn,

their remains spattering against the rear wheel wells, the sudden takeoff throwing Vicky against her seat restraints.

"Is that...?" she began, but I didn't have to answer her.

What did answer was a thunderbolt straight from some ancient Greek god, tossed down from Olympus. The proton beam was a broad swathe of plasma-hot fire, so bright it hurt to look at, after-images from the blast blinding me with starburst of purple and white. I could still see well enough to watch it slam into the center of Dave Clines' house and blow it into kindling.

The shock wave from the blast hit our rover half a klick away and lifted us up onto two wheels for a heart-stopping second. I jerked the wheel in the other direction, letting off the gas, and releasing the breath I'd been holding when we touched back down, the suspension groaning and creaking in protest.

And I was back in the war. The screams of overtaxed turbo-jets ripped apart an alien sky and death rained down around us, indiscriminate, killing soldier and civilian alike. A small body lay half-buried in the wreckage of a Tahni row house, one of the last victims of a war that had left millions of dead and homeless, left permanent scars in places that couldn't be reached by the finest medical nanites.

But this wasn't a Tahni dual-environment fighter. The shuttle wasn't military, not originally. It lacked the sleek, dagger-sharp lines of a Fleet assault shuttle, instead rounded at the nose and the front of the delta shape, patchwork armor welded into place where a military bird would have been seamless and baby-smooth. But the proton cannon was military grade, there was no doubt about that. I'd been close to the hellfire touch of the weapons myself, though they hadn't been targeting me, not on purpose. Incoming friendly fire has the right of way, though, as the saying goes.

"How the hell did they find us?" Vicky was yelling over the

racket from my open window, the wind pouring in and the wheels thumping solidly off the rutted road.

I squeezed my eyes shut, risking taking a detour into the corn to clear the explosions of color from my vision. When I reopened them, the flashes had faded, but nothing else about our situation had improved.

"Can you see it?" I asked, trying to look over my shoulder and not run off the road. "Where did it go?"

"I think it went high again." She had the window open on her side now and was leaning out, searching the sky. "They're looking for us."

I didn't have the lights on, not that it would have made any difference. Unlike my piece of shit, bare-bones rover, their shuttle had IR and thermal, and God alone knew what else. They were up there and they were going to find us eventually. The question was where we wanted to be when they did.

"I'm heading back to our property," I told her. I jammed the gas to the floor and winced at the concussive vibration from running over the rough dirt road at nearly sixty kilometers an hour.

It was impossible to talk with the bang-bang-bang of the wheels slamming into the suspension and I didn't try. Vicky knew what was going on. If they caught up with us before we reached our house, at least we'd know where we were, know the layout of the land. And I convinced myself that even if they'd known who Clines was, maybe found his ID on his 'link and traced it back to his house, they wouldn't know about Vicky and me. The only one who'd seen either of us and lived was Zan-Thint, and he hadn't recognized me.

Sure, I was fooling myself, but the thing about a plan is, you have to have one. You have to come up with a course of action and even if it's not likely to do anything but buy you another ten minutes of life, that's ten minutes when things can change.

Captain Covington, my CO for the whole of my time in the Marines, from private to second lieutenant until his death in the penultimate battle of the war, had told me that every minute alive is another minute you can fight, and every minute you fight is another chance to win.

Somehow, I doubted he'd had this scenario in mind when he'd said it.

"I don't see them," Vicky yelled in my ear, having ducked back inside, her hair wind-whipped and wild, the tie around her ponytail having been blown off. "Maybe they went back to their landing field."

As it turned out, she was right, the shuttle had turned back. Because they didn't need it anymore.

The road back to our house from Clines' place took us through a stand of transplanted Earth trees, genetically-engineered oaks twenty meters tall, a sort-of natural barrier between properties, meant as a convenient dividing line and also an aesthetic barrier, trying to avoid the impression of endless rows of crops. Or so we'd been told when we moved in and found them waiting for us. I didn't know how they'd got them to grow so quickly, but I was sure they had, since there was no way they'd brought them here and transplanted them fully grown. I didn't know why they hadn't kept growing at that rate, but they didn't seem any taller now than when we'd first moved in. Just tall enough to hide what was happening on our property until I cleared the first break in the groves and took the connecting road onto our land.

We were only a kilometer from our house, plenty close enough to see the hoppers circling. They didn't even bother to black out their running lights, confident no one here would have anything that could bring them down, and they were probably right. I slammed on the brakes when I saw them, biting off a curse.

"They know," Vicky said, echoing my own thoughts. "They know who we are."

She didn't sound frightened. Her tone was flat, her expression neutral, as if she'd accepted her fate, as if the reality of our situation had beaten down the conviction which she'd been keeping alive that we would survive this. I couldn't, though. The Cameron Alvarez who would have accepted this, would have welcomed it, had died in the war.

"I'm heading for Brad and Kayla's." The rover jumped into a screeching lunge forward, like the thing was sentient and had just been waiting for my command.

"They'll see us."

"They would if we took the road," I agreed.

I twisted the wheel to the left and plowed into a row of cornstalks twenty meters across, pressing the accelerator to the floor and holding it there. The stalks flogged the hood of the rover, an energetic drumbeat from a never-ending synth dance number, the kind that used to be hot in the clubs on Earth twenty years ago and were still making the rounds across the colonies. The rover flung itself into the thrash pit, ignoring the flagellation until some of the stalks wrapped themselves around one of the axles. The car jerked and skidded, but for all the stark, cheap simplicity of the design, the rover was a durable, powerful vehicle and the plant material gave way before the metal.

Rows of corn were mown down by our bumper like grass, and if anyone had happened to be looking our way, they wouldn't have been able to miss our passage, whether they had night vision or not. But they were watching the road, watching the house. Watching for us.

How had they known it was us? How had they tracked us down? Even barreling through the corn field, knuckles white on the wheel, locked in a desperate struggle to keep the rover going straight, the questions burned in my thoughts.

Eld knew our names, of course, had found them out the night of the crash. Had he just assumed it was us tonight, after the shootout? Hellnick could have told him where we lived. Or had Eld just decided he couldn't risk trusting any of us anymore and was going after everyone at the meeting who hadn't voted to go along with him? If he had....

"Try to get Brad and Kayla on your 'link," I told Vicky, realizing I'd left Torrey hanging when the shuttle had destroyed Dave Clines' house. "Tell them we have enemy troops on the ground at our property and that they should make sure Eld's people aren't coming after them, too."

I wasn't even sure if she could hear me over the racket from our drive through the field, but she began patting around on her belt for her 'link, bracing herself against the door column with her other hand, letting her rifle jump around in her lap because she didn't have a spare hand to hold it down.

"No signal," she told me.

She didn't have to elaborate. Either the enemy around our house had disabled the re-trans antenna or they were jamming us. It was the least of our problems; the row of corn that had been concealing us ended. I'd known it would. I knew the width and length of each of the rows by heart, having programmed the auto harvester to plant and reap each every one of them, and I knew there was a gap between them, twenty meters of hard-packed ground for hauling out produce in cargo trucks. I thought, so far as I'd considered it at all, that it would be two seconds of exposure, maximum, and then we'd be back in the concealment of the fields of corn.

And it would have been if I hadn't slammed into the rear quarter of a cargo truck and flipped the damned rover end for end.

[13]

The spatter of cornstalks against the front of the truck had become constant, something I'd gotten used to over the two or three minutes we'd been wading through the rows, and when we came out of the last row and into open air, it was like running indoors out of a rainstorm, a sudden shock. That's the only excuse I had for not seeing the truck.

Its lights were on because Eld's forces weren't concerned about concealment. Their only concern was finding us, and while I knew they'd be looking on the paths between the rows, I hadn't envisioned the sort of shitty luck that would put one directly in front of us. Vicky had time to get out half of a warning, and then a cricket bat slammed me in the chest.

Or at least that was what it felt like when the seat restraints bit. I'd never been in a vehicle accident, unless you count the time my suit landed in a lake from a thousand meters up, and this didn't compare to the impacts I'd experienced in the Vigilante battlesuit. Even being kicked by a pissed-off Tahni mecha hadn't had the pure, naked concussion of smashing the front end of our rover into the cargo truck.

If we'd skimped when it came to the night vision features on the rover, we'd at least splurged when it came to safety. Airbags popped open so quickly, it was as if they'd been there all along and I just hadn't been focusing on them. Back in Tijuana, when I was about four years old, my brother had been playing soccer with his friends and I'd just *had* to join the game. That had lasted about thirty seconds, until one of Anton's friends had kicked that old, rubber soccer ball right into my face. I'd cried for a half an hour and hadn't asked to play again.

The airbag slapping me in the face reminded me of that soccer ball, although I didn't have time for crying, and definitely couldn't run to my mother for comfort. It did distract me long enough for me to miss the exact moment the rover's passenger's-side wheels came off the ground, though I realized it the instant we hit the point of no return and I knew we were going to flip.

The side airbags inflated a second time when my door hit the ground, bouncing my head back up and filling my vision with stars. I could feel the car grinding to a halt, sliding up to the edge of the opposite line of cornstalks, but I couldn't see it, couldn't make out anything except the ringing in my ears and the dull ache that seemed to come from every part of my body at once.

I don't remember making the decision to move, don't remember thinking the problem through and coming up with a course of action, but my hands were in motion as if some cosmic puppet-master was working through me. My belt knife was in my hand and I had no idea how it had gotten there, but I knew instinctively what I had to do with it. The seat restraint quick-release was jammed.

Had I tried it? I didn't know, I just knew it was jammed. It was dark, the interior lights in the cab smashed, and I had to find the base of the straps by feel, then slide the knife blade between my body and the straps, somehow keeping the blade facing outward. The pressure against my shoulders slacked off with the first cut, then disappeared with the second, and I nearly fell into the side of the car, which was now down, stopping myself with a grab at the wheel, keeping the knife stretched out safely away from me.

"Vicky," I croaked, my mouth filled with cotton. "Are you okay?"

"Wha' th' fu' happ'n'd?" she murmured, shaking her head, hands feeling around her chest for her restraints.

I didn't try to answer, just cut her free and caught her by the shoulder before she could fall head-first toward the left side of the cab. She staggered, off-balance, and I grabbed her face gently between my thumb and fingers and made her look at me.

"Honey, are you okay? We gotta get out of this car right now. You understand?"

"Don't call me 'honey,' you dork," she said, her voice firming up along with her legs.

I breathed a sigh of relief and ducked back down into my side of the car, feeling around until my hand closed on a gun. It wasn't the one I'd been looking for, I could tell immediately. The Gyroc pistol had a distinctive, curved grip, but this one was squared-off and fat in my hand, front-heavy and bulky. It was Dave Clines' slug-shooter, which I didn't know how to operate or even how to aim, but it was all I had time to grab.

The windshield was cracked and splintered, designed for safety rather than invulnerability, another compromise we'd made between price and features when we'd visited the industrial fabricator to have it made. This particular compromise I was happy with, since it let me kick the windshield out of its frame and gave us a route for a quick escape. The plastic sheeting folded outward at the impact from the sole of my boot and I squeezed through, putting my back against the hood of the rover, bringing the handgun up to high-ready in both hands.

The night hit me like a cold splash of water to my face, as if

I'd still been insulated from the universe outside the vehicle even after the rover had been broken and battered around me. Now, the chirp of crickets and the rush of the wind were deafening in the absence of the wheels thumping on ruts and cornstalks slapping against the front of the rover, and punctuating those background noises were footsteps and confused groans.

And the gabbling sing-song of the Tahni language. It was on the other side of the rover, where the cargo truck had spun out from the collision, and I had the sudden revelation that the cargo truck had been a makeshift personnel carrier and I was now facing a whole squad full of Zan-Thint's Tahni soldiers, probably armed with KE rifles that could rip us to pieces.

Just stay alive for another ten minutes. Shit. Just stay alive for another minute.

Vicky pushed through the warped sheet of splintered plastic that had used to be the windshield, coming out behind me, one hand on my shoulder, the other somehow filled with her rifle. I don't know how she found it in the midnight chaos that was our truck cab, but I wasn't going to question the luck that had provided it.

"We're going into the corn to lose them," I whispered to her, pointing straight ahead.

There was only about three meters between the nose of the rover and the next row of cornstalks, which doesn't seem like much until you run the risk of getting shot while crossing it.

"Then you know that shit is concealment, not cover, right?" she said, eyeing me with obvious skepticism.

"We can have one or neither. I'll take the one. We go in and angle off to the right and hope they shoot the other direction. It's the only plan I have that doesn't involve the two of us trying to shoot it out with a squad of Tahni." I was getting a bit strident and a bit too loud and I took a deep breath and tried to control myself. "We go together on three."

She looked as if she wanted to argue, but she didn't. She just nodded and raised the rifle to low port. Behind us, the voices were moving, shifting from far to our right, coming left and behind us. The Tahni were circling around the rover.

"One," I whispered, using the light from the headlights of the cargo truck to give Clines' gun a quick once-over, finding a manual safety and disengaging it.

More gibbering Tahni language, directly behind the back of the rover. I wondered if they could see us through the back window.

"Two." I recalled that a gun like this would need a round chambered off the magazine in order to fire. I pulled the slide back a centimeter or so and saw a glint of what might have been metal inside, some sort of cartridge case. I'd read about weapons like this in history texts, but metal cartridges were hard-core antique.

I'd just let the slide ride back into place when the first of the Tahni came around the back of the rover, KE gun probing ahead of him. Like the ones who'd been guarding the warehouse, these weren't equipped with helmets, which I thought was particularly short-sighted of them. Since I had no idea whether the rounds this handgun fired would penetrate the light, armored vests they were wearing, I aimed the handgun instinctively at the first one who cleared the back of the car and shot him in the head.

"Three!"

The discharge of the handgun had been an explosion of light twenty centimeters across and the pistol bucked in my hand like it wanted to jump free in protest of being used in this manner. I held on and squeezed off another three rounds, not aiming so much as hoping, then took off on Vicky's heels.

If the cornstalks whipping against the car had been annoying, their impact on my face was absolutely painful and I raised a protective arm over my head to fend them off. I'd said we were cutting right, and Vicky had taken me at my word, rushing in straight barely three meters before she took a forty-five-degree angle to the right. She was only a couple meters ahead of me and I could still barely register her passage in the darkness, but she'd been right. This was concealment, but we only had seconds before....

The hum-snap of the KE rifles firing was nearly drowned out by the smack of the tantalum needles slicing through the cornstalks, starting behind us and to our left and moving steadily our way. They were the hounds of hell snapping at our heels and the panicked animal in my hind-brain wanted to throw myself to the ground and roll into a fetal position, but experience and instinct told me something else, something just one half-step further away from giving into panic. I ran faster, almost blindly, catching up with Vicky and passing her, grabbing her by the arm more to make sure I matched her pace than to propel her along.

The needles chased us, but I had the conviction that if they actually knew which way we were heading, ducking to the ground would accomplish nothing—the things were travelling at a couple thousand meters per second and could chew downward through the corn and into us just as easily if we were on the ground. I had to take the chance that they were firing at random, hosing back and forth in an effort to get lucky and hit us. I also had to take the chance they wouldn't rush headlong into the stalks after us, in the dark, after at least one and maybe more of their comrades had been gunned down.

The Tahni didn't lack for emotions of their own sort, but I'd never known one of their soldiers to seek personal vengeance during the war. As far as we knew, they viewed death as part of the will of their spirit-Emperor, and even if this group had abandoned the religion and philosophy of their homeworld, casting aside habits you'd learned from childhood wasn't nearly so easy.

Which was why I prayed silently as I ran, despite experiences in my life that might have led a more rational man to question the existence of a merciful God. Whether God was listening, or I'd guessed right, or maybe fate was simply toying with me, the gunfire slewed back the other direction and we kept running.

To where, I wasn't so sure.

"I think we might have finally lucked out."

Vicky cast a baleful look at me.

"You weren't an officer *that* long. You know better than to say shit like that when the universe is listening."

But she wasn't whispering the words or trying too hard to stay low against the edge of the cornfield. Brad and Kayla's house was only two hundred meters away and there was no sign of Eld's people or his Tahni allies, no hopper running lights in the night sky, no scream of shuttle engines. The outside lights were on and the only vehicles present were the family rover and a small cargo truck he'd bought with part of his separation bonus. Torrey was a bit freer with his than we'd been with ours, maybe because it didn't seem as if he could ever picture himself leaving this world.

"I guess there's no use trying to sneak up on them," Vicky said with a shrug, rising from a crouch and walking toward the house, slinging her rifle over her shoulder. "It's gonna be dawn soon and I'd rather not wait out here for the mosquitos to come out and start doing their thing."

I followed her, Clines' gun still weighing down my right hand. I'd had to shift it from one hand to the other on the five-kilometer walk out here, as my palms became sweaty in turn and the grip began to get slippery. I was ready to lay it down, ready to lie down myself. The planet's gravity might have been a hair lighter than Earth-normal, but you couldn't have proved it by me. I was being dragged toward the ground by the pull of a neutron star, my legs a mass of aching muscles, every step a supreme effort.

It didn't seem to bother Vicky as much, but I'd always been convinced women were better at ignoring discomfort than we men. Or maybe she was just as burned out as I was but too proud to show it. Either way, her step was brisk and my heels were dragging, and when we reached the porch of Brad and Kayla's house, I leaned against the railing for a second before I was able to climb the steps.

"Brad! Kayla!" Vicky called, pounding on the door. "It's us! Let us in!"

She sounded as if we'd arrived early for a dinner party rather than showing up as fugitives with legions of enemies on our trail, but I wouldn't have even had the voice to yell. I was seriously considering just lying down on the porch and falling asleep right there when the door banged open and Brad Torrey emerged, rifle at his shoulder, eyes flickering around behind us as if he expected the Tahni to be right behind us.

"Jesus, Alvarez, Sandoval," he sighed, relaxing slightly when he saw that we were alone. "You broke off right in the middle of talking to me and the last thing I heard was a Goddamned explosion! I thought you two were dead."

"Night isn't over yet," I said. It almost was. The skies were getting a lighter grey with each passing minute as the primary star creeped upward on the other side of the eastern horizon. I estimated we had about a half an hour until it became light enough to see. "Can we come in?"

He waved us inside, though from his deep scowl, he didn't seem very happy about it.

The light was on in the kitchen and Kayla was waiting there, pacing, hugging herself as if the pre-dawn chill had penetrated through the stone walls and insulation and past the central heating. I thought at first that she was scared, but the expression on her pinched face was more anger than fear.

"What in the living hell is happening out there, Cameron Alvarez?" she demanded. "David got himself killed? Tahni soldiers? Has everyone gone insane?"

I frowned, then realized I still had the gun in my hand and set it down on their table. The heavy metal made a deep, authoritative thump on the wood and I winced.

"Sorry," I said, though I wasn't sure if I was apologizing for scratching her table or for the insanity of the situation. My hand was palm-down against the cold, wood surface and I leaned into it, suddenly unable to stand unassisted, the exhaustion crashing down on me.

"Oh, for goodness sake," Kayla clucked, emerging from the walled-off funk to grab me by the shoulders and push me into one of the chairs. "Sit down before you fall down. Both of you."

I let my head tilt backwards against the padded chair, my eyelids sneaking down like stealthy little ninjas. I forced them back open.

"If I sit down," Vicky told Kayla, "I won't be getting up again for a while. Could I use your bathroom first?"

"Of course, girl!" Kayla seemed to have reverted to her normal mother-hen self. "Come on, I'll show you where it is."

The two of them vanished down the hallway, Vicky still toting her rifle over her shoulder. I realized abruptly that I would probably never see my own rifle again and I felt an odd pang of loss for the weapon. I snorted amusement. I'd never been sentimental about any of the Vigilantes I'd gone through in the Marine Corps. They were tools, a hammer I used to pound the enemy, and if one hammer broke, well, there was another waiting in the tool kit to do the job.

Now, though, when everything I owned I had to buy with my own money, when everything that broke had to be fixed or replaced by me instead of DXing it and pulling another out of inventory, the tools seemed to have taken on an almost sentient quality. My rover was a piece of shit, but it was *my* piece of shit. It was gone, too, though it could probably be salvaged and repaired.

Not by me, though. I had an intuition that no matter what happened, repairing broken-down vehicles was going to be a low priority for quite some time. I realized that Torrey had said something and I shook my head clear and tried to focus.

"Sorry?" I said, a yawn nearly interrupting the word. "What was that?"

Torrey was over in the cupboard, rummaging among the shelves there.

"I said," he repeated, "I think I have some coffee in here if you want some."

I almost said no. I had never been a big coffee drinker, even in the Marines, and I used it even less out here, where all you could get was the locally-grown shit. The soil here gave it a strange, bitter taste. But caffeine was a handy substitute for sleep I wasn't likely to get, and beggars couldn't be choosers.

"Sure, thanks."

"I'm afraid you've really stepped in it this time, Alvarez," he said, shaking his head. He glanced back over his shoulder from the cupboard. "Knocked over a fucking big hornet's nest. But then, I suppose that was your specialty."

"What do you mean?" My brows furled in confusion, but the expression devolved into another yawn.

"Back in the Corps," he elaborated. "I saw your record. You

were always agitating, weren't you? Trying to get shit done your way instead of accepting the situation and soldiering on."

I think I was smiling, but it was a reflection of confusion rather than amusement.

"What the fuck are you talking about, Brad?"

Whatever his answer might have been, it was cut off by a shout from down the hallway, a pained cry, pitched high enough that it was assuredly female, though I couldn't tell if it was Vicky or Kayla.

"No!" That was Vicky, not frightened but angry. "Cam! Get out!"

My exhaustion disappeared in a surge of adrenaline and I lunged across the table for the handgun. Brad Torrey moved faster. When he turned from the cupboard, there was a pistol in his hand, something fat and bulbous, with an emitter so broad I could have stuck my fist into it. My mouth dropped open in an incoherent attempt at a question, and Torrey answered it by pulling the trigger.

[14]

I floated in limbo and waited to pass on to the other side.

That was how it worked, I thought. You died, your body rotted, and your soul made its way to Heaven or Hell, or maybe Purgatory if you listened to Father Gomez, the old priest. Mama didn't believe in Purgatory, though. She thought there were just two choices. I'd asked her once, in the infinite wisdom of a six-year-old, if being in a big lake of fire for all eternity wouldn't just get boring after a while. She told me she didn't believe hell was a lake of fire. She said she believed Heaven was being in the presence of God, sharing community with all the saints and angels, while Hell was being alone, just you and the darkness and no one else.

That hadn't seemed so bad to me, making my way through the foster care system in Trans-Angeles. I'd spent most of my time *trying* to find a place where I could hide in the darkness, away from everyone. Then I'd repeated the process on the streets, hiding in shadowed alcoves and niches in the cracks of the system and finally thought I'd found the perfect hiding place in the arms of a Vigilante battlesuit.

And now, finally, it looked as if I'd found my nook of darkness, one that would last me for all eternity. And I had no illusions I'd be going to Heaven, not after the life I'd led. I just wished I'd been there to help Vicky...

"Goddamnit, where the hell did the girl go?"

The voice came from light-years away, and I wondered if Mama had been wrong, if there were other people around in Hell after all, someone to share the suffering with. Not good people, though. Good people wouldn't be swearing in Heaven. Mama didn't like swearing and I was sure that meant God wouldn't care for it, either.

"This was your fault, you fat bitch!"

Oh yeah, this had to be hell. No way would anyone in Heaven talk like that. But the voice was clearer now, piercing, clear, and familiar. I couldn't place it through the haze over my thoughts, but I was fairly sure it wasn't someone I wanted to spend eternity with.

"I tried!" I *did* know this voice. It was Kayla Gruhl. What was she doing in the afterlife? "But she still had the rifle and I had to be cautious. Sandoval is nobody's fool...neither of them are. The only reason Brad got the drop on Alvarez was that he was half-asleep."

Kayla? Brad? They'd done this to us?

I wasn't dead. With that realization came a wash of intense pain, spearing into my skull like the blast from a plasma gun and spreading outward. What had happened to me? I tried to remember and received for my effort a mental image of the last thing I'd seen. The handgun Brad Torrey had held had been fitted with a bell-shaped muzzle, a miniature transmission dish. It was a sonic stunner.

Where would have gotten one of those? And *why*? Not just why had he and Kayla betrayed us, but if they were going to betray us, why bother to knock me out when he could have just put a bullet in my chest and been done with it?

My face twitched, an involuntary muscle spasm, and I tried to keep my eyes shut, stay still, pretend I was still unconscious until I figured out where I was and what was happening. I was seated in a wooden chair, possibly even the same chair I'd been in when Torrey had shot me, except now my arms were pulled around the back of it, my hands fastened together at the wrists by something hard and unyielding but slightly pliable, feeling of plastic. Zip ties, maybe.

My ankles were likewise restrained to the legs of the chair and I tried to picture the construction of the furniture, wondering if I could slide the ties at my ankles down off the end of the legs and get free. But I had a sense there was a cross-piece there that would prevent that. They'd trussed me up good, a turkey ready for the oven.

"You did the best you could, honey," Brad assured his wife, sounding absurdly domestic given the circumstances. His tone changed with the next sentence, directed at someone else. "It's not as if she has any military training! You knew that! I asked you to come take care of it yourself, but you had to make me try to take them down first before you came!"

"They would have bolted if they'd seen us coming." The same voice as before, a bit less harsh, as if the man was admitting Torrey was right. "Hell, they scooted through our perimeter three times on the way here. They know this land better than we do. All this fucking corn looks alike to us."

"Why didn't the Colonel come himself?" Torrey demanded. "This is his operation. His people are soldiers. No offense, Captain, but Alvarez and Sandoval aren't some Pirate World smugglers who you can have your muscle push around. They don't scare that easy."

Eld. It was Captain Eld. I knew I'd heard that voice before. Torrey and Kayla were working with Eld...and with the Tahni. My breath started to come heavier, my pulse speeding up in time with the rage in my chest. And the rage betrayed me.

"Because Zan-Thint and his people are busy making sure what happened with these three doesn't spread to the rest of your veteran friends. They're out there now, going from farm to farm, house to house."

His voice was moving, getting closer to me.

"Is he going to...kill them?" Kayla asked, the hesitation in her voice almost convincing. Did she really care or was she trying to soothe her conscience?

"Not unless they put up a fight. The whole point of this operation was *not* to attract attention, but that's all right buggered now." He was directly in front of me. "Thanks to you, Alvarez." He snorted a laugh. "You can stop pretending to be unconscious. I know exactly how long that stunner lasts...I'm the one that gave it to Torrey in the first place."

I opened my eyes and saw the smuggler captain looming over me, seeming even taller now than he had when I'd first met him. A Gyroc pistol hung loose in his left hand, his trigger finger tapping absently along the side of the receiver.

"I know what you're thinking, jarhead," he said, the corner of his mouth turning in a sneer. "Why did I keep you alive? Why didn't I just have Torrey here finish you off?"

I glanced over at Brad and Kayla. Neither of them could meet my eyes.

"I figured you'd get to that part," I said, trying to work saliva into my mouth. Waking up from a sonic, I found, was a lot like waking up from an auto-doc, except for all the pain. "I was mostly wondering why they'd do it."

"They abandoned us in this fucking wasteland!" Brad Torrey blurted, anger flashing over his features, and I thought he was probably angry at me for putting their actions into unflinching words. "After all we'd given to them, everything we'd lost, they exiled us here! The Corporates are bleeding us dry with their fees and surcharges! All they want is to drain our separation bonuses and then buy us out!"

"You sound like Dave," I told him. "Did you warn them we were coming? Did you get him killed?"

"Enough," Eld snapped, leaning over, and grabbing me by the back of the neck, forcing me to face him. He smelled of must and oil, his breath stale. "We kept you alive because I need your authorization for your 'link."

He pulled the device out of his pocket and I thought he must have fished it out of our rover, because that was the last place I'd seen it.

"Torrey here isn't going to pass your little spy video on to anyone else, of course," Eld said, the smile he threw at Brad and Kayla chill and merciless. "But I don't need it floating around the ether here, hopping from one server to another. So, you're going to delete the fucking thing for me, permanently."

He held the 'link up to my face.

"You can either do it now, of your own free will, or I can start carving bits off of you until you beg me to do it."

I would have shrugged if I'd had the range of motion available. The recording wasn't going to do us any good, anyway. Even if it remained in the system for the next year and some CSF investigator eventually stumbled across it, we'd be long dead.

"Cameron Alvarez authorizes open access," I said into the audio pickup. If I'd been holding it, all it would have taken was my biometrics, but he wasn't trusting me to operate the thing myself. Maybe he was afraid I'd send it to someone else if I had it in my hand.

Eld grunted and began scrolling through menus, tapping now and again until he smiled with what I took for satisfaction and tossed the device aside. It clattered on the floor against the far wall and he eyed me with disdain.

"I thought you'd put up more of a fight, Marine."

"Well, I'm a little tired," I told him.

"Cap'n!" The front door burst open with the golden glow of morning, and one of Eld's crew stomped inside, the scarred, shaven-headed man out of breath and looking more than a little afraid to tell Eld the news he had. "We have a watch along the perimeter roads. She hasn't slipped through, I'm sure of it. But we can't find her. We're scanning the fields with thermal scopes, but all she's gotta do is keep moving ahead of us and we won't be able to pick her up that way."

"Use the fucking hopper then!" Eld said.

"Colonel Zan-Thint called the last one away to help him secure one of the other properties, Cap'n."

"Oh, that fucking flat-eared son of a bitch." Eld's teeth clenched as if trying to keep any further imprecations private. "All right, then. She wants to play Little Miss Commando, I can fucking play that game, too." He motioned to the bald man. "Grab him, chair and all, bring him out on the fucking porch where his bitch can see him."

I had a vague idea of where this was going and I didn't much care for it. I yanked at my restraints, trying to remember the tricks I'd learned for getting free of zip ties on the streets of the Underground, but most of them required me to have been conscious when the ties were put on, which hadn't been the case. Eld didn't even bother to warn me against it, supremely confident in his own precautions, eyes out on the fields in the distance as he walked out the door ahead of us.

Baldy grabbed the back of my chair and tilted it backwards, scraping the back legs against the wood floor. The squeaking, grinding noise set my teeth on edge and I caught a glimpse out of the corner of my eye of Kayla wincing at the damage to her floor. A couple hours ago, I would have felt bad for her, but at the moment, I would have gladly urinated on her prized throw rug. Brad Torrey was staring at me as the interior of their house withdrew from sight and I was dragged through the door and into the morning light, and I thought maybe there was shame in his expression.

It disappeared into the glare of the morning sun as baldy spun me around and set my chair facing east across the front yard into the crops. More of Eld's people wandered around the edge of the field, carbines held at the ready, staring into the corn, looking as if they were ready to shoot the first thing that moved.

"Your wife is a real hellcat," Eld told me, hands on his hips as he joined his men in a careful scan of our surroundings. "Killed two of my crew already, and now all the useless pussies are too scared to go into the stalks after her." He shrugged, giving me a look that was almost apologetic. "I know, I *should* really kill one of them myself as an example for the others, but would you believe it? It's not that fucking easy to get good help, and there won't be any more coming this way for a while. Thanks to you backwoods fucks, I don't have any people to spare."

I glared at him.

"I'm from the Trans-Angeles Underground," I corrected him, grinding the words out. "I'm not any kind of backwoods fuck."

"Well, pardon the hell out of me, Mr. Big City Slicker." He chuckled. "If you're so fucking cosmopolitan, why are you out here a hundred light years from the edge of the Commonwealth?"

"If you'd ever lived in the Trans-Angeles Underground, you wouldn't have to ask why anyone would want to leave it."

He grunted appreciation, but when he spoke again, it was a bellow, projected outward so Vicky could hear.

"Sandoval! We have your husband! If you don't surrender in the next thirty seconds, I start cutting off bits of him and feeding them to Torrey's dogs!"

He pulled a sixteen-centimeter knife from a sheath on his belt in illustration and took a step closer to me.

"Run, Vicky!" I yelled, hoping she'd listen to me. "He'll kill us both anyway!"

Eld spun into a backhand, catching me across the face, the blow hard enough to knock the chair over sideways with me in it. Fireworks exploded in my vision, a sharp pain in my cheek transitioning into a dull ache. Suddenly I was back in the group homes, in yet another fight I wasn't going win and instinct tried to bring my hands in front of my face, draw my knees to my chest in a protective ball. But I was strapped down, and when the chair hit the porch, so did the side of my head.

It wasn't much as thumps on the head went, certainly not the worst I'd received even since I'd joined the Marines, but it was enough to make my vision go hazy and my ears start ringing. Despite the incipient tinnitus, I could still hear Eld's words clearly as he bent over and hauled me up by the shoulder, the tip of his knife floating in front of my face.

"All right, bitch, time's up! You stand your ass up right now with your hands empty and your arms in the air or I start cutting!"

"Cap'n!" It was Baldy, I thought from the accent and the inflection, though I couldn't see him from where I was sitting. "There's something moving out there!"

Eld's knife pulled a few centimeters away from my face, his head coming up, scanning the fields, and I did, too.

Don't do it, I begged Vicky silently. *Just get the hell out of here.*

I caught sight of the movement Baldy had reported, a rustle in the corn maybe a hundred meters away. It could have been anything. The colonization crews had brought Earth animals along with crops and insects, not giving much of a shit about the local ecology, and I had seen coyotes, rabbits, bobcats and deer in the crops alongside the rock dragons, water-lizards, bore worms and a dozen other native fauna. I prayed I was seeing the track of one of those animals making its way through the crops, searching for food. I prayed Vicky had been smart enough to leave me behind.

"Is that you, little miss?" Eld yelled, squinting against the glow of the primary star. "Don't make me ask again!"

Eld grabbed a fistful of my hair, the first time in years it had been long enough for anyone to accomplish that, and pulled my head back. I tried to keep my eyes on him, but all I could see was the roof of the porch, support beams stained with moisture from the earlier rains, insects buzzing around under the eaves.

But I felt the tip of his knife digging into the side of my neck, felt a drop of blood making a runnel through the dirt caked there, heading down my collar onto my shoulder.

"All right, Marine," Eld sighed, sounding as if he was genuinely going to regret what he was about to do, "guess she wants to make this difficult."

It wasn't that difficult, at least not for me. Eld's head exploded.

I had a very clear view of it in the split-second before the blood reached my eyes and I squeezed them shut and looked away by instinct, and I wasn't sure if I'd ever get the image out of my mind no matter how long I lived.

I saw nothing for long seconds, and what I heard wasn't what I expected. I heard neither the sharp crack of a gunshot nor the hiss of a Gyroc round, just a distinctive hum-snap, something I hadn't heard in years. It was the sound of a Gauss rifle, the issue weapon of the Force Recon Marines during the war and still a restricted firearm, not something anyone out here would have been able to legally acquire.

Whoever *had* managed to acquire the guns were very liberal about using them. The hum-snap discharges of the electromagnetic slug shooters merged into a single, rhythmic harmony, lasting a good ten seconds, punctuated by the smack of tungsten slugs into flesh and wood, and the tinkle of shattering windows and falling glass.

Dozens of the projectiles were slicing through the air, leaving miniature sonic booms in their wake, and I tried to shake the blood out of my eyes, knowing one of them had my name on it and not wanting to go out blind. But the barrage ended as abruptly as it had begun and everything was dead silent except the huff of my own labored breath in my ears.

Footsteps, running across the ground, up the steps to the porch, light and agile, and then soft fingers rubbing the blood and God knew what else out of my face, and Vicky was standing above me, a look of disbelief passing across her features, as if she couldn't quite accept that we weren't dead.

"You're okay," she assured me, as if I might have some doubts about the nature of reality myself. "I'll get you out of this shit."

She pulled her knife off her belt and knelt down, slicing through the ties around my ankles, and with her out of the way, I was finally able to see past her, to the corn field. A dozen dark shapes had emerged from the stalks, clad in black armor, their faces hidden behind mirrored visors, their Gauss rifles held at low port, muzzles sweeping back and forth as they searched for anything else to shoot.

Through their ranks walked a single figure, outfitted the same as the others, but his helmet off, held under his left arm. His head was shaven bald, shiny, the interface jacks implanted in his temples clearly visible, flaunted even. I had once thought those gleaming, dark eyes cruel and stupid, but I'd learned that he was not that much different from me, just a scared, lonely kid trying to fit in and not succeeding very well. We'd drifted apart, assigned to different platoons and eventually, different companies, but by the end, I'd considered him a friend.

God knows, I was happy to see him now.

A grin split Wade Cunningham's broad, ugly face as he stepped up onto the porch, offering me a hand.

"Cam Alvarez," he said. "Fancy meeting you here."

[15]

I stared into Kayla Gruhl's dead eyes, unable to look away. Somewhere in the sightless blue, I thought, were the mysteries of the universe, the answers to all my questions. Or maybe there was just peace and rest. I wondered if I should feel envious of her.

One of the black-armored Corporate Security Force troopers zipped the body bag over her face and the black plastic broke the spell, cutting loose my attention and allowing it to drift back to the woman's husband. He was flex-cuffed into a chair in an ironic reflection of my own position only a few minutes before, but I hoped my reaction had been a bit more stoic. Brad Torrey was sobbing uncontrollably, his shoulders shaking, tears streaking his face.

The man had confronted death before, had seen his men die, seen civilians slaughtered just as I had, but the death of his wife had broken him. I couldn't blame him for that, though my sympathy was constrained by the dull anger I felt at his betrayal. At *their* betrayal. The two canceled each other out and I sagged in my chair, sinking into numb exhaustion. Vicky's hand on my shoulder roused me from the stupor, reminding me there were questions I hadn't yet asked.

"Wade," I said to our old comrade in arms, "not that you don't have some hellacious timing, and it's nice as shit to see you again, but how the hell did you wind up here? And how the hell did you wind up in the Corporate Security Force?"

Wade was grinning, as if the blood and the corpses scattered between the living room and the porch didn't bother him, as if he was still used to wading ankle-deep through that sort of shit and it hadn't been over a year since the end of the war. He stood with his feet precisely shoulder width apart, parade rest, though his arms were resting across the top of his Gauss rifle, the sling spreading the load across his tactical vest and over his shoulders. The rest of his team still had their helmets on, their visors down, their radio communications trapped inside the soundproof material, and they might as well have been robots for all I could tell.

"That message you sent," he explained, "probably would have gotten ignored, because I'll be honest with you, man, there ain't too many people at the Corporate station who woulda paid attention to whining by the settlers here. But lucky for you, *I* was there, and I recognized your name." He shrugged, as if it was just an everyday indicator of exactly how awesome he was. "I brought down a shuttle and took a pass over that farm you talked about, that Hellnick asshole. Couldn't see anything, and it might have ended right there...except we couldn't see *anything*. Not farm equipment, not animals, not workers, not nothin'. It was pretty clear they had a camo net stretched over everything. They must have eyes on the station and they saw when we launched a shuttle."

"Did you land on Hellnick's farm?" Vicky asked, her grip on my shoulder tightening, an edge to her voice. She hadn't forgotten Dave's death and neither had I.

"I thought we needed some intelligence first." Wade sniffed as if the idea was insulting. "So, I decided to visit you guys. And when I got to your place, I stumbled across a shitbag trying to hide inside your barn with his rover, and he didn't look like no farmer."

"He talked?" I was surprised. Not that the smugglers would give up their boss but that it could happen so fast.

"Fuck no!" Wade snorted a laugh. "He took a shot at us and we put him in the ground. But he left behind his 'link and we heard them call for reinforcements to search for you." He indicated who 'you' meant by pointing at Vicky. "I didn't want to rush on in and get you two killed, so we flew nap of the earth and landed as close as we could without twigging them to us being there."

"And you found Vicky before they did," I finished. Vicky punched me on the shoulder.

"The hell they did. I found *them*."

"As for why I'm here...," Wade trailed off, the corner of his mouth turning up. "That's a long story, and I think we got better things to do." He nodded toward Brad Torrey. "He's your friend. Sort of. You want to take a run at him before we do this the hard way?"

I didn't ask what the hard way was. But Brad was vulnerable right now and I thought he'd feel guilty about giving us up, and since Eld was dead, maybe he wouldn't feel any particular loyalty to the Tahni. I felt like ten kilos worth of hammered shit and I'd never been any sort of intelligence type, but I was a fellow officer. It might mean something to him, still.

I pushed out of my chair, my quads protesting at the motion, and limped over to where Brad was sitting, dragging my chair with me. It scraped against the wooden floor and I wondered if the sound still bothered him. If it did, he didn't show any sign of it as I spun the chair around and sat across from him. He didn't even look up at me, his head still bowed, sobs still racking his body. His wife's blood was splattered across the right side of his chest, staining his shirt, and a few drops were smeared across his cheek. I couldn't tell which of the holes through the front wall was the round that had killed her. There were too many. I wondered how he'd survived without getting hit.

"I'm sorry about Kayla," I told him. I don't know if it was the right way to start, but it felt right, and I was going with my gut. "She didn't deserve this."

"I did this to her," Brad said, an agonized moan that was nearly a wail. "This is my fault." He finally met my eyes, and I'd seen that sort of pain and loss before, on colony worlds we'd freed from Tahni occupation. "For the love of God, Alvarez, just kill me. I can't live without her."

"If you want to die, I know these guys would give you the chance," I said, glancing aside at the mirrored visor of one of the CSF troopers. "But before you do that, I want to know what the hell is going on. I think you owe me that much."

He glanced at me sharply, his expression firming up, eyes flaring with anger.

"Why would I owe you a damned thing?"

"Semper Fidelis, Captain Torrey," I reminded him. "Did you never think about what the words meant when you learned them at the Academy?"

That seemed to hit him, and I wondered if it might have been striking below the belt. The man's wife was dead on the floor beside him, after all.

"Eld didn't tell us much," Torrey said, the words slow to emerge, dragged out against their will. "He didn't trust us enough for that. He just told us this was going to happen with or without our help and if we agreed to be his eyes and ears, keep him apprised of any plans the other veterans were making, that he'd try to avoid hurting anyone if he didn't have to."

"Except us," Vicky said, glaring at the man. I shot her a quelling look, understanding the anger but lacking the time for it.

"I know you didn't want anyone to get hurt, Brad," I said, soothing, the way I'd talked to privates who were one fuck-up shy of being sent to the brig when I badly needed them for the next mission. "But things didn't turn out that way, and now you have to make it right. What did you hear? I know you kept your eyes and ears open. You were too good a Force Recon Marine to not pay attention."

He made a face like he'd bitten into something sour and finally spat it out.

"His guys weren't exactly careful about talking in front of us," he admitted. "They were smugglers, hijackers, not soldiers. Not the Tahni, but Eld's crew. Most of them hated Zan-Thint, the Tahni commander. He's in charge, not Eld, they all figured out that much, though Eld would never have admitted it. He was paying Eld, using him as a go-between."

"Why?" The question came out a bit more strident than I'd intended and I reminded myself I was trying to play the "good cop" here. "I mean, if he wants to hire a human as a go-between, why would he bother with a bunch of Pirate World thugs? Or did they ever say?"

"I don't know. But he's a Tahni. Maybe no one else would be willing to work for him. I know it was his idea to go to Hellnick's farm first, though. They were complaining about that, about how much they had to pay Hellnick, how it would eat into their profits. There was something there he wanted."

Yeah, I could believe that. I'd seen it, though I still had no idea what it was.

"Do you know what kind of defenses Zan-Thint has out at the Hellnick place? Is there anything besides dismounted infantry?"

"I've never been out there," Torrey insisted, then went quiet, as if I had flipped a switch and he didn't intend to say anything else.

"Don't get stubborn on me, Brad," I warned, leaning toward him, close enough that I could smell the lingering stench of alcohol on his breath. He'd been drinking while I was unconscious. Maybe out of guilt. "I feel bad for you, but not bad enough to forget the part where you were going to let Eld slice me into bits on the front porch. You think you want to die, but I'm telling you, these guys...." I gestured around us at the CSF mercenaries. "...they're not soldiers. They're not Marines. They don't have no Uniform Code of Military Justice and there're no cops out here to make them behave. You can talk to me or you can talk to them, and if you talk to them, you won't be *asking* me to kill you, you'll be *begging* me."

And I was talking out of my ass because I had no idea if the CSF troops would even lay a hand on the man. They had a reputation for making their own rules out on the edges of the Commonwealth where there was no other authority, but rumors were worth as much as you paid for them.

Torrey licked beads of sweat off his upper lip, appearing worried more about himself than his dead wife.

"They said something about a cargo shuttle they put one of those proton cannons on," he said. "If there was anything else, they never talked about it."

"I've heard enough," Wade declared, stepping closer to us, hand going to the pistol grip of his Gauss rifle. "We know they have an armed lander, Vicky already told us that much. But it's no match for our assault shuttle. I'm going to order my crew to blast the whole place with proton cannons and we can sort through the rubble afterward."

"You can't," I insisted, coming to my feet to face him, exhaustion forgotten in the heat of urgency. "Zan-Thint sent his troops out to round up the other veterans. He might be keeping them there as hostages."

"Some of them have children," Vicky added quietly.

I could see the struggle playing itself out across Wade Cunningham's rough features as he weighed our words against his better judgement, and likely his orders from his superiors.

"What's your idea, then?" he asked us. "You two were the officers."

"We could sneak in on foot, like you did here," Vicky suggested. "We know a way through the sensors...."

"That's no good," I interrupted, shaking my head. "They're going to have blocked that way off with either increased electronic coverage or live patrols now that they know about it. But you could have the shuttle drop us off close enough for a dismounted assault on the place, then it could attack the warehouse. There's not room for the settlers in the warehouse—they'd have to be in the barracks-type buildings they put up beside Hellnick's house. You threaten the warehouse, you'll draw their attention and their fire and we can sneak in and secure the hostages."

"We?" Wade asked, noticing my phrasing. "Us?"

"Well, you didn't think we were just going to sit this out, did you?" Vicky asked him, hands on her hips, feet squared off like she was getting ready to fight Wade. "No fucking way. Those are our friends and neighbors the Tahni bastards are holding out there."

"They killed Dave," I said, not quite as enthusiastic about it as Vicky but just as resolute.

"Your friend got killed," Wade countered, "because you all got in over your heads and thought you were some kind of half-assed commando squad. You're not Force Recon and neither one of you belonged out there."

"And you do?" Vicky snapped, stepping up nose to nose

with the man. "Last I checked, both of us had more time outside the suit and under fire than you did."

Well, that might have been stretching it for Vicky. She'd been out of her armor for a grand total of maybe ten minutes compared to the days I'd experienced, but I didn't argue the point.

"The CSF trained me."

The answer was a bit sullen and defensive, but I was fairly certain from the shifting of Wade Cunningham's eyes, a subtle glance at the squad of corporate mercenaries moving through the room, that it got under his skin, and I wondered if it had been a sore spot with the men and women he was leading.

"Then you can keep an eye on us," I suggested. "We'll stick next to you and you can make sure we don't get in the way. But we have to be a part of it. What else are we gonna do? Stay here and hide in the cellar?"

"Yeah, that's about what I had in mind," he admitted. "I mean, someone has to stay here and keep an eye on this piece of shit." He glared at Torrey to let me know to which piece of shit he was referring. "And I can't spare any people to baby-sit him."

"I'll take care of him."

Vicky and Wade both stared at me, uncomprehending, as I hunted around on the kitchen table and grabbed my sheathed belt knife. They'd taken it off me after Brad Torrey had stunned me. I pulled it out of its sheath then picked up the thing beside it on the table and walked back over to where Torrey was tied to the chair. Torrey's eyes went wide at the sight of the naked blade and I did nothing to alleviate his fears because he didn't deserve it.

"What are you...?" Wade began, but trailed off when I buried the knife blade in the seat of the chair, behind the backrest, just within reach of Torrey's bound hands.

Torrey frowned, feeling at the hilt.

"You'll be able to get yourself free," I explained to him, "once you wake up."

Then I levelled the sonic stunner at him and fired from point blank.

A banshee screeched inside my head, talons ripping and clawing at my nerves, but it was so much worse for Torrey. His face screwed up in agony for just the briefest of moments before his features went slack and his eyes rolled back in his head before closing. I wasn't sure if holding the trigger down that long would damage his ears or his brain or whatever, and I didn't much care.

"That should put him out for long enough," I decided, tossing the stunner back onto the table. "Now get us some armor and a couple of those Gauss rifles and let's get in the air."

[16]

"No Gauss rifles, huh?" Vicky lamented, checking the magazine of the pulse carbine she'd been handed as we boarded the assault shuttle.

"We didn't bring any spares," Wade admitted, turning and waving a finger at the crew chief, signaling the woman to raise the bird's belly ramp. He still hadn't put on his helmet, and I wondered if he'd left it off so he could talk to us or because he just didn't like wearing it.

I'd never been inside an assault bird before and it seemed cramped, particularly with almost a platoon of the CSF troops inside. The seats were narrow and uncomfortable even with just the armored vest I'd been provided along with my laser weapon, and I had to think the bird had never been intended to hold so many acceleration couches.

"Last time I fired one of these," I said quietly, not caring if anyone heard me over the hum of the belly ramp closing, "was on Port Harcourt. I was in the car with the Skipper and Top and some Tahni civilians were throwing rocks at it, so I shot at their feet, scattered them."

"The Skipper was a good man," Wade said, crossing

himself. I blinked. I never would have guessed that Wade Cunningham was Catholic. "I couldn't believe it when I heard he died."

Around us, the shuttle crew was squeezing past the acceleration couches, checking each of us to make sure our restraints were secure before they passed the word up to the cockpit that we were ready for take-off.

"I was there," I told him. His eyes were wide. I suppose he hadn't heard. "I was there when Lt. Ackley died, when Scotty died, when the Skipper died. Henckel. Delp. Now Dave. I thought when the war ended, I was done watching people I care about die."

Vicky leaned against me, just a touching of our shoulders, but I could feel her warmth and appreciated the reminder that she was there and the unspoken promise she wouldn't go away. Below and beside us, turbines began screaming to life, swallowing up whatever reply Wade might have had. I could see his sigh even if I couldn't hear it. He reached into a pouch on his vest and pulled out a pair of ear buds, handing one to each of us. As we slipped them into place, he finally fastened his helmet to its yoke, his face disappearing behind the mirrored anonymity.

"Can you hear me?" His voice sounded tiny, distant in my ear, fighting a losing battle against the jets.

"Yes," Vicky confirmed.

"Barely," I added, and I could hear myself through the audio pickup but not in my other ear.

"Close enough. It's a short flight, so listen up now while we have the time. I'm staying behind our point team and you two are staying behind me. Don't go past my position unless I tell you. I know you were both officers and you're used to being in charge, but this is my show and if you want to come along, you do what I say. Clear?"

"You're the boss, Sgt. Cunningham," Vicky told him,

somehow managing to sound respectful and mocking at the same time.

He *had* been a sergeant, hadn't he? I'd lost track of him after he changed companies in a reorganization, sometime between the time I left for OCS and the time I'd returned. E-6, I thought he'd ended up. Acting platoon sergeant for Charlie. Used to giving orders himself.

"Sure thing," I said. He could have saved his breath. I had no desire to order anyone into the line of fire now or ever again. "What's the plan?"

The jets roared and boost pushed me into my seat, a giant sitting on my shoulders as we rose straight off the ground. I couldn't see the outside and I missed having a Heads-Up Display to show me the fire of the engines and the dust clouds roiling up around us. Trapped inside this tin can, isolation and claustrophobia clawed at the edges of my brain. Once upon a time, the sight of an open horizon would have thrown me into a panic, but now, after spending so much of the war and the time since on backwoods colony worlds, I was used to the great wide open and the once-comforting enclosure of the shuttle had my nerves on edge.

Or it could have been the whole flying into combat thing.

We didn't ascend very high, not more than a hundred meters up before the rear engines took over and the pressure shifted from my shoulders to my chest. It hadn't been quite as long since I'd flown in a military shuttle as it had since I'd fired a pulse rifle, but it was close. This was a life I thought I'd left behind, yet here I was. Here *we* were.

"We're doing it your way," Wade answered my question once the acceleration had settled into something more tolerable. "The shuttle is going to come in low, drop us close enough to run in."

Run in. Great. My legs already feel like they're about to fall off.

I didn't dare complain though, not after badgering Wade into taking us along.

"The crew is going to take the shuttle in and make a run at that warehouse you talked about, draw out their forces, while we circle around behind them and free the prisoners. Once they're out, you two are going to lead them to safety while the rest of us sweep through and take out those Tahni troops."

I nodded. It was a solid plan, simple and hard to fuck up. Something a couple of former platoon leaders and a platoon sergeant might come up with. God help us if a colonel had been involved.

I held the buttstock of the pulse carbine between my hands as if its emitter was welded to the deck, like it was keeping me stable rather than the straps holding me to the seat. The polymer and metal and ceramic was smooth and cold, impersonal, and foreign. It wasn't my weapon of choice. I belonged encased in BiPhase Carbide, bounding into combat in great leaps, seeing the battlefield in chunks of data. But that was another life. I wasn't a drop-trooper anymore, despite the interface jacks implanted in my temples. I was straight-leg infantry, Force Recon but less useful.

"You know what this reminds me of?" Vicky asked. I shook my head. "You didn't go to school much, from what you told me, but I went to the Housing Bloc school start to finish, from the time I was old enough to talk right up to the day I enlisted, and I used to have this nightmare that I'd gone to school and I was walking around the hallways in my underwear because I'd left the house and forgot to get dressed first."

I laughed, not just at the absurdity of the story but at the fact she'd grasped exactly what I was feeling without me having to say a word.

"Two minutes," Wade announced, and I wondered if he'd understood her reference. Probably not. Wade wasn't a bad guy, but he'd never been the brightest bulb.

"No spare helmets, either I assume?" I asked him.

"Just stick with me," was his answer, "and you won't need one."

Great.

The deck fell out from beneath us, or that's what it felt like, and I knew what it meant. We were descending fast, and the next thing was going to be...

"Shit!" I blurted, the exclamation leaving me along with my breath as the shuttle's belly jets slammed me against my safety harness, decelerating us with abrupt brutality for the space of a few seconds before the landing gear slammed into the ground.

My chin smacked into my chest and the restraint straps bit into the sides of my neck, my shoulder joints, and my waist, gripping so tightly I was sure they'd never let loose. But then the landing gear popped back up on its hydraulics and the restraints relaxed and Wade was already yelling in my ear.

"Out! Out! Out!"

I yanked at the quick-release and tumbled forward, awkward and unpracticed, keeping my pulse carbine pointed in a safe direction only through a supreme effort of will. My instinct was to pile out of the opening belly ramp the moment light leaked in from the outside, but Wade didn't move, so I steadied myself against the back of the acceleration couch in front of me and waited. The few seconds it took for the rest of the platoon to un-ass the shuttle dragged into hours inside my head, but finally, Wade lurched out into the center aisle and down the belly ramp, and Vicky and I raced to be the first to follow him.

I won, simply by the virtue of being one seat closer and nearly collided with his back on the way down. It felt unnatural to be rushing into a tactical movement in the late hours of the morning, with the primary star beating down on us like a spotlight, but I knew better than anyone how illusory a shield the darkness was. If the Tahni had drones out and they happened to be looking where we were, they'd see us whether it was high noon or a cloud-veiled midnight. But it still felt wrong.

The CSF mercenaries were throwing themselves to the prone in a half-circle perimeter around the belly ramp, and Wade took a knee at the center of them, holding his Gauss rifle at the ready, scanning the horizon. We were in a hollow, the end of an ancient and dead riverbed, with the highlands rising above us, the plateau where Hellnick's farm had been built. We were on the other side of the property from where the three of us had infiltrated last night, a section I'd never seen except once from the air when we'd first arrived at the colony. But I knew from the terrain that we were close, not more than a few kilometers from his house, and suddenly, the fatigue I'd felt in my legs and back was gone, vanished in a wash of adrenaline.

Adrenaline would only last me so long, I knew that from experience, and there'd be a price to pay when it was gone, but for now, I'd take it and be grateful for it. My heartbeat was a trip hammer in my chest as I crouched beside Wade, pointing my pulse carbine outward, making sure I wasn't sweeping any of the friendlies with the muzzle.

Friendlies. Odd word to use for a bunch of men and women I'd never met, whose faces I had never seen. But in this case, the enemy of my enemy was definitely my friend, at least for the moment, and I didn't want them to think I was about to shoot them in the back.

The shuttle's turbines were still roaring, throttled down to drop us off but not shut off, and once the boarding ramp began to motor back into the belly of the aerospacecraft, the engines spun up and a windstorm lashed at us with a hail of dust and debris. I turned away from the sharp-edged, streamlined attack craft, slitting my eyes against the assault, so I didn't see the bird raise off the ground, but the shrinking shadow it cast and the Doppler effect of its engines drawing away told the story. I urged it on with my well-wishes, since its presence was an advertisement of our position, and the farther away it got, the better off we were.

"Move out," Wade ordered. "Double-time."

I'll say this for the corporate mercs: they didn't waste time. The words were still buzzing in my ear, but the man walking point was already up and jogging, his armored combat boots flashing high out of the tall grass with each step. Wade didn't wait for the whole platoon to precede him this time, darting in after the last trooper in the first squad.

I cursed under my breath, knowing that meant Vicky and I wouldn't have the luxury of hanging back and dragging ass. I took comfort in the fact that I was carrying a lighter load and knew the terrain, but mostly I knew Vicky wouldn't let herself be seen as holding Wade and the others back, just out of pure, stubborn pride, and I refused to let her down.

I didn't want to look as if I was imitating the mercs, but with the tall grass and the unknown dangers of rocks and chuckholes concealed beneath it, the whole high-knee look of boot camp recruits running the tires was the only practical way to make time, so I surrendered to the inevitable. My breath was coming in labored chuffs after only a few hundred meters, the muscles in my butt and lower back burned with each step threatening to tighten up into cramped uselessness. My whole body screamed in outrage, and I snuck a glance at Vicky to see if she was feeling the same way, but I might as well have been looking at the carved face of some ancient stone idol. I knew she wasn't in any better shape physically than I was, but the woman was as obstinate as a mule.

Hell, if Wade Cunningham could keep up the pace, I sure could. I told myself that, but when Wade raised his fist to call a security halt, I went down to one knee a half-second before everyone else and hoped they wouldn't notice. We'd reached the crest of the rise and the point trooper had stopped out of what I would have recognized earlier as SOP if I'd actually had any training in tactical movement on foot since Boot.

Wade moved up to the front in a low crouch and, since he hadn't told us to stay back and had said we were supposed to stick with him, so did we. I tried to keep my eyes glued to Wade's back, since I lacked a helmet with a HUD or any sort of IFF transponder reader and he looked almost identical to the other black-clad CSF troops. I would have looked like a huge moron if I wound up tagging behind the wrong guy, and as much as Wade Cunningham and I had made peace from our initial acrimony, I wasn't ready to give him something that ridiculous to hold over my head.

Wade came to a halt just before the crest of the hill, then went down to elbows and knees and high-crawled over to the position of the point man, behind a rock outcropping that would give them both a glance over the rise. I took a knee at the spot where Wade had gone to his belly and waited there, not wanting to give away our position by sticking my head up in the wrong place, but Vicky eeled past me, nearly disappearing into the grass as she crawled up to Wade and the point man. I sighed and went down on my belly, fronds of prairie grass tickling at my neck and face as I scrambled up the hill, my pulse carbine cradled across my elbows.

I moved up beside Vicky and found out what they were looking at. Below us, laid out like pieces on a sand table, were Hellnick's farmhouse, ornate and overbuilt, like a recreation of an English farmhouse of the Elizabethan era by an architect whose only exposure to the design was a ViR-drama of a Jane

Austen novel, and behind it the barracks buildings. They were low-slung and sprawling, built as cheaply and quickly as possible, I thought, white-washed wood planks and sheet metal roofs. Boxes for people.

Who was inside those boxes, I couldn't tell, though I could see a handful of Tahni soldiers clomping around the entrances to the buildings, their armor a dull, matte grey and brown, KE guns carried at the ready.

"Do we think the civvies are in the buildings?" Wade asked, and I thought the question had to be directed at Vicky and me, though how we were supposed to know was a mystery.

"If they're here," I ventured, keeping my voice low since I didn't have a soundproof helmet to contain it, "the barracks are the only place that makes sense. The warehouse wouldn't have room for them all and I don't see Hellnick wanting them in his house."

"There looks to be at least a couple dozen Tahni down there," Vicky said, edging forward beside the point man. "How many do we think Zan-Thint has? I don't know if he'd be able to spare enough to keep a guard force at everyone's farm individually. He might have taken them to Gamma Junction, but that would mean keeping a fair-sized portion of his troops an hour's flight-time away."

"There are hoppers down there," Wade noted, pointing with the barrel of his Gauss rifle. I followed the gesture and just made out the silhouette of the aircraft against the woods beside the farmhouse. "He can't have that many of the things. I don't think he has enough to send to your town and still have half a dozen of them sitting around here."

On the other side of the barracks was the warehouse, and beyond it, the airfield. I assumed the armed cargo shuttle was out there, though I couldn't see it, but I did notice a smaller passenger lander just sticking out from the edge of the field past the warehouse.

"What are those?" That wasn't Wade's voice, so I assumed it was the point man's and that he'd switched over to the net Wade shared with us to take advantage of our local knowledge of the terrain. The sound of his voice was a shock, the first sign I'd had that the CSF troops were real people and not automatons.

"Can't tell," Wade admitted. "Alvarez, you see those?"

"What are we looking at?" Vicky asked, sounding annoyed she hadn't been asked. I was happy she'd spoken up since I had no idea either.

"You see those...I dunno, *lumps* out there, past the barracks?" Wade said, pointing with his weapon again. Which I suppose wasn't technically a safety violation since he wasn't pointing it at anything he wasn't ready to destroy.

Now that he described the things, however vaguely, I spotted them. Lumps might have sounded inexact, but it was what they looked like. Grey and shapeless, maybe three or four meters wide and nearly as tall, but lacking any sort of detail. There were four of them that I could see, scattered around between the barracks and the warehouse.

"It's some kind of camo netting," the point man decided. "Like what they used when we had our fly-over before."

"But what the hell are they hiding underneath them?"

"Where's the shuttle?" Vicky wondered. "It dropped us off nearly half an hour ago. Hasn't it had time to sweep around the other side of the plateau yet?"

"It's right on time, Sandoval," Wade assured her. His face was invisible beneath his visor, but if I could have seen it, I was sure he'd be wearing that smug smile I had so often wanted to punch when we first met. "I told them to give us time to get into place first. Unless you'd rather charge right down into the enemy guns."

"Charging into enemy guns is what we do, Cunningham."

"It's what we *did*. Ain't none of us Marines anymore. In the CSF, we're more about discretion being the better part of valor, you know?"

Vicky grunted in reply, more disdain in the monosyllabic utterance than a soliloquy from someone less eloquent. I reserved judgement, mostly because I kind of agreed about the whole not running headlong into a bunch of Tahni KE guns with nothing between me and thousands of hypersonic tantalum needles but a skimpy tactical vest.

"Here it comes."

That was the point man again. I wished I knew his name. I wished I knew any of their names, not just so they'd feel like real people to me, but also because interacting with them would have made our relationship more personal and maybe given them something of a sense of responsibility for our lives. It would be easier for them to just watch their own asses, and let us both die if we were nameless local yokels.

He was right about the shuttle, though it took me a whole extra second to pick up the sound of the engines. I figured his helmet must have had audio enhancement in it. The distant hum was the buzz of a mosquito, and by the time I'd found the black dot on the horizon that was the shuttle, it was already growing into the size of a raven on the wing. The whine turned into a roar and I thought the Tahni would have to be stone deaf not to hear it.

"Yeah, they're taking the bait," Wade announced, bloodthirsty eagerness in his breathless tone.

I followed his stare and saw the Tahni running off to the edge of the clearing, the muzzles of their KE guns swinging upward as if they could shoot the bird down. Maybe if it had been a commercial shuttle, they'd have had a chance, but even those tantalum darts weren't going to penetrate the centimeters-thick BiPhase Carbide hull of the assault craft. They'd have to find that out the hard way.

"All right," Wade said, rising to a knee. "That's our distraction. Over the top, boys and girls." He waved the troops forward, looking for all the world like a wartime recruiting poster. "Let's kill us some fucking Tahni. Just like old times."

[17]

I was flying down the hill, legs moving so fast that I didn't dare try to slow my pace for fear of tripping and tumbling head over heels, unable to even swing my arms for added balance because I needed to keep my pulse carbine pointed in a safe direction, praying to God not that I would survive but more that I wouldn't embarrass myself.

But at least I wasn't tired anymore.

Once upon a time, I'd complained about the flood of data that I'd had to endure in the Heads-Up Display of the company commander's version of a Vigilante battlesuit. It had seemed I knew everything and nothing at all simultaneously. Too overwhelmed with information to make sense of it all, I'd wished for a simpler time when a Marine or a soldier was only responsible for the facts they could confirm through the gate of their senses.

Be careful what you wish for. I could see little or nothing on the periphery of my vision, entirely focused on Wade and the CSF troops ahead of him and trying to keep my position behind them because they had the bigger guns. Straight ahead, past the mercenaries and the far too open, far too long stretch of grass-covered meadow, were the Tahni. They were running from our right to our left, barely two hundred meters away, but seemingly oblivious to our presence, absorbed with the approach of the shuttle. I wasn't worried about them seeing us as much as I was one of the CSF mercs deciding he just had to take a shot at them and attracting their attention.

But I guess Wade hadn't been lying about the corporate types not being eager to die, because they kept with the plan and let the Tahni throw themselves into the threat they expected; the assault shuttle. I wondered how long it would take the shuttle crew to decide there were enough of the bad guys gathered together to be worth a firing run, and as it turned out, it took another five seconds.

I hadn't seen the Gatling laser turret mounted on the port-side delta wing of the shuttle when we'd boarded, but the evidence of its existence ripped through the morning air with crackling lines of plasma, the high-power pressure pulses channeling the hyper-explosive cartridges in the hopper through multiple lasing rods to avoid burning any one of them out too quickly. The laser pulses were invisible, not in the optical spectrum, but the sheer heat energy off the blasts was enough to ionize the air around them, and when the laser was past, leaving behind an evacuated tube where the air had been, that same superheated plasma rushed in to fill the vacuum with a rolling peal of thunder that echoed through the hills.

The sound wasn't the most important side-effect of the light amplification by stimulated emission of radiation for the Tahni troops, though. Most of the shots didn't hit the Tahni soldiers, not in the split second the shuttle had to fire at them before it was past, but that much energy hitting the towering oak trees that shaded Klaus Hellnick's farmhouse was enough to liberate the water vapor trapped inside the bark...violently.

If I'd ever seen an oak tree explode before, I'd been in armor and it hadn't had quite the impact it did at that moment. The flash threw white and purple scars across my vision, the concussion reverberated through my sinuses and chest, and the sound slapped me in the face nearly hard enough to knock me over. A fragment of smoking wood whizzed just a few centimeters past my head and would have taken it clean off if it had hit, since I wasn't wearing a helmet.

The Tahni were fully armored, and I doubted the tree shrapnel would have been able to penetrate their protection, but it took a few of them off their feet and, more importantly, kept them disoriented and not looking our way. The assault shuttle was curving around the other side of the farmhouse, about to make a gun run on the storage building and really stir up some shit. The Tahni were being drawn out in the opposite direction from our approach, we were maybe a hundred meters from the barracks and I let myself entertain the idea that everything was going to go exactly as planned.

God must not have liked that sort of overconfidence.

I'd expected the Tahni or what was left of Eld's crew to launch their armed cargo shuttle in response to the gunship, but she'd remained on the landing pad, and if anyone had tried to get her in the air, I hadn't seen the attempt. I hadn't had time to wonder why, merely been thankful for the opportunity for our assault shuttle to continue the air support. Now I knew why, and I also knew what those camo-covered lumps were between the house and the barracks buildings.

The covers slid aside, pulled down by Tahni crews, revealing a familiar sight, something I'd become all too accustomed to encountering on Tahni worlds during the war: coil guns, air defense artillery.

"Oh, fuck me!" Wade exclaimed, and I could appreciate the sentiment. "Shuttle One, get the hell out of there! We have ADA, un-ass the AO!"

Un-assing this Area of Operations was a good idea, but as

fast as the shuttle was, lidar-guided tungsten slugs from an electromagnetic launcher were even faster. Multiple guns opened fire at once, so I couldn't tell which of them had hit the bird. I didn't even see the actual impact. One moment, the assault shuttle was banking low, less than fifty meters off the ground, and the next, it had disappeared in a cloud of smoke and dirt and debris.

The sound of the crash was dull, anticlimactic, an authoritative thump, as if a judge were slamming down a gavel. The cloud of smoke rising from the wreck was from trees and brush catching fire, I was sure. There was nothing on the actual shuttle that could burn. The fusion reactor had scrammed on impact, just as it was designed, and the ejected plasma had the same effect on the foliage as the laser blasts had, enough to set the whole stand of trees on fire, maybe enough to burn across the grass fields to the crops if no one bothered to extinguish it.

The squad on point had slowed their approach at the crash, whether from some tactical judgement or perhaps simply out of shock, I didn't know, and I dug in my heels and came to a halt as well, lacking any other choice. That was when the first of the Tahni troopers noticed us. I couldn't see their eyes through their visors, but the body language was clear, even from an alien, and half a dozen KE gun emitters swung our way.

I knew what we *should* have done. Not that I was Force Recon like Brad Torrey, but some tactics transcended branches or divisions or how thick your armor was. We should have charged through, gotten into the middle of them, using their buildings for cover and forced them to think about blue-on-blue fire when they shot at us. But Wade was in charge and trying to get the others to follow me, instead, would have accomplished nothing but confusion.

"Form up!" Wade yelled, the order high-pitched and a little desperate. "Lay down suppressive fire now!"

It was a close second as ideas went, but I had the cynical thought that they didn't hand out silver medals for combat just before I threw myself flat and the rounds started going downrange. From both directions. I twisted around to make sure Vicky had done the same, worried she might have succumbed to the same instinct to attack that I nearly had, but she was hugging the dirt, trying to work her pulse carbine around to where it could do some good.

I hadn't even thought about my own weapon because it seemed superfluous compared to the metal death ripping through the air only centimeters over our heads. The Tahni were pouring in streams of tantalum needles, not well-aimed as of yet, since they'd been taken by surprise, but that wouldn't last. Return fire came in more measured doses, the military-grade Gauss rifles the CSF mercs carried snapping out heavy, tungsten slugs at a rate of around one per second. The deep-throated hum of the internal magnetic coils ended in a higher snap as the rounds broke the sound barrier, heavy and authoritative against the lighter crack of the smaller tantalum darts.

Tahni troops went down, projectiles the size of my little finger spearing through their armor as if it wasn't there, and more of the platoon filtered in behind us, filling gaps in the line, falling into the prone in a semicircular formation, each squad firing in turn to keep the rate of fire constant. Tahni troops abandoned their positions at the ADA turrets, unable to depress the coil guns far enough to fire at us, rushing forward to meet the new threat and many catching a round before they had a chance to shoot back.

"Wade," I yelled, trying to be heard over the endless crack of electromagnetically-launched projectiles going supersonic. "We have to get to the hoppers before they do!"

I didn't elaborate, hoping he was smart enough to understand on his own. If the Tahni or Eld's crew got the hoppers in the air while we were still out in the open, we were toast. Even if the ducted-fan helicopters weren't armed, a couple of Tahni troopers with KE guns could still wipe us out firing from an open canopy.

"Bounding forward by squads!" Wade ordered, proving the intervening years since the war hadn't turned him into an idiot. "Get us to the shelter of the farmhouse! We're making for the hoppers!"

I snuck a quick look back at Vicky, making sure she hadn't been hit, but she scrambled to her feet along with Wade and me and the lead squad. It was a light platoon, only three squads, lacking any sort of heavy weapons, but the other two squads did an admirable job of laying down covering fire. Most of the Tahni had been out in the open and were too far from the buildings to seek any sort of real cover, but natural selection culled the ones not bright enough to go to the ground and kept their return fire to the spray-and-pray variety.

They'd been that way in the war, I'd noticed, a mindset reflected in their choice of weapons. Our Force Recon Marines carried Gauss rifles that fired heavy slugs at one per second, but their KE guns went for quantity over quality and accuracy, hosing tiny darts by the dozen instead. Not that just one of those darts couldn't ruin a guy's day, but as my old marksmanship instructor at Boot used to say, "You can't miss fast enough to win."

We reached the lee of the nearest barracks, covered at least from two sides, and those who could took up positions behind a small stand of cottonwood trees and put down a barrage of suppressive fire to give the next squad the time to join us.

"What about the prisoners?" Vicky asked, motioning toward the barracks.

If our friends and neighbors were inside the buildings, they were either guarded or restrained, or perhaps just hugging the floor, hiding from the gunfire, but either way, I hadn't seen them.

"We can't get them out of here on foot, under fire," Wade said, not letting the words interrupt the shot he was taking. His right shoulder jerked backwards at the recoil from the Gauss rifle.

The second squad was moving, maybe not as fast as they had before. It was close to noon on a cloudless day and it was getting nice and warm, and that armor had to be dragging at them. I knew just the vest was weighing me down and trickles of sweat were collecting at the small of my back, cold and uncomfortable.

"Hell," Wade went on, yanking out a spent magazine and slapping a new one home with an ease that spoke of constant practice, most likely since the war, "*we* aren't getting out of here on foot! And there's what? Five or six of those hoppers? That's barely enough to pull the whole team out. We don't even know that they're in those buildings and us going in there and trying to break them out would just draw fire."

"We can't just leave them here!" Vicky insisted. "We don't know what that Zan-Thint will do to them! There are fucking *children* in there!"

Her face was flush with righteous indignation and I shared the sentiment, but I had to agree with Wade, maybe because I'd been an officer longer than Vicky had and understood that no amount of wanting something to be true would change the facts, no matter how unpleasant they were. Or maybe I'd learned that much earlier.

"There aren't that many of them." It wasn't the point man. This was a woman and I assumed she was in the lead squad because everyone else would have been too busy running or trying not to get shot to listen into our conversation. "And they can't shoot for shit. We might be able to take all of them down."

Almost as if the ancient gods of war had heard the boast and decided to punish her hubris, something big, loud, and ugly burst right through the roof of the warehouse in a spray of burning insulation and smoking sheet metal, and nearly landed right on top of us, jump jets screaming their outrage. There were, I realized in retrospect, only four of them, but with the roar of the jets in my ears and the sun in my eyes and the ice-cold talons of sheer terror gripping my chest, there might as well have been a hundred.

They were gargoyles, ancient golems with faces frozen in an inhuman grimace, three meters tall and two meters wide, a ton and a half of alloy and ceramic powered by an isotope reactor, and for years, killing them had been my purpose in life. They were Tahni High Guard battlesuits, and suddenly I remembered the eight containers I'd seen in the warehouse last night and knew exactly what had been inside them.

I should have moved immediately, should have reacted on hard-won instincts, and ran. My pulse carbine wouldn't even scratch their paint, and neither would the Gauss rifles the CSF mercs were carrying, and running was my only option. But I couldn't. I was frozen, but not with fear. Fear I'd grown used to. Fear was an old friend, a confidante, the angel on my shoulder whispering when it was time to get my ass out of there and live to fight another day.

No, this was something different, a claustrophobia I'd never felt before, the conviction that I was trapped not in a space too small to breathe, but in a loop I couldn't escape. I was back in the war, a war that would never end, in my own private version of Hell, where I would keep fighting, keep killing, keep watching people I cared about die in a struggle against an enemy who would never surrender.

Vicky saved me. She grabbed my arm and I knew it was her because I knew her touch better than I knew my own reflection, knew the voice urging me on even though I couldn't hear the words over the thunderous carnage. Metal arms were swinging and KE guns large enough to have been crew-served if they hadn't been mounted on a three-meter-tall battlesuit were chopping into the ground, the trees, and the CSF troopers. Bodies and pieces of bodies were spinning away in crimson clouds and there wasn't a damned thing I could do about it except run.

One of the CSF mercenaries was right in front of me, trying to aim his Gauss rifle at a battlesuit, just within arm's reach of me. I hooked my fingers inside the neck yoke of his armor and yanked him along behind us as we ran. There was only one place to go, one avenue of escape worth trying, and we had already identified it, which kept me from having to debate the question in my mind. The hoppers. We had to get to the hoppers and hope to God we could make one of them fly.

I didn't bother dodging or weaving or following a serpentine pattern because our only defense against the metal titans was speed, getting away before they noticed us. It was a cynical, self-serving gambit, hoping the enemy would be too busy killing the other Corporate mercenaries to have time to shoot at us, but there was absolutely nothing we could do to save them.

"I've got to go back!" It was Wade. I hadn't been sure when I'd pulled him along with us, though it made sense. He'd been closest to me before the battlesuits had landed, and none of us had the time to move before the attack had begun. "They're dying!"

"And so will we," I wheezed the words out, barely able to breathe, my boot soles digging up bits of dirt and mud and throwing them out behind me like rocket exhaust. "Run, you idiot!"

I was ready to let him go back if he wanted to. Not that I wanted him to die, but there was no time to wrestle with the man, no time to argue. He could take his chance with us or take his chances with the Tahni. The choice was his and he made the right one. Another of the mercs was running up behind us, amazingly fast for someone weighed down with that much armor, sprinting so hard I thought they were going to pass us until a burst of heavy KE gun darts ripped through their chest and they were suddenly gone, fallen away.

Something tugged at my right sleeve just above the elbow, just a sting and then a wetness trickling down toward my wrist and I knew I'd caught a graze. Just a graze, though, because if one of the darts had hit me square, there'd be nothing left of my arm. I didn't stop to look at it, didn't try to stop for the dead CSF trooper or look back to check if the Tahni battlesuit was still shooting at us. The arm wound would wait, the merc was dead and if I was about to die, I figured I'd rather not know.

The hoppers were at the edge of a stand of trees, but there was cover along the way and the three of us took advantage of it, ducking behind one of the anti-aircraft turrets. My back rested against the footrest where the gunner stood to operate the thing and I sucked in a few lungfuls of air, holding onto my gun like a totem despite the fact I had yet to fire the thing. KE gun rounds smacked into the other side of the emplacement, a handbell choir ringing through the metal and if I'd had any thought of trying to take the controls of the coil gun and see if I could depress it enough to take out one of the suits, it died aborning, realizing how exposed I would be to fire from the others.

"Go!" Vicky urged, then set the example by leading the way.

I couldn't let her get too far ahead, though I wasn't sure if that was because I was afraid she'd run into Tahni along the way and need help, or simply because I didn't want to get left behind. More supersonic projectiles ripped into the dirt and mud around us, but none of the battlesuits came after us, maybe too busy with the mercenaries to abandon the fight to pursue us.

The hoppers had seemed kilometers away, but now they jumped up to meet us, impossibly close, and I nearly slammed my shoulder into the canopy of one of the things, feeling around for a catch, desperate to get inside even though the safety the plastic bubble offered was illusory. Anything was better than standing outside, waiting to get shot.

I found the catch just as Vicky and Wade were both running up, looking as if they meant to push me out of the way and open the thing themselves. The canopy swung upward and I leapt into the cockpit, climbing behind the controls despite the fact that I had never flown one of the things, only watched training videos and paid attention to the pilots who took us into Gamma Junction.

It didn't seem that hard, or at least it hadn't from the comfort of my own home, watching the vids. The power button was right where it was supposed to be, and pushing it rewarded me with a whine of rotors spinning up.

The throttle. I needed to find the throttle. There it was, a touch control on the main screen, simple, meant to be operated by someone with no real pilot training. They'd *tried* to make the thing easy to fly, although they probably hadn't considered the possibility of someone trying to figure it out while being shot at. Distractions kept trying to draw my eyes away, flashes of motion, CSF troops running across the yard between the barracks and the farmhouse, trying to reach some cover, *any* cover from the withering fire of the battlesuits.

They were still shooting; I'll say that for them. They had to know the Gauss rifles were useless against the High Guard suits, but they had nothing else and either they couldn't think clearly enough to run, or were too stubborn to admit defeat.

"Get out of there!" Wade screamed at them. "Get to the aircraft! Jesus Christ, get out!"

But it was too late.

Streams of tantalum swept across the mercenaries, blowing them into tumbling, bloody chunks of human, removing the doubt I'd had about them being automatons. Whether they'd chosen to fight or run, it affected their fate not one bit, because death had come for them in the form of a metal demon and wouldn't be denied.

One of the battlesuits hesitated for a beat as the last of the CSF mercs went down, very manlike in its motion, searching for a new target. And finding us. The heavy KE gun mounted along the thing's right arm swung toward me in slow motion, teasing, daring me to do something about it.

I did the only thing I could and fed power to the throttle, pulling up on the steering yoke and hoping to hell I hadn't forgotten something. As it turned out, I had. The canopy wasn't closed all the way, and when the hopper shot up out of the clearing, the air rushing in slapped me in the face, forcing my eyes shut, and I twisted the yoke hard to the left, remembering the trees on the right, unable to see if I was actually going the right direction. Dirt or debris had gotten into my eye and I squeezed it shut and tried to look out the other one, but it was filled with tears. Something slapped into the hopper's airframe hard enough to send a shudder running through the fuselage and the wheel vibrated in my hands like it was trying to get away and let someone more qualified fly the aircraft.

"Cut right!" Vicky yelled in my ear, hand gripping my shoulder like an iron vise from the rear passenger's seat. "To the right!"

She didn't say how far to the right or how long to keep it that way, and my vision was a distorted kaleidoscope of light flares and indecipherable blues and greens, so I threw the hopper into what I thought would be about a ninety-degree roll. Did I mention I had never flown a hopper before? We went into a spin. The canopy had closed and my vision had cleared, but now that I could see, the only thing I was seeing was the world outside the cockpit tumbling out of control.

Someone was screaming at me to level the bird out and I think it might have been me.

"Holy God, we're gonna crash!" Wade screeched.

I am not a big man, was never a gym rat like Wade had been, but even Drop Troopers in the Marines have to stay in fighting shape, and the last year as a farmer had given me muscles in places I didn't know there were muscles, and an appreciation for pain. I used every Newton of force I had in me to grab that steering yoke and force the hopper back level.

The ground and the sky settled into their proper places, but the former was way too damned close. There was maybe room to fit one of those High Guard battlesuits between our belly and the dirt, but it would have been a tight squeeze. I pulled up, but not too much, not wanting to turn us into a big, floating target, and twisted around in my seat to figure out where we were.

The warehouse was directly behind us, and off to the right was the landing field, with the armed cargo shuttle and the passenger lander still on the ground, and hopping high over the roof of the warehouse were the four High Guard battlesuits. The jets could take them up a hundred meters and keep them in the air for a few seconds, but there was no way they could catch up with the hopper...but they didn't have to. They could send thousands of those hypersonic darts out to do the chasing for them.

The hopper was very responsive, reminding me of my Vigilante battlesuit, and I tried to keep the comparison in mind as I shifted the wheel from side to side, keeping a gentle hand on the wheel. The thing fought me, rebelling at the random shifting back and forth while still at full throttle, and my knuckles were white on the wheel, the muscles in my forearms beginning to cramp up.

The hopper had a rearview camera, but I was afraid to look at it and check on the enemy, afraid to take my eyes off the horizon, sure the slightest faltering of my attention would send us nose-first into the ground. My teeth were grinding and I didn't bother attempting to relax, sure we'd catch a burst of hypervelocity slugs right through the cockpit any moment. It seemed we'd been flying for minutes, but I knew how time seemed to stretch out in combat, so I didn't give that much weight until I felt Vicky's hand fall gently on my arm.

"It's okay," she told me, her voice hoarse and strained. "I think we're clear."

I steadied the steering yoke, keeping it straight but not slowing down, and finally checked the rear camera. Nothing. Just blue sky and green fields. I snuck a glance behind me and saw Wade pulling off his helmet, his face pale and beaded with sweat.

"They're dead," he whispered, as if it had just hit him. "My whole platoon. I got them killed."

"What the hell do we do now?" Vicky wondered. "Where do we go?"

"We gotta call for help," Wade declared, an edge of fear to his tone. "We gotta get word to the station. They have to get us out of here."

"Gamma Junction," I decided. "It's the only place with a comm antenna."

"And if they destroyed it?" Vicky asked.

"Then," I said, "I have no idea."

[18]

"I have no idea."

Gamma Junction was deserted. I'd been prepared to land the hopper in one of the open lots at the center of town and try to blend in with the crowd, but there was no crowd. We'd seen it from the air. No civilians, no pirates, no Tahni.

When I was a kid in Tijuana, there was this street preacher who would stand on a corner near where the gangs sold dope and ran hookers, and he would hold a Bible in one hand and a meter-long cross in the other and tell them all how judgement was coming. He said Jesus would return and take the faithful up to Heaven with him and they didn't want to be the ones left behind, because it would be the most hopeless existence imaginable, knowing all they had to look forward to was suffering, death and Hell.

Gamma Junction had been raptured right the fuck out of town and the three of us were left behind in hell.

"How many people lived in this place?" Wade asked, his boots crunching against gravel, his eyes hunting around at every click or clack echoing from an alley or a storefront, and the muzzle of his Gauss rifle following his eyes. He'd left his helmet in the hopper, which had seemed odd to me. It gave him a tactical advantage. But maybe it also reminded him of the people he'd lost.

"Not many," Vicky answered, speaking softly, as if she thought someone might be skulking in the shadows, listening to our conversation. "Not on a permanent basis. A few hundred."

"Most of them were civilians," I pointed out. "Only maybe a third were veterans. They wouldn't have had to move everyone out themselves, just ordered the civilians to shelter in place out on the farms and then grabbed the vets and took them...somewhere."

At least, that was what I was praying had happened. Because the alternative was not only too horrible to contemplate, but it was also right in line with what I'd expect from a rogue Tahni colonel. Even a Pirate World scumbag like Eld would have balked at executing hundreds of colonists in cold blood, but to the Tahni, we were the enemy, the ones responsible for bringing down their government, their religion, their way of life for the last thousand years.

None of us said it, though. No one wanted to be the first to put it into words.

We'd been silent as we landed in the square at the edge of town closest to the spaceport. The hopper had done that much, at least, on its own, the autopilot perfectly capable of landing itself and happy to be of service. The antenna's physical structure was intact, we'd seen that much on the flight in. I'd dared to let myself hope it might actually prove to be our salvation until we'd come close enough to see the charred, blackened section near the base of the tower, where the operations shack had been.

The shack had been obliterated right along with the computer hookups, the electronics, the wiring, the power source...everything else we would have needed to send a message to the Corporate Council space station.

We didn't walk straight back to the hopper, although we should have and every second we spent out in the open made me feel like I was wearing a target on my back. But it felt like the answers should be here somewhere and none of us wanted to leave without them.

"There's no way we could rig up another transmitter?" Vicky suggested, checking in another of the shops, pulse carbine at the ready. It was empty, just like the rest had been. "There's gotta be equipment somewhere around here, maybe in one of the warehouses. We could find the hardware and a power source."

"We could," I agreed, "but I have no idea how to do it. Unless you've been trained on comm gear, Wade?"

"We had technicians for that." He wouldn't meet my eyes, and if survivor's guilt had taken corporeal form, it would have looked exactly like Wade Cunningham.

"We could check the local nets for a tutorial," Vicky said, her tone excited for just a heartbeat as she pulled out her 'link. Then the breath went out of her in a sigh and the hope escaped with it. "Except they shut the nets down. Of course."

Her arm tensed as if she wanted to smash the 'link to the ground and stomp on it, but instead, she put it back on her belt.

"They might still be here, you know," she said, the words almost an accusation. "Just hiding out or something. We don't know they've been...taken away."

"They might," I admitted. "But if they are, it doesn't change much. We can't ask them to go against Tahni battlesuits with a few Gyroc carbines and hunting rifles. If they are hiding out, we should let them stay there until this is all over."

"But *we* can't stay here," Wade said, flinching at another stray sound. I'd heard it, but it was probably the wind, or maybe one of the many stray cats in the little town. "They're going to come here looking for us."

"Yes, they are." An idea nagged at the back of my mind and I tried to open my thoughts to it, give it some space and time to grow. "And that might be our best bet."

The door latch gave way on the second kick, slamming inward and ricocheting off the inner wall. I caught it with my left hand, the right extending the emitter of the pulse carbine ahead of me.

It felt wrong, breaking into George Johnson's shop. Vicky and I had split rounds of beers with the retired Fleet engineer and his crew of technicians whenever we'd spent the night in Gamma Junction and while we weren't exactly close, he was definitely a friend. I had hoped Vicky had been right, that he was hiding inside the shop, waiting out the insanity, but I quickly found out that was fantasy rather than reality.

George Johnson was slumped face-down behind the counter of his shop, his shirt matted with dried blood. There were a dozen pinprick holes in the wall behind him where the tantalum darts had passed through his body, decorated with a splatter of crimson that had dripped downward long after he'd taken his last breath. A short-barreled shotgun lay on the floor only a couple meters from his outstretched hand, telling the story of his death. He'd kept it behind the counter to deal with pushy off-worlders, but it hadn't been nearly enough against armored Tahni. They hadn't even bothered to unload it or take it with them, so little did they respect the weapon.

I nearly gagged on the smell, covering my mouth with my hand, and moving past the counter back into the storeroom. One thing about a battlesuit, it filtered out the smell of death. Ivan and Ken, George's employees, were nowhere to be found, and I held out hope they'd been taken alive or, better yet, gotten away to somewhere. Though it would have been very handy to actually have one of them around, because they might know how to do this for real instead of just faking it.

Finding the transmitter parts wasn't that difficult. George labelled everything compulsively, as if he and the two men he'd worked with for nearly two years might forget where they'd stored the things they'd fabricated themselves and put together by hand. The gear was in a pair of metal storage boxes, each about thirty centimeters on a side. I tried lifting one experimentally and estimated that it weighed twenty-five kilos and I didn't want to carry both of them out by hand.

I checked the storeroom for a powerloader and found a wheeled dolly instead, which, I suppose, made sense. Powerloaders needed maintenance, replacement power cells, and spare parts, and all that cost money. Wheels and bearings could be fabricated cheaply, even out here. George had always complained about how low his profit margins were, how expensive it was to have anything shipped to Hausos, and how the Corporate Council and the government should hurry up and bring the Tahni into the Commonwealth so we could open up production facilities there and cut down on shipping costs.

He'd never complain about it again, though. The thought punched me in the gut, making me pause for a sharp intake of breath as I maneuvered the dolly under the stacked crates. Not just for George's death, though I knew I'd see his bloody face again in my nightmares, not just for Dave, but for the whole colony. Even if we found everyone else alive and unharmed, this place would never be the same again. More than half the settlers here had turned against the others, betrayed them. No one would ever trust each other again.

And if many more had gone the way George had, had been killed resisting capture, it might be even worse than that. A day ago, I'd reluctantly thought of this planet as home. Now, it was just another war zone. I needed to get out of this building before I threw up.

The dolly's wheels caught on the doorstep and I had to drag it over the threshold and back out into the afternoon glare, as if it knew that the skies had cleared and the primary star was beating down mercilessly. I'd unfastened the front of my borrowed tactical vest, but the improved ventilation didn't do much to dry the sweat collecting in the small of my back and under my arms.

"You got it?" Vicky asked me.

She was standing beside the wreckage of the little radio shack, unfolding a table she'd salvaged from another of the shops. Beside it were two crates of electronics, none of which I could have identified with a gun to my head. And off to the side, in the shadows, was a smaller case, thick metal, with warning labels printed all over it. It had been the hardest to find, the hardest to get to, and the most important. Wouter Pistorius' shop sold and rented mining and construction supplies, a little bit of everything, from diggers to bulldozers to buildfoam dispensers and the chemicals to fill them. But he only had one safe, and it had taken a full magazine from Wade's Gauss rifle to blow the hinges off the thing.

I nodded my answer before I broke the news to her.

"George is dead."

"Fucking bastards," she spat, slamming a palm against the flat of the table, then leaning against it, her head bowed. It wobbled but stayed upright beneath her weight. When she looked back up at me, there was agony in her eyes, and I wondered if it was from the news of the man's death or from having the same realization I'd had a few minutes ago. "Anyone else?"

"No."

I set the crates down beside the table and pulled open the top of one of them, then began placing its contents on the table.

Wade was coming, a toolbox under one arm and a second hanging in his other hand, his rifle slung across his back. His steps were short and labored and he was gritting his teeth by the time he reached us.

"What's the point of all this?" he asked plaintively, dumping the two heavy-looking tool chests on the pavement, then leaning against his knees, sucking in a breath.

"They have to think we're trying to repair the transmitter," Vicky snapped, her tone that of an impatient mother dealing with a dense teenager. "This won't work otherwise."

"But why did we have to go to the actual shops and grab all this specific shit?" he elaborated, waving at the gear we'd gathered. "They wouldn't know the difference. And it's not as if any of us know how to actually put the shit together. We could have just pulled a half a dozen boxes from the place next store and pretended we were fixing the thing."

I tried not to let the embarrassment show on my face, because the real answer was, I hadn't thought of that. But now that I did...

"Because that felt sloppy and half-assed," I told him, sending my impression back through time to when I'd made the decision. "And the Skipper told me that any time you half-ass something, you make a bad habit."

Which had the added benefits of both being true and being the wisdom of someone Wade respected, so it would keep him from arguing.

"How do you know they'll see us?" he asked, instead, at least shifting the conversation to something I could answer honestly.

"If you'd kept your helmet on, you'd have seen the drones." I nodded toward the landing field. "They're small, but they don't fly like the local birds."

"They're not birds," Vicky reminded me pedantically.

"Avians," I corrected myself. "Anyway, I've spotted it three times since we landed and, if I spotted it, you can bet your ass it spotted us."

"And what happens if they do the sensible thing and just send hoppers after us?"

Wade, I realized with a blinding flash of the obvious, might have been put in charge of a CSF platoon, but the man was still an NCO at heart, and a junior NCO at that, maybe even an enlisted man. Not that enlisted or junior NCOs were less intelligent than officers, but their priorities were different. A corporal or a buck sergeant wouldn't hesitate to ask the same questions over and over until he or she understood the answer, but an officer would be afraid of being annoying and looking stupid, and would pretend to grasp the concept even if they didn't.

If anything scared Wade Cunningham, it sure as hell wasn't being annoying or looking stupid.

"Because they're Tahni," I said. "Because they never use the smaller hammer when the bigger hammer is available. Because when they were faced with an assault shuttle, they didn't try to shoot it down with their own shuttle, they blew it out of the sky with coil guns. And when they see us here trying to fix this antenna, they aren't going to use a hopper that takes an hour to get here, they're going to hop that shuttle up and be here in ten minutes."

"You think we have just ten minutes?" That idea seemed to rattle him, and I suppressed a sigh.

"Probably. Why don't you go grab your helmet out of the hopper and get into position?"

"You know this ain't gonna be like stealing a hopper, right?" he said, shifting his rifle back to the front, pausing before he went to retrieve his helmet. "A shuttle has security interlocks,

ID plates, codes...you're going to need the pilot alive. And cooperating."

"Yeah, I know," I assured him. When I offered nothing more, he shrugged and jogged off toward the hopper.

"He's right about that," Vicky said, once he was out of earshot. "If the pilot is one of Eld's crew, we can probably pressure him into unlocking the controls, or maybe even offer him a deal. But if it's a Tahni...."

She didn't have to finish the thought. The Tahni we'd taken prisoner during the war had proven less than cooperative, at least if the rumors were true. Scuttlebutt had it that many had committed suicide rather than remain in captivity, considering it dishonorable or even sacrilegious to allow themselves to be taken prisoner by us, a lesser race. I hadn't personally witnessed *that*, though I'd seen enough to believe it.

As if on cue, a sonic boom echoed from one side of the plains outside the town to the other and it only took a few seconds of hunting before I found the shuttle coming in from the direction of Hellnick's farm. Relief made the talons of stress loosen their grip on my chest. It was the passenger lander, not the armed cargo shuttle. Which meant it was regular ground troops coming after us, not the battlesuits. That had been the worry I hadn't brought up around Wade, knowing he would have seized on it and let it chew away at his confidence.

I nestled the buttstock of my pulse carbine into the crook of my shoulder and grinned at Vicky with much more confidence than I actually felt.

"I guess," I told her, "we'd better hope it's a human."

[19]

Why the hell did I volunteer for this?

The question echoed in my head, almost drowning out the tromping footsteps of the Tahni soldiers, but not quite. They couldn't see me, not tucked away in the intact corner of the burned-out radio shack with tons of metal antenna structure blocking their thermal and audible sensors, but they knew I was here. I pulled my right hand off the pistol grip of the pulse carbine and wiped it against my pant leg, drying off the sweat before wrapping my fingers back in place.

I was the highest ranking of the three of us during the war, the one with the most leadership experience, the one who'd come up with this dumbass plan in the first place, so why had I volunteered to be the bait?

Because Wade wasn't about to do it and Vicky would have.

I glanced around at the bare metal surrounding me, wondering again if it was thick enough to protect me from KE gun rounds. I just had to keep the Tahni troops' attention on me for a couple minutes, keep them looking away from the shuttle, not searching for other threats.

But there was a whole squad of them, eight. I'd counted them as they'd unloaded from the shuttle, not feeling so grateful anymore that they hadn't sent battlesuits. The suits were deadly, of course, but they were also huge and clumsy when they tried to target something as small as a dismounted human. Crunchies were easy to miss, beneath contempt of the armored knight of a battlesuit trooper, at least that was how I had felt when I'd been the one inside the suit.

These guys were leg infantry and they wouldn't miss me. Which was fine, since I didn't want to be missed, but the plan also involved me not getting shot, and that part I wasn't so confident about.

I had suffered from nightmares, flashbacks, sensitivity to bright lights and loud noises for the better part of a year. It hadn't been debilitating, just an ever-present fact of life, an annoyance I'd had to deal with, the price to be paid for living so close to death for so long, like a toothache that never went away. It was gone now. I was scared, but it was a reasoning fear, a manageable one. Dying was a thing I could understand, unlike living.

I touched the trigger pad of the pulse carbine lightly and the optical sight lit up with a circular targeting reticle, simple and lacking the hold-over hash marks of the scopes on our hunting rifles because there was no bullet drop for which to compensate. The laser would go straight where the reticle floated, until something absorbed or reflected its energy, or until it went long enough for the inverse-square law to turn it into harmless light.

The Tahni were wearing armor, but not the two-centimeter thick plates so heavy they had to use a powered exoskeleton to move around in it like their shock-troopers during the war. This stuff was light, the sort their ordinary line soldiers had been equipped with, and it might have been enough to absorb the energy from a pulse pistol, but whether it could stop a blast from the heavier cartridge of the carbine was an iffier proposition. They were close enough that I wasn't going to take the chance. I'd aim for the visor of their helmets.

What if they have grenades?

I didn't believe they had, hadn't seen any evidence of it, but that's the sort of thing my mind whispered at me, a mental version of Wade Cunningham, still an enlisted man down in the lizard brain. I shushed it and ducked further behind the mass of a heavy, metal toolbox, one of the few things to survive the destruction of the shack.

I couldn't help it. I flinched when they fired through the opening where the door had been before most of the front wall had been smashed. Tantalum darts ripped through what was left of the splintered wood, sending bits of it spinning across the room, smacking into the metal of the antenna base with a dull tone in contrast to the higher-pitched pings of the darts disintegrating against that same material, some leaving behind tiny craters, others barely a scratch.

Bits of debris showered down onto my head and I wished for a helmet, any helmet to protect my eyes from ricochets, even one of the Tahni kind that wouldn't fit my head right. Some of the partisans on places like Demeter and Brigantia had refitted the things to make it work, and I would have been willing to give it a try. My instinct was to squeeze my eyes shut against the rain of particles, but I couldn't. I knew they would keep shooting as they came in and I had to be able to aim.

The muzzle of a KE gun was the first thing to emerge around the jagged edge of the front wall, the darts still spitting out so fast they were invisible except as a slight wavering of the air just ahead of the emitter, as if the snap-snap-snap of microsonic booms was unrelated to the presence of the rifle. My trigger finger cramped, wanting to pull on its own and fighting against my intent not to shoot until I saw his helmet. It was a second, a second and a half, the space between breaths, and then the mottled grey armor of the Tahni trooper came into view, the shoulder pauldrons first, then the oversized neck yoke, bigger and broader than the one on the armor of a Force Recon Marine or Wade's CSF mercenaries, and finally the helmet.

The visor was smoke-black, a chevron a few centimeters wide across the middle of the helmet, nothing visible through it to indicate there was a living thing inside. I'd studied military history in OCS, seen how soldiers and Marines used to be equipped, with open-faced helmets, eyes wide and faces exposed, very human. We'd changed the design once we took our wars into space and the helmets needed to be capable of being sealed against a vacuum, and by the time we'd encountered them, the Tahni had done the same. Now we were all faceless demons, The Enemy, and there was none of the hesitation there had once been for a human to take the life of another. I wondered if it had been a mistake.

I touched the trigger pad and a flash of man-made lightning connected me to the Tahni for a fraction of a second, the side-effect of the burst of invisible pulses that did the real damage. The visor disappeared in a spray of sparks and a flush of steam and by the time I could see through the ceramic material, there was nothing to see, no face behind it, just the brutal evidence that we were all meat puppets.

The first one hadn't even had the chance to fall when the next Tahni came through, banging his shoulder into the dead male's back and knocking him forward, throwing off the second one's aim just long enough for me to shift mine. My breath threw my aim off, the reticle and the initial burst hitting low, sparking off that broad neck yoke, like the collar of some dress jacket long out of style. I didn't know if the shots penetrated the armor or not, but I didn't take the chance, keeping the trigger depressed as I elevated the emitter upward by a few centimeters. He fell quicker than the other one had, going to his knees then slumping onto his chest.

The next soldier in line was neither stupid nor suicidal and jerked backwards out of the doorway before I saw more than the muzzle of his KE gun, and the incoming fire died off for a beat, but I knew it was just the calm before the storm. I ducked behind the toolbox before the storm came.

The storm was metal, blown by an electromagnetic wind at thousands of meters per second, smashing wood and plastic and smacking against metal in a hail of sparks. I wasn't going to wait this one out. There were at least three of them firing and they weren't going to stop until they'd sprayed every millimeter of the remains of the shack with tantalum needles. I'd done my part, drawn them to the antenna, now it was time to get out.

If I still could.

We'd planned for this, but our strategy session had been a grand total of about five minutes, our prep time had been less than ten, and there'd been way too much wishful thinking involved in it for my tastes. Breaking the hole through the corner of the shack hadn't taken more than a couple minutes, hiding it behind a pile of rubble and debris just a few more, but kicking it all aside and squeezing through was a matter of seconds...plus two extra seconds to reach back and yank the priming cord.

This was where the wishful thinking had come in. The Tahni wouldn't have arrayed themselves in a circular firing squad, so *one* side of the place was going to be open, but which had been the guess. I'd made the best one I could, and if I'd guessed wrong, I was about to crawl out of the shack right into the feet of a Tahni soldier and get my un-helmeted brains blown out.

I didn't. I was greeted by the narrow confines of the alley

between the antenna and the town's perimeter wall, which was there more to keep out the intermittent flooding from the artificially flat plane of the landing field than it was for any sort of security. I turned right and ran, ducked over as if crouching would save me from enemy fire, the impact of tantalum on steel audible in regular half-second intervals between my labored gasps. I was running not just from the Tahni but against the clock, counting down from twenty in my head.

Twenty seconds had been cutting it close, but I knew I wouldn't have more time than that before the Tahni stormed into the radio shack and if they saw that I was gone, they would pull out and start looking for me...and looking away from the antenna.

When the clock in my head reached twenty, I threw myself to the ground and covered my head with my hands.

I'd heard a lot of explosions during my military career, both from inside my battlesuit and out of it, but this one was qualitatively different. Wouter Pistorius didn't keep much of the blasting compound in his safe, but we hadn't needed much, just enough to cut through the support columns for the antenna. Civilian blasting charges designed for cutting through granite hillsides had a different timbre to them than military HpE, deeper and full-throated, a whump I felt down in my chest before the higher-pitched crack that bounced off the buildings around me.

I couldn't see the effects of the ten kilos of blasting compound at first, because I couldn't see *anything.* Smoke billowed out from the base of the antenna and swallowed up all light, all detail. I squeezed my eyes shut against the smoke and dust, trying to keep my breathing shallow but coughing fitfully despite the precaution.

My ears felt as if they were filled with water and even the

high-pitched whine that was all I could hear sounded as if it was being filtered through a kilo of cotton, but when the crash came, I felt it right through the pavement, and I knew the charge had done its job. Even more dust washed out from the impact of the massive metal framework of the antenna structure and I didn't know how much the damned thing massed, but it sure felt substantial filtered through the shaking pavement.

I wanted to see it, wanted to wait until the dust cleared and see the destruction I'd wrought, make certain of how many of the Tahni troops I'd taken out, but there just wasn't time. This wasn't the big show, this was a distraction, and I had to get to the main event.

I made my way down the wall by feel, not quite running but shuffling as quickly as I could without tripping over debris. I knew my pulse carbine's magazine had to be close to empty and I patted at the pouches on my tactical vest, finding a fresh one and yanking it out, ejecting the spent one from memory of ancient training. It clattered to the ground, the sound right at the edge of audible in my battered ears and I slapped the full magazine home.

The refill made my breath come easier, maybe because it was something familiar and comfortable or maybe because the thought of being able to shoot back was reassuring. Or maybe the dust was just settling back to the ground and I wasn't breathing in bucketsful of it every second. By the time I reached the gate, I was certain no one was chasing me and I took a moment to sneak a look over my shoulder.

The antenna, so long a fixture of this town, a landmark we would see first thing as we came over the horizon in one of the regular hopper flights, was gone, a cloud of grey smoke shot with the brown dust off the road its only memorial. The building across the street from it was smashed to kindling by the wreckage and a pang of guilt squeezed my chest at the realization I couldn't remember who owned the place or what sort of business it was. Someone had cashed in what the Commonwealth owed them for putting their life on the line in an interstellar war and sunken all their hopes into this tiny storefront on an isolated colony, taking the chance that it would grow into something important. And now it was gone and it had been my hand that destroyed it, even if Zan-Thint and Eld had been the ones at fault.

I turned away from the carnage and back toward the purpose behind it. The passenger shuttle was stock, unexceptional, and might have been ten years old or a hundred—the design had been around since the first ships had navigated the first wormhole we'd discovered, starting us on a path that had led to two full-scale interstellar wars with the Tahni and one police action against the same sort of pirates who'd brought Zan-Thint and his people to Hausos.

Maybe we'd be better off if that freighter hadn't stumbled across the jumpgate.

But no, then people like me would have been stuck in the undergrounds of the mega-cities with nowhere at all to escape. And right now, escape was what was on my mind, and that shuttle was the only avenue.

Wade and Vicky were already moving, having been in position before the Tahni had gone after me in the transmission shack, but I couldn't find them against the gray fusion-form pavement of the landing field and that was a good thing. If I was looking for them and couldn't see them, maybe that would mean the shuttle crew, who would be distracted by the explosion and the collapse of the tower, wouldn't see them either.

I held out hope they wouldn't notice *me*, but that was a longshot, so I didn't try to curve around behind them or anything nearly as stealthy as that, just ran straight at the shuttle. It was still sitting on the landing field, its belly ramp open, engines inert. I knew it wouldn't last, and I hadn't made it more than twenty or thirty meters toward the aerospacecraft before the ramp began to lift off the tarmac, the turbines whining softly at first but with building intensity.

I wasn't going to make it in time. Luckily, I didn't have to. I hadn't spotted Wade and Vicky, but that was because they'd looped around the other side of the shuttle and been blocked from my view by its landing gear. The two black-clad silhouettes moved out from behind the left-side rear landing treads, one leaner, sleeker than the other, moving with lithe grace to hop onto the slowly closing ramp before it could raise half a meter off the ground. Wade grabbed the end of the ramp and pushed himself onto it, following Vicky with a good deal less agility since he was hauling around nearly half again her mass.

The ramp kept raising, closing with a hiss of escaping air while I was still ten meters away, leaving me crouched beneath it, flinching at the scream of the turbines, squinting against the dust and dirt being stirred into a cyclone by the jets spinning up. The shuttle was a dragon out of myth, its hot breath scorching against my exposed face and I ducked away from the exhaust, taking refuge behind the nose gear.

I clutched at the grip of my carbine with helpless desperation, taking on faith that the damned shuttle wouldn't take off and roast me like a chicken. I trusted Vicky. I sort-of trusted Wade. Well, I trusted Vicky, anyway. My heart trusted her, but my feet were edging away from the shuttle, getting ready to take off in case the thing actually began to boost.

Just as suddenly as they'd spun up, the turbines began to throttle down, and my heart slowed right alongside them. I leaned a hand against the nose gear's hydraulic piston and tried to bring my respiration back to normal, then jumped again when the motor for the belly ramp hummed back to life. Vicky's head peaked out from the gap between the ramp and the hull before it was halfway down, a grin splitting her face.

"We lucked out," she told me. "The troops were Tahni, but the flight crew belonged to Eld. They're human."

I returned her smile.

"Then let's go have a talk."

[20]

"Are you sure they're gonna let us go?" the pilot whined. "I don't wanna go to jail, man."

Wade and I exchanged a look from the acceleration couches on either side of the smuggler shuttle pilot and Wade rolled his eyes.

"Trust me," he told the man, "the CSF has better things to do than worry about shipping a nobody like you off to the nearest Patrol base. You get us to the station, we'll put you on the next freighter back into the Commonwealth and you can do whatever the hell you want from there. Don't you need to concentrate on flying?"

It wasn't a bad question. The jets were rumbling steadily and the sky outside the viewscreens was turning from deep blue to black, and I would have thought it would be a great time for the shuttle's pilot to be paying attention.

"Naw, this thing basically flies itself unless I'm trying to avoid getting shot at."

The pilot was a heavy-set man, which was something of a shock to me. You just didn't *see* fat people in the colonies...or much of anywhere. Back in Tijuana, most of us had barely had enough to eat and the only fat man I'd ever seen was a gang boss who ate more than everyone else as a sign of his power. In the cities, the basic health care systems had kept even the poorest of us at an ideal weight and it was no different in the Marines. But this guy was from the Pirate Worlds and basic health care out there away from the Commonwealth was probably lacking. His jowls hang down like a hound dog, despite an unsuccessful attempt to hide them beneath a bushy beard and mutton chops.

And he sweated. A lot. Which didn't make it any more of a pleasant experience to be in the same, cramped cockpit as the man, but we didn't trust him enough to leave him alone.

"What about them?" the pilot asked, nodding back toward the rest of the flight crew, two men and a woman, secured by flex cuffs from Wade's kit and stuffed into acceleration couches in the passenger compartment. And gagged, because the woman had kept yelling at the pilot, warning him what Eld would do to him if he betrayed them. It had been my pleasure to let her know Eld was dead, but that had simply changed her script to nonstop profanity. Some of it had been impressive in its imagination and scope, but it had been distracting from our negotiation with the pilot, whose name we hadn't bothered to learn but whom the woman had called "you useless, limp-dicked fuckface."

It was a well-thought-out name, but not one I wanted to try to repeat.

"Them?" Wade repeated. He didn't twist around in his seat because we were still accelerating up through the atmosphere and sharp movements were contraindicated, but his eyes darted that way. "My first instinct is to just leave them tied up in this piece of shit and cut it loose to coast into the primary star." One of the men made a desperate squawk through his gag, shaking his head, eyes wide. Wade sneered at him. "But since they're your friends or something, I guess I could send them back to the planet or something. Or maybe just hang onto them until we hook up with the military and hand them over."

The man who'd squawked seemed relieved, but the woman still looked mad enough to spit nails. The other was still quiet, not showing any emotion, probably the most dangerous of the three. Vicky sat in the row behind them, Wade's sidearm in her hand, watchful.

"All right," the pilot said, as if we were still in the negotiation phase of this relationship. I was of the opinion that the negotiations had ended the minute he'd lifted the shuttle off the ground, but we were flying so I didn't press him on the issue.

"You guys do know this thing won't make it all the way to the station, right?" he asked. "I mean, I guess we *could*, but it would take like, *weeks*. We don't carry enough reaction mass to get there quick."

"Yeah, we know," Wade assured him. "Just get us into fucking orbit. This thing has a transmitter, right? They don't make you shout out the window?"

"Sure!" The fat man pointed at the console in front of Wade's position. "It's right there. You know how to operate it, man? I mean, I kind of do, but it ain't my specialty."

"I'll figure it out."

He'd have to do it soon, I judged. Nothing but stars through the front screens now, and nothing pulling me towards the shuttle's deck, just the acceleration from the drives pushing me into the back of my seat. The scream of the jets had faded, and the rumble of the drives through the fuselage was deeper, a subtle difference but one I recognized as the transition from the air-breathing jets to the on-board metallic hydrogen fuel supply. We were in space, low orbit, almost clear of the atmosphere.

"Oh, dude...," the pilot said, almost a moan, his jowly face going slack, eyes fixed on the sensor screens in front of my position.

"What?" I tried to see what he was seeing, but I knew next to nothing about crewing a shuttle.

"That's like, our ship, man." He pointed to a large, delta-shaped icon at the right side of the screen that I had thought until that very second was supposed to be us. "I mean, like, it's the cargo ship, the *Dryad*. She was supposed to be off getting another load of weapons for the cache, but I guess she's back."

"And she's armed, right?" I assumed.

"Oh, yeah, man. She's got, like a big-ass coil gun and a proton cannon. She could blow us right out of the sky if she wanted to. But I don't think she'd do that."

"Why not?"

"Because she's like, launching an armed shuttle, man." He pointed at the screen again, as if the arcane markings there would mean anything to me. "She's probably gonna try to board us."

"Fuck," Wade commented, punching at the controls of the communications console like it owed him money. "Fuck, fuck, fuck."

"Yeah, well put," I murmured.

"Corporate Council station Zebra Four," Wade said, enunciating every words carefully, "this is Task Force Leader Cunningham, authorization code Gamma Alpha 2397640 Hotel. Do you copy?" He shot a glare at the pilot. "You just keep flying this thing, you hear? Don't slow down, don't acknowledge them."

"Okay, dude, but they're like, already calling us, right?"

"They are, and I'm ignoring it. Keep flying."

I had rarely felt this useless. Even when I'd been in my suit, riding a drop-ship into a space battle, I had, at least, been able to tap into the tactical net with my HUD and get some idea of what was going on. But the sensor suite on this thing was ancient, and it bore little resemblance to the tactical display of a Commonwealth Fleet cruiser.

"We copy your transmission, Cunningham." The voice was calm and business-like, a woman, I thought. "What is your status?"

"I am in a passenger bird heading for high orbit around Hausos," Wade said, speaking quickly, one eye on the sensor screen. "We have Gomers approaching fast, an assault bird coming off that cargo ship at point nine-zero. I need armed support and I need it quick or they are going to open fire."

"Roger that. I will pass it on to the watch commander. Hold tight."

"Hold tight, she says," Wade murmured. "What the hell else am I gonna do?"

"You want me to keep going?" the pilot asked, looking between the two of us.

"I want you to point us at the coordinates I gave you," Wade snapped, not even looking at him, "then take this piece of shit to however many gees you think it can stand and keep it there until your damned reaction mass runs dry."

"Like, sure, man." The fat man shrugged. "It's gonna like, hurt, though, you know?"

"Oh, trust me," Wade said, shaking his head, "I know."

"Put the gun away, Vicky," I told her. "In a second, there won't be much chance of any of us moving on purpose."

Her eyes went wide and she began looking around for someplace to stow the pistol, finally settling on a cargo pocket in the back of the acceleration couch in front of her barely a second before the pilot called out a warning.

"Boosting!"

And we were indeed boosting. I was no sort of spacer, just a passenger for all that I'd spent more time in spaceships than 99 percent of humans alive, but I judged our acceleration right at about seven or eight gravities, right at the threshold of human endurance. Pressure on my chest like a shuttle was parked on top of it, tunnel vision, a roaring in my ears, consciousness pulling away from me, all were familiar side-effects of high-gee boost and the only difference now was, I didn't have the comforting embrace of my Vigilante to make it all better. I don't know why that made a difference, but it did. The cold slap of the shuttle's ventilation drying the sweat on my neck, the bright lights of the controls, the openness of the cockpit all conspired to compound the misery, the agony.

Wade was moaning, an incoherent sound from deep inside his chest, and it took me a second's concentration to make sure it wasn't coming from me. But the pilot was, somehow, unbothered by the discomfort of his body weighing as much as a full-grown bull rock dragon. His face was flattened out from the push, his eyes bulging, but his fingers were still moving, nudging controls, I assumed to adjust our course though I couldn't even feel the lateral burn of the maneuvering rockets, and if there was a shift in the stars on the screen, I couldn't see it past the starbursts in my vision.

The ruthless boot of Newtonian physics crushed me beneath it for what seemed like forever, but realistically, I couldn't have stayed conscious for that long and neither could have Pilot Tubby, no matter how much of a hotshot he was. More significantly, the little shuttle didn't carry enough metallic hydrogen in her small fuel supply to maintain this sort of boost for more than a few minutes. I was wondering if those few minutes might be enough to give me burst blood vessels or internal injuries when the acceleration cut off abruptly and threw us all into free fall.

I went from weighing close to 600 kilos to weighing not a damned thing in a fraction of a second and I clenched my jaw shut to hold back the uncontrollable rush of bile that was my stomach's reaction to the shift. Wade couldn't quite keep his in and globules of something yellow-green splattered against the view screens, rebounding and reforming. I watched them with horrified fascination, convinced they were going to bounce back and hit me right in the face, but the ventilation system came to the rescue, drawing the droplets into the overhead vents.

"That's it, man," the pilot lamented, waving his hands in an expression of impotence. "We're out of gas. Not even anything left to brake if we wanted to. No one comes to rescue us; we'll drift into interstellar space...eventually. We'd die of starvation first. Or maybe the cold."

I peered at the sensor display, trying to make sense of what I was looking at, getting the idea that the armed shuttle which had launched from the pirate cargo ship was still boosting toward us and didn't look to be anywhere near out of fuel or reaction mass.

"Oh, I don't think we're going to get the chance to die of anything that pleasant," I said.

"Shit, man," the pilot moaned. "They're still accelerating. That's gotta be a cargo boat and she ain't carrying nothing but guns and fuel. They'll be on us in a few minutes."

"I called it in," Wade said, wiping at his chin, sounding as confident as a man with vomit staining his face could. "They're coming."

"They're coming from the fucking gas giant, dude!" the pilot exploded, sounding as if he was upset about us failing to keep our side of the bargain we'd made, although I didn't recall anyone promising him we'd be able to get away clean. "It'll take them fucking two days to get out here even at high-gee boost."

"Maybe," Wade admitted, his smile a bit wan and green around the gills. "If they were flying an assault shuttle. Or a system patrol boat."

"Task Force Leader Cunningham." The voice came over

the comm's cockpit speakers as if on cue. "This is Intercept One. Armed response has been approved and we are on our way."

"Roger that, Intercept," Wade replied. "Be advised we are bingo fuel and coasting unpowered. We will be unable to maneuver or decelerate."

"We'll figure it out, Task Force Leader. Wait one."

"Told ya," Wade said, shooting me and the pilot a satisfied grin.

"Told us *what*?" the pilot asked.

He tapped out a series of commands on his control panel and the view on the main screen shifted from the star-filled black out of our nose camera to the curve of Hausos out the stern. I hadn't seen the planet from space since we'd arrived over a year ago and it struck me how beautiful it looked now; how beautiful it had looked then. The beauty faded as the pilot fiddled with the console again and the camera zoomed in to its optical and computer enhanced limits. And there it was, the converted cargo shuttle pursuing us, not a computer simulation or a sensor blip, but the actual optical image of the ship, backlit by a flare of fusion fire.

"That thing is in visual range, dude! They're going to open fire on us in like a minute, and if they don't, it's only gonna be because they want to match velocities, board us, and then torture us *before* they kill us! You know the shit Tahni will do to a guy, man?"

"The Tahni don't torture humans," I corrected him, and my voice sounded almost alien to me, cold and distant. "They'll starve them, cage them outdoors in the cold, execute them like rabid animals, but they don't torture anyone. For that, you have more to worry about from your friends."

"They ain't my friends, dude," the pilot insisted. "I just needed the fucking money."

"Just keep watching that picture," Wade told him, still seeming unworried.

Me, I was worried. Now that I could move again, I twisted around in my seat and checked on Vicky. She'd been uncharacteristically silent and I had thought maybe she'd passed out from the heavy boost, but her eyes were wide open, her face pale. The gun was back in her hand.

"You all right?" I asked her.

"We should get our long guns out of the locker," she said. "I'm not letting them take me."

"What the hell is that?" the pilot demanded, pointing at the screen.

It was a flash of light, a prismatic ring that would never have occurred in nature without the intervention of a Teller-Fox warp unit twisting reality into submission with raw gravimetic energy. Inside the ring was nothing, the most intense concentration of nothing anywhere, a glimpse into another reality so alien humans couldn't even perceive it. One of the instructors at OCS had tried to explain it to us, though it had seemed to go over a lot of heads.

"You know how you think you see something out of the corner of your eye," he'd said to the class, his dark eyes flashing manically, "but when you look, there's nothing there? Transition Space is that nothing."

And it was nothing, but it was a Nothing that pretty much was a whole universe. Human eyes hadn't evolved to make sense of it, so they slid off it without seeing it. The silvery delta shape that emerged from the whole, though, that I could see just fine. I'd seen its like before, during the war, flown by the Fleet Attack Command. It was the smallest ship built that could be fitted with a Teller-Fox warp unit to travel through Transition Space.

"Is that a missile cutter?" Vicky gasped.

"It used to be," Wade said, practically beaming with pride.

"We bought up a bunch of 'em after the war and refitted them. They ain't got missiles anymore, but the proton cannon..." he trailed off as the cutter's fusion drive ignited, spurring it toward the cargo shuttle.

The shuttle's main drive cut off and its maneuvering thrusters flared as it tried desperately to shift its course, but it was far too late. The cutter had come out of T-space only a few hundred klicks away from the shuttle, well within range of the proton cannon that was now its primary armament. The particle beam was invisible in the vacuum, and the shuttle's display lacked the software to simulate it the way the military ships I'd been on had done, but its effects were obvious.

Burning oxygen shot out of the gap in the shuttle's fuselage where the cockpit used to be, and maybe I just imagined that I saw tiny human figures tumbling out of the rent in the hull or maybe I didn't. Either way, I didn't feel bad for them.

The cargo bird might have kept on coasting on the same course, unguided, its controls turned to burning metal gas along with its crew, but the CSF cutter wasn't taking any chances. The proton cannon lashed out again, and this time it speared through the tail of the bird, right into the metallic hydrogen fuel stores. The shuttle disappeared in a glowing ball of white fire, pieces of it scattered at angles along its original course, propelled by the blast.

I blew out a breath I hadn't realized I'd been holding and would have sagged in my chair if there'd been gravity to allow it. Instead, I went limp against the restraints and felt tension drain away from me.

"This is Intercept One," the speakers announced, the voice male and cocky, a typical pilot. "You doing okay in there, Task Force Leader?"

"I am now." Wade cocked an eyebrow at the pilot as if to

say, “I told you so.” “You think you can match velocities with us and get us out of this piece of junk?”

“Hey man,” the pilot complained. “That’s like, not nice.”

“Roger that, Cunningham. You boys and girls hold tight. This’ll take some high-gravity maneuvering, but we’ll dock with you in a half an hour, tops.”

“I gotta hand it to you, Cunningham,” Vicky said, shaking her head, “your people really came through for us.”

“Yeah.” The man seemed to deflate now that the danger was over. “Let’s hope they’re still my people in a couple hours.”

“Why?” I wondered. “What happens in a couple hours?”

“That’s when I get to tell my boss that I got my whole platoon killed.”

[21]

If I thought the inside of the assault shuttle had been cramped, I quickly found out how spoiled I had been. A missile cutter was built to comfortably hold a crew of three, though someone had told me that most of them had flown with only two during the war. There were ten of us crammed into her, and even though the smuggler crew was jammed into the two incredibly small cabins—barely closets, the rest of us couldn't all fit into the cockpit.

"Welcome aboard Intercept One, ladies and gentlemen," the pilot said as his copilot and crew chief both floated back into position beside him in the cockpit, having left to help us secure the prisoners. "I'm Flight Officer Dunstan and I will be your captain today, and on behalf of the crew, the Corporate Security Force and the Corporate Council, I hope you have a comfortable five-minute trip back to our base."

Dunstan was a garrulous type, good-natured for all that he still reminded me of the Attack Command pilots I'd met in the war, who were mostly dicks. He didn't look up or move from his chair as he talked to us, though, not from any attempt to be rude, but because he was plugged into it. He must have been Fleet, because he had the same sort of implant sockets as Wade, Vicky, and I, though his wetware was undoubtedly optimized for flying small spacecraft. The superconductive wires connecting him to the control console seemed extrusive and fragile compared to the shorter, thicker ones in the helmet of a Vigilante, but I had to assume they functioned just fine or they would have been redesigned before the end of the war.

The crew chief spared us a wan glare, glancing back and forth from the single spare seat in the cockpit to the three of us.

"I'm afraid two of you are gonna have to ride in the utility bay," the woman said. "There are a few fold-down acceleration couches back there."

"Aw, come on, Ruthie," Dunstan said, grinning, eyeing us sidelong. "We're just gonna jump back and then maybe a couple minutes of maneuvering thrusters. They'll be fine."

"CSF regulations, *sir*," she replied, the words sharp, belying the respectful form of address. "I'm afraid I have to insist."

"Sorry, guys." The pilot shrugged, possible in the microgravity only because he was strapped in. "Guess someone is going to miss seeing our base for the first time...."

"One of you take it," Wade said, still sounding as if we were flying back to his own funeral. He pushed off without another word, heading back to the utility bay, barely larger than the cabins, with most of the space taken up by equipment lockers.

"I'll go back with Wade," I told Vicky, then leaned in close to try to keep the next few words private. "He probably needs to talk to someone."

"He does," she agreed, "but it's not you."

"Why not?" I asked, my face falling despite the lack of gravity. "We were friends."

"You were brothers in arms," Vicky corrected me. "Tell me the two of you ever hung out for one second off-duty."

"Well, no," I admitted. "Not after the son of a bitch got us into that fight with Force Recon...."

"Exactly." She started to move past me, but I raised a hand to stop her.

"Wait a second. You two weren't even as close as that. You hated Cunningham."

"But I'm also not a threat to his self-image." I started to object, but she cut me off. "Cam, you won the Silver Star in a battle he missed because he was trapped in his suit with a broken back. You were made company commander while the highest he ever got was platoon sergeant. And I'm a woman, which *shouldn't* matter, but this is Cunningham we're talking about so it probably does. Let me talk to him."

I didn't argue this time, mostly because the CSF crew chief was giving me a dirty look. I just let Vicky pass and moved into the last acceleration couch in the cockpit and strapped myself in.

"So, you and Cunningham served together in the Marines?" Dunstan asked, hands dancing across the controls.

The cutter shuddered under the hammer-blows of the maneuvering thrusters, jolting me in my seat. I nodded without thought, unused to microgravity, and felt the motion moving me against the restraints.

"Yeah. When I first joined up."

"What'd you say your name was again?" the crew chief asked, frowning.

"Cam Alvarez."

"Oh, yeah, I heard that name before. Brigantia, right? I was there with the Fleet. I heard you blew up the deflector shields."

"More or less." I'd blown up the communications antenna, causing a feedback into the fusion reactor, shutting down the deflectors long enough for the cruiser in orbit to destroy them, but she wasn't writing a dissertation.

"Boy, you couldn't have paid me enough to land in one of those damned suits," she opined. "Those drop-ships were flying coffins."

For some reason, I found her suddenly irritating and fell back on old habits.

"Why do they call you a crew chief?" I asked her. "There isn't much of a crew on this ship and they're both pilots, right? What do you do besides making sure everyone is obeying in-flight regulations?"

Her expression soured, but Dunstan chuckled.

"It's from the Attack Command," he explained. "There were only two people in the missile cutters, one officer, one senior NCO. They were going to call the NCO the flight technician, but they figured a bunch of them would get killed so they named it something with more prestige to get people to volunteer for the job." The copilot laughed. The crew chief did not. "Naw, I'm just being a dick. It was actually a hold-over from pre-spaceflight days and no one bothered to change it when we went from shuttle crews to cutters. But Crew Chief Amendola here is a first-class technician who can repair anything on this ship if you give her the right parts and enough time."

Amendola still didn't smile, but her frown evened out.

"Hold onto your lunch, we're Transitioning again."

My lunch had been a hastily-consumed, months-old protein bar I'd found in the utility compartment of the hopper we'd stolen, and it had already made two trips down my gullet with an intervening ride to the back of my throat. This time, it stayed firmly in place. I wouldn't call myself a *fan* of jumps into Transition space, but it hadn't hit me as hard as some of the Marines in my platoon.

This time felt less extreme than the jumps I remembered from the war, which made some sort of sense, I suppose. I had heard that the larger the wormhole the Teller-Fox drive opened up, the more drastic the gravimetic tidal effects, though I was no sort of physicist and didn't know if that was science or wishful thinking. Either way, I didn't feel the urge to puke and called it a win.

We were in T-space for less than a minute and when we emerged again, Hausos was gone, a faint star in the view from the rear cameras on the edge of the main display, and the mottled, grey face of Perkunos scowled down at us as if the gas giant were the ancient wind god it was named after and he was upset at us for disturbing his millennia-long sleep. I'd never seen the planet up close, but I'd watched videos on the system before we emigrated and the presence of the Corporate Council mining facility had been a feature touted by the recruiters from the Colonial Authority. A Council base meant Corporate Security Force troops and aid in case of trouble. And I suppose it had.

It took a moment for me to notice the base itself, despite the fact we'd jumped in almost on top of it. The slowly rotating cylinder had to be over a kilometer long and nearly as wide, but it was lost against the massive sweep of Perkunos, a speck on the swirling yellow clouds of the giant planet. The gas mines weren't visible from this far away, but I knew they were down there, buried in the wisps of the upper atmosphere, automated because the radiation in that close would have been fatal to a human.

The whole thing could have been automated, but it wasn't. Maintenance pods swarmed around the outer surface of the station and a freight hauler floated off her polar docking port, two bulbous cargo shuttles mated to the non-rotating umbilical, loading or offloading. There had to be hundreds of personnel on board, and I wondered what for?

"What the hell are all of you guys doing out here?" I asked

the question aloud because Dunstan seemed chill enough that he might answer it.

He shared a look with Amendola and shook his head.

"Sorry, Alvarez. That's gonna be up to the boss."

I didn't ask who the boss was. I figured I'd find out soon enough.

"What in the living fuck is going on down there, Wade?"

The woman's hands were clasped behind her back, almost as if she was in parade rest, though I was fairly certain she'd never been in the military. She didn't seem the sort. Oh, her clothes were uniform, dark grey and utilitarian in a designer sort of way, like something she'd spent a lot of money on to get that nondescript and yet still fashionable. They weren't exactly military, at least not Commonwealth military. They reminded me of old history videos I'd watched about World War Two, an impression not ameliorated by her short, severe bob of dark hair or the blood red of her lips. She was a good four centimeters shorter than me, but I still felt as if I should be looking up at her, and it was all I could do to restrain myself from snapping to attention at the bark of her voice.

Wade had. He'd braced like a Boot Camp maggot in front of a whole shark attack's worth of DI's.

"Chief Investigator Dukanovic," he said, his voice stiff and formal, "I'm not sure we can speak of the issue in front of people not cleared for it."

The woman rolled her eyes, pacing across the large conference room and looking the two of us up and down like a cattle vendor checking a couple of prospective beef cows. I'd been surprised that we'd been called into the conference room at all. When we'd arrived in the station, Wade had warned us we'd probably have to sit in a waiting room and cool our heels while he talked to his superior, but we'd barely made it off the cutter before a uniformed CSF trooper had confronted Wade and told him in no uncertain terms that all three of us were to report immediately to the Level One Executive Conference Room.

The place, I had to admit, was swanky. I'd expected something akin to the military space stations I'd passed through a few times during the war, Spartan, pragmatic, and unadorned metallic grey. This wasn't the military though, for all that the CSF played at it so hard. The walls were a tasteful beige, decorated by well-fabricated copies of what I recognized as famous pieces of art from Earth. The offices we passed by looked comfortable, the furniture a sort that would have been at home in any of the colonial governors' offices I'd walked through the wreckage of on so many worlds.

The conference room itself was afforded a rare luxury on a space station: a picture window. It could, I supposed, have been a holographic view screen set into the wall to make it look like a real window, but when we'd stepped inside, I had risked Wade and Vicky's ire and the wrath of Chief Inspector Dukanovic of the Corporate Security Force to step to the side and actually tap against it with a knuckle. It was solid and the image didn't waver with the presence of my skin. It could still have been a flat-screen monitor, but the outside image was slowly shifting along with the procession of the spinning drum and I just had the sense that this was exactly the sort of extravagance the Corporate Council would go for.

"I took the liberty of looking into the background of your friends," Dukanovic said, finally, sniffing at the last word as if she found the concept of friends to be frivolous. "I would say they're trustworthy enough to be read in on a Bravo Level clearance."

"Yes, ma'am," Wade said, breathing out what might have

been a sigh of relief or maybe one of concern as he cast us a sideways glance. "It was what we were worried about. Colonel Zan-Thint has led a splinter group of disaffected Tahni out into the Hinterlands...."

"The Hinterlands?" Vicky repeated, squinting at Wade.

"The systems the Tahni Imperium considered off-limits to colonization," Wade explained.

"Oh, you mean the Forbidden Zone."

Restraining the snort of laughter trying to force its way out of my chest was painful. Wade's throat bobbed as he swallowed hard, gaze flickering toward his superior as if he was waiting for a blow to fall. But the Chief Inspector just regarded Vicky with a thin smile, which my wife returned. Vicky was purposefully fucking with the woman to see how she'd react and, probably, to show her she wasn't impressed. I was simultaneously cheering her inwardly while also wishing she'd stop, because I wanted to be included in whatever this planning session was rather than waiting in the break room. I compromised and said nothing.

"Yes," Dukanovic said drily, "the *Forbidden Zone*. Go on, Cunningham."

"They were working in conjunction with a smuggler out of the Pirate Worlds, a Captain Eld. I didn't have a file on him, but that doesn't mean anything. Most of them were born off the grid, never had as much as a pre-natal screening, much less an ID scan into the system. He was a weapons smuggler, from what Cam and Vicky have told me."

"Was?" Dukanovic repeated, arching an eyebrow.

"We closed in on him and his people at the farm of one of his collaborators, a former Force Recon officer named Torrey. He'd sold out Cam and Vicky when they sought shelter there and Eld was holding a knife to Cam's throat to try to force Vicky to surrender. I had one of our sharpshooters kill the man."

"That's unfortunate." She scowled, hands on her hips,

regarding me with a look that said she thought it had been a bad trade. "He might have proven a useful source of intelligence."

"They've constructed a warehouse on the property of a refugee settler named Klaus Hellnick," Wade went on. "Cam went inside. Tell her what you saw, Cam."

Interesting. Rather than repeating what I'd already told him, and maybe letting slip what he knew, Wade was getting me to report it. That was a slick move, smarter than I would have given him credit for. Maybe he deserved his position after all.

"It's full of munitions," I told Dukanovic. "Small arms right up to proton cannons and at least a full squad's worth of High Guard battlesuits."

"They used those to take out my platoon," Wade told her, face set in a grim frown. "Just tore through us like we weren't there." He sucked in a breath, closing his eyes for a moment as if he had to reset his brain before moving on. "Tell her the rest, Cam."

The rest, huh? I had a feeling 'the rest' was why I was in here.

"They'd dug something up from behind Hellnick's farmhouse. Something big. Ten meters by twenty, I think. It was in the center of the warehouse, like the place had been built for it." I didn't hold back what I thought. It might get me in trouble, but I wanted to know what was going on and there was always the chance they'd let something slip. "They had it covered under a tarp, so I couldn't see what it looked like exactly, but there was a...vibration coming from it. Like a sound but not one I could hear."

Dukanovic's reaction was subtle, something a lot of people might not have picked up on, people whose continued existence hadn't depended on reading the mood and intent of group-home bullies, gang enforcers and drug mules. Her eyes narrowed almost imperceptibly, her lips parting by a millimeter at a tiny, abrupt intake of air too soft to be a gasp, too smooth to be a hiss.

"I get the feeling," I said, eyes locked on hers like a targeting laser, "that the thing, whatever it was, was the reason they were on Hausos. It doesn't seem like a particularly desirable place for a Tahni insurgency to set up shop otherwise."

"Oh, I wouldn't be sure of that, Mr. Alvarez," she said, as if the reaction had never occurred. "It's isolated, far from any military bases and even farther from the Patrol or any other law enforcement. And there were, quite obviously, fault lines in your local society which Zan-Thint and Captain Eld could exploit."

"We need to go back," Wade said, conveniently cutting off the discussion of whatever it was that the Tahni had dug up. "We can't let them get away with this. They have a starship in orbit. If we don't get back there, we're going to lose Zan-Thint and...." He stumbled over the words, and I could tell he was forcing himself to not say what he wanted to say. "...and everything he has on the planet."

"Except you don't have a platoon anymore, Wade," she pointed out. I winced at the brutality of the statement, as true as it was. "And none of the CSF personnel who are left on this base have nearly the amount or quality of training they did." She shrugged, as if the matter were of little import. "Yet, you're correct. We can't let him get away. Send the cutter. Strafe the farm with the proton cannon. Kill all of them."

"There may be innocent people being held captive on that farm!" Vicky cut in, taking a step forward, fists clenching as if she was about to start a fight with the older woman. "You can't just destroy everything!"

"Then give me an alternative, Ms. Sandoval," Dukanovic snapped, leaning into Vicky's aggressive stance, nearly nose to nose. "All the tender feelings in the galaxy aren't going to stop a squad of High Guard battlesuits, as you should know better than anyone. If we don't take them down from the air with the cutter, what the hell would we do about them?"

"Actually," Wade said, cocking his head to the side like a little boy who's gone behind his parents' back and is about to beg forgiveness, "I might have something we can use."

[22]

"Holy shit," I murmured, running a palm down the BiPhase Carbide of the armor's chest plate, the cold smoothness of it as familiar as the touch of an old lover. "I never thought I'd see one of these again."

Much less three. The cargo storage bay was small, tucked away in the middle levels of the station, and the centripetal gravity felt lighter, as if any step could carry me to the ceiling if I wasn't careful. The lights were dim, dust bunnies spinning in the breeze from the ventilation proof that even the cleaning 'bots didn't get here often.

It had been the perfect place to store something you didn't want your bosses finding out about. The shipping containers were large, but not large enough to draw attention, three meters by three meters, just small enough for a powerloader to work them into the interior storage from the docking elevator. Now they'd been cracked open and what had spent however many weeks or months gestating inside those cocoons had burst forth to become a beautiful butterfly.

Three Vigilante battlesuits rested in the grip of the storage racks, matte grey, sullen, and stone-faced, and yet they were the most beautiful things I'd seen in years.

"Task Force Commander Cunningham," Dukanovic said, her voice stiff, the words as formal as if they were the prelude to a court-martial hearing, "what in the hell is this and how did it get into *my* station?"

"They were up for auction," Wade explained. I'd expected him to talk fast, trying to wheedle his way out of trouble, but instead, he seemed proud of the acquisition. "Restricted usage of course. Us or one of the new registered private military companies. No one else bid on them and I had some discretionary funding left from the expense account for the task force, so...." He shrugged. "I didn't know if we'd ever use them, but I felt better having them around. I guess I can't explain that to someone who hasn't been in one. But if the cutter can get us in there, drop us on top of Hellnick's farm, the three of us can take on those Tahni suits."

"There are *eight* of the Tahni suits, Mr. Cunningham," Dukanovic reminded him, still an edge to her tone, but a different set to her eyes as if she was willing to be convinced. "And I may not have been in the Commonwealth Fleet Marine Corps, but even I can tell that these suits are unarmed."

She was right about that. It wasn't the first thing I'd noticed, but it had been in the top three. Where the missile launch tubes had been on either side of the "backpack," the extrusion that housed the isotope reactor, were empty concaves. Where the plasma gun had been mounted along the right arm of the things, there were empty ports and hardpoints and the lack of an articulated right hand made the suits seem deformed somehow without the gun to cover them up.

"They're unarmed *now*, ma'am. But the hardpoints and the power and targeting connections are still operable. We don't have plasma guns to mount on them, but we got other stuff. Gatling lasers, Gauss rifles. It'll be enough."

He sounded damned confident. And I didn't contradict him because I was, too. I didn't know if that was realistic or if it was simply being beside a Vigilante again, getting the chance to wear one was a drug-like high. I tore my eyes away from the suit, sensing Vicky's frown. I thought, for a moment, that she didn't share my confidence, that she was scared and unsure we could pull this off, but the intensity of her focus on me belied the idea.

"Are you sure about this?" she wondered. Her voice was soft, meant only for me, though I was sure Dukanovic had picked up the exchange. "You know what happened the last time you were inside one of these."

I did. Delp had died. Vicky had almost died, had been in the medical bay stuck in an auto-doc for days. And I'd wound up with flashbacks, nightmares, insomnia...

She wasn't worried about us dying, though that might have been a residue of the cocky Marine she'd once been, and probably still was at her core. She was worried about me. She was worried I would climb into the Vigilante and all the ghosts of my past would come back to haunt me, that I'd lose it and curl into a ball and die.

But I *wasn't* worried about that. Because I knew that everything that had been missing, everything that had been stripped away and left me bare and defenseless over the last year was standing right in front of me.

"Yeah, I'm sure," I said. "Get me some guns, Wade, and plug me in." I offered Dukanovic a wintery smile. "If there's one thing your file should have told you about me, ma'am," I told her, "it's that the one thing I'm good for is running a Vigilante... and killing Tahni. You get us down in that compound, and we'll take care of those High Guard suits."

Dukanovic eyed us in silent consideration for a long, awkward moment, but then she slowly nodded.

"Very well, Cunningham. Since you created this mess, I'll give you the chance to get yourself killed fixing it. But understand this." She raised a finger in warning. "If you fuck this up, no one's coming to the rescue. That cutter is going to blast the whole place into atoms and then I'll send a recovery team to salvage what's left. I don't give a damn if there's a hundred babies and the President of the Commonwealth in that compound, it's getting torched. Am I clear?"

"We won't let you down, ma'am," Wade assured her, which wasn't exactly an answer to her question, but she let him get away with it.

"You launch in two hours," she declared. "Get those obsolete pieces of shit ready to go."

She spun on her heel and exited the storage room without another word.

"By obsolete pieces of shit," Vicky said slowly, frowning after her, "did she mean the suits or us?"

"Probably both," Wade admitted. "Come on. We need to get these things gunned up and we don't have much time."

"There's something else going on down there, Wade," I told him, stopping him in his tracks as he was about to retreat from the storage compartment. "Something you're not telling us."

He glanced the way Dukanovic had gone, paranoia in his stance and the whispered answer he gave us.

"There is," he confirmed. "And if we live through this, I swear to God, I'll brief you on the rest. But not here."

Vicky sniffed, shooting me a skeptical glance.

"That good enough for you?"

"It'll have to be." I gave the Vigilante one last pat, a silent promise to come back, and followed Wade out the door.

"You know," I said, grunting with effort as I cranked the handle of the torque wrench, tightening the fastening bolt of the Gatling laser, "theoretically, we could have carried these things during the war. They were always one of the equipment options. But I don't believe I ever once saw a Vigilante armed with anything but a plasma gun."

The Gatling lasers were odd weapons with the air of something cobbled together. And in a way, they were. Military history had been one of the required courses for OCS and I'd developed a bit of a fascination with the development of the weapons we used. Laser weapons, our instructors had told us, had long been the brass ring that weapons designers had been grasping for since the early 21st Century. Oh, large, artillery-sized weapons had existed since the middle of that century, fragile and dragging a huge bank of power cells along. It was impractical for anything but fixed positions or ships, both surface navy and space variety, and only large ones of those.

Then some research group led by a guy named Shockley had figured out the two problems that had been holding back development of battlefield laser weapons: the optics and the power source. They'd developed a method of funneling the heat energy from chemical Hyper-Explosives ignited in a specially-designed chamber through lasing rods, doing away with the power source altogether. The optics had required decades of experimentation using zero-gravity crystal growth and new composite materials until they'd finally settled on a complex arrangement of nanostructures that could focus the lasing energy into something tight enough to use as a weapon.

Ironically, they wound up with the exact opposite problem as they'd had before. The new nanocrystal focusing lenses were easy to make in sizes compact enough for small arms, and the new lasing rods would handle the rates of fire an individual weapon would generate, but that left a gap between the pistols and carbines that were now ubiquitous in the military and law enforcement and the reactor-fed lasers on cruisers and no obvious way to fill it, since manufacturing nanocrystal emitters and lasing rods of that size and durability would have been prohibitively expensive.

So, some genius had looked back at the early history of cartridge firearms on Earth and discovered the Gatling gun and had an inspiration. Instead of making one large lasing rod and one large nanocrystal emitter, they packed eight, or ten, or twenty smaller ones together in a ring around a motorized hub and spun them past the ignition chamber, firing off thousands of rounds per minute. It was a kludge, but it worked and no one had come up with anything that worked better.

"That's because of the ammo," Vicky informed me, sounding distracted as she worked on securing a heavy Gauss rifle to the left forearm of her Vigilante. It was fed from an external drum and would be useless once she fired off the last round, since there was no way to reload from inside the suit, but beggars couldn't be choosers. And there were only eight of them. "Even with the feed umbilical...." She gestured at the articulated metal feed arm extending from her suit's Gatling back to a hopper mounted where the missile launcher would have been. "...we've got what? Two thousand rounds? A shuttle can carry ten thousand, and we can't reload without retreating back to a service bay. That's why no one wanted to mount anything except a plasma gun as the main weapon. It carries enough metallic hydrogen for more shots than anyone would have the chance to take in one engagement."

"Jesus Christ," Wade murmured, sliding a belt of Hyper-Explosive cartridges into his hopper. "Does getting a commission automatically make you physically unable to stop blathering on and on about everything?"

"Knowledge, Sgt. Cunningham," I told him, doing a poor impression of one of our old battalion commanders. "Battles are won with knowledge just as much as weapons."

"What *I* know," Wade shot back, slapping the hopper's maintenance cover closed, "is that we have about a half an hour to seal these fucking military surplus jobs up and walk them down to the hangar bay." He tossed his wrench into an open toolbox and dusted his hands off theatrically. "And this dumbass NCO is done. How about you smartass officers?"

One last turn of the wrench and I dropped mine beside his, returning his grin with one of my own. "Ready when you are, unless you got some more ammo I can squeeze into this thing."

"'Fraid that's it," he lamented. "I had to strip this shit off the station's missile-defense turrets, and let me tell you, the Chief Inspector liked that even less than me coming back here without my platoon."

"Were you close with them?" Vicky asked. I winced. I had avoided asking Wade about the people he'd lost because I knew exactly how raw that wound would be, and I hadn't wanted to press him on it. But Vicky was always more of a people person than I had ever been, so I had to assume she knew what she was doing.

"Not really." Wade leaned against the chest of his battlesuit, as if drawing comfort from the contact. "They'd just gotten back from training a few weeks ago. I could barely remember their names. We were the first of a new sort of CSF task force and I was the first commander." He sighed, shoulders sagging. "Guess that didn't go so well, huh?"

"It's not your fault," I assured him. "What else could you have done? What your boss wanted? To strafe the place from a thousand meters up and kill everyone? You were trying to do the right thing. You're *still* trying to do the right thing. And now, we're going to help you do it. Right, Vick?" She cocked an eyebrow at my use of Dave's favorite nickname for her, but nodded her support.

"I don't know, man," Wade said. "I mean, there's *eight* of them. And we ain't exactly gonna be able to call for air support, not with those coil guns covering the whole compound. The cutter can't land, can't hover, can't do anything for us until we take them out." He banged a knuckle against the housing of his Gatling laser. "We got these, however long the ammo holds out, and that's it."

"It rains on the just and the unjust," I reminded him. "That's all they're going to have, too. All they were mounting was heavy KE guns, no missiles, no electron beamers. They're just as much surplus as these things are. And I guarantee you, not a one of them is as good inside a suit as we are."

Well, as Vicky and I were. Wade had never been more than passable in a Vigilante, but now wasn't the time to be bringing it up.

"They killed your platoon because you weren't expecting them, Wade," Vicky said. "Now, it's our turn. Because they're sure as hell not going to be expecting this."

He nodded gratefully, then hit the control to open the chest of his armor and clambered into it, as awkward as a virgin in a brothel. I tried not to seem quite as unpracticed, though I wasn't sure who I was trying to impress. I had one foot braced on the interior chock of the folded chest plastron when Vicky's hand on my arm stopped me.

"I'm scared, Cam."

"Of what? You think I'll have a flashback, freeze up?" I pushed myself up into the Vigilante, squeezing my legs and arms into place, smiling at her from inside the opened shell of the thing. "It's not going to be a problem. I never had any trouble in the suit. It's stepping outside of it that's the problem." I fished the leads of the interface cables out of the inside of the helmet and unspooled them, giving myself enough slack to reach the jacks in my temples. Metal clicked against metal and I plugged into the suit for the first time in what felt like a lifetime.

"I know," she said softly, her words nearly drowned out by the hum of the servos as the plastron swung shut at my command. "That's what scares me."

I wasn't sure what she meant and I didn't give myself the luxury of trying to figure it out now. I had more pressing matters. The interior of the Vigilante was dark, the chill embrace of a coffin or the security of a womb, depending on how you thought about it. I didn't. Think about, that is. I wasn't thinking about anything, I was meshing with the suit's systems.

It took a while. The things had been decommissioned, shut down, and it wasn't as simple as simply tripping through a few menus to establish my authorization. This was a full reboot, like setting up your 'link for the first time, and I worried I wouldn't finish setting the thing up in the time we had left. But only two or three dozen selections and twenty minutes later, there were greens across the board and I felt the slight give in pressure as the joints unlocked.

I don't remember taking my first steps as a toddler, but I'm sure it felt something like this. Unsure, unsteady, unfamiliar. Yet also working from instinct because I was born for this.

I was born for this.

The words echoed in my head as if shouted into an empty cathedral, the blasphemy of a fallen priest screaming into the eaves of an abandoned church the horrible truth, that he no longer believes in God.

I still believed in God. I thought. Maybe. But what I no longer believed in was Peace. I no longer believed I was suited for it, no longer believed I could put down the metaphorical sword and pound it into the equally metaphorical plowshare. I wasn't a thief anymore, I wasn't a con man anymore, I wasn't a criminal...that had been something I'd done to survive, but it wasn't who I was.

But a Marine...I was beginning to believe that was more than just a Faustian bargain I'd made with the government to stay out of punitive hibernation, more than just another unpleasant thing I'd done to stay alive. It was, I'd decided, what I was, *who* I was. I'd made a mistake thinking I could transform myself into a farmer.

I was born for this.

I clomped out of the storage room, every motion feeling more and more natural, more and more like I'd never left the suit.

And I knew, I thought, why Vicky was scared.

[23]

"We're not going to be able to offer you any support until and unless you take out those coil guns," Flight Officer Dunstan reminded us yet again, his voice much less bantering and good-humored coming over my helmet speakers. "You do that, I'll stop-and-pop and let that platoon of ground troops out for the clean-up, but you're on your own until then."

"You keep saying that as if we've forgotten between now and the last time," Vicky snapped. She hadn't spoken a word the whole flight back to Hausos, but I could feel her stewing even through the armor of her battlesuit.

If it had been cramped on the flight out to the CSF base, it was sheer lunacy now. The three of us were sitting on our fat, metal asses in the utility bay, anchored to the hull with the magnetic soles in our heels, with the CSF platoon crammed into bolted-on emergency seats crammed into every spare niche. They'd ripped out the equipment lockers to make room for them and it was still a claustrophobe's nightmare.

"Sorry," Dunstan offered, clearly not. "But three of you going against all of them...."

"We know the odds," I said, cutting off the line of discussion. "Talking about them won't make them better."

"Well, here's something that might make the odds better," he told us. "You know that freighter y'all saw in orbit? The one that launched that half-assed assault bird after you?"

"The *Dryad*," I said, nodding even though he couldn't see it. "Yeah, I remember."

"Well, it's gone. Like, nowhere to be found. I guess they could be tucked into the far side of the moon, but the base's spy drones would have noticed that, so the most likely scenario is that she just cut and run. So, at least we ain't gotta worry about her taking potshots at us on the way in."

"Shit," Wade muttered, sounding as if Dunstan had just pissed in his breakfast.

He didn't have to explain why. Vicky and I were in this thing to rescue the hostages, but Wade's job depended on bringing in Zan-Thint, and if that ship had taken off, the odds were pretty good he was on it.

"He might have gotten away," I said quietly to Wade, making sure to switch to a private channel since I didn't know how much Dunstan and the flight crew knew. "But whatever the thing is that you don't want to tell me about, it was *huge* and probably weighed tons. It would have taken them days to load it on a cargo shuttle. You'd have noticed the activity even from orbit."

"Yeah," he allowed. "Maybe you're right."

I hadn't said it just to comfort him, though. We needed him and his people to make this happen, and while I didn't want him suddenly deciding that Dukanovic was right and he should just blow the whole place up. The Wade I remembered had been no sort of coward, but he also hadn't always been a stand-up guy. He'd back-stabbed me until I'd earned his respect, and it was great that I *had* earned it, but those colonists down there hadn't, and I didn't know this version of Wade Cunningham well enough to be certain he felt any sort of responsibility to a bunch of civilians he'd never met.

"We got some thermal readings from those barracks," the copilot told us. "Good news for you guys, it looks like they're packed with people. Humans, according to the analytics, so probably those neighbors of yours you were talking about."

At least there was that. I'd been fretting over the possibility that they'd been moved or worse.

"We're going to have to be extra careful about where our rounds go," I said. Those barracks are just wood and sheet metal."

Wade awarded me with a grunt and from Vicky, I got nothing.

"Atmospheric entry coming up, boys and girls," Dunstan announced. "Hold onto your hats because up is gonna be up and down is gonna be down and I think we're about to ride straight through a thunderstorm."

"Why couldn't we ever have dropship pilots as entertaining as him?" I wondered. "All I remember is a lot of warnings about incoming ground fire." No one thought that was amusing enough to answer. I sighed and got down to business. "I'm going out first, then Vicky, then you, Wade."

"I should be on point," Wade said, sullen and withdrawn and not making me feel any better about the whole thing. "It's my mission."

"It *is* your mission," I acknowledged. "You're in command. That's why you're in the rear. You don't lead a mission from point. Maybe they didn't teach you that at NCO school, but it's one of those things they pound into your head at OCS. I have the most combat experience of any of us, so I go first. That's the great thing about being a civilian now, I don't have to act like an officer, but you do."

"Man, I never knew how much that must have sucked." He sighed. "Okay, you go first."

At least there was that.

The cutter began to rock like a boat on a rough ocean, jolting now and then with the shock of an updraft. If I'd been strapped in beside the others, it might have made me airsick, but inside the Vigilante, it was a mother rocking her baby to sleep. I'd felt the motion before, so many times it was almost a comfort. I wasn't in a drop rack, but it was close enough, and if the cutter wasn't a drop-ship, it would do the job for just the three of us.

"Two minutes to drop," the crew chief said, much less winsome about the whole thing than the pilot. "Make sure everyone not in a battlesuit has their safety restraints tight."

"Cameron." I jumped at Vicky's voice. I didn't think she was going to talk to me. "Tell me something."

"Sure. Anything."

"Tell me if you can go back once this is over."

"I don't think any of us can go back to the way it was," I said. "Not after what the refugees did, after what Brad did."

"Not here," she corrected me. "Not on Hausos. I know that. I mean, anywhere. Can you go back to the life we were living?"

I thought about lying to her. I hadn't ever, hadn't ever intended to, but she was about to head into combat with a force more than twice our size in jury-rigged, surplus armor and I didn't want to distract her. But I couldn't bring myself to do it. She deserved more—I'd promised her more. When we'd been married in front of the Catholic priest on Brigantia, we'd written our own vows, and beyond the usual love each other forever—which we both knew was probably bullshit since we had no idea how long we were going to live and who the hell knew if any relationship could last for hundreds of years. We'd promised we'd always be honest with each other, which seemed a more realistic goal.

"No," I admitted. "I can't. I don't know that I could have even if this hadn't happened."

"We're over the drop zone," the crew chief announced. "Opening the belly ramp. Get ready."

The position we were in was an impossible one for a human to have muscled their way out of, our legs curled up beneath us, no leverage at all, but the suits weren't humans and they had lots of extra muscle to work with. I rose to my feet, the magnets still gripping the deck and stepped out onto the ramp as it lowered. The scream of the belly jets was a dull roar through the insulation of the armor, the howling jetstream of the air outside the ramp a whisper. We were three kilometers from Hellnick's farm and two hundred meters off the ground.

I jumped.

The first time I'd done it for real, not in the simulators, it had felt unnatural, like suicide. My hind-brain had rebelled against it, insisting it was an unsurvivable drop, but of course I'd done it anyway. This time, the dropping was easier than the staying and for the first time since this whole thing had begun, I felt as if I had control over it. Gravity pulled and my jumpjets pushed back, and I flew.

It was night outside. I couldn't swear to which night it was, to whether we'd been gone one day or two, but it was night and it made no difference at all. Inside the helmet, it was always day, the computer's software taking the input from the infrared and thermal filters, the sonic sensors and every other bit of data the suit took in, and painting a picture from it, an illusion for my senses of brightest day. The plateau was laid out like a topographical map beneath me, antiseptic and clean, not as much as a harvester to break the clean lines of the crops. Hellnick hadn't bothered to send it out. Guess he didn't intend on making a living from selling his crop.

And then I *did* see something rising above the hill, a wash of hot, fusion-fed jets against the dark, cold of the night. It was the cargo shuttle, the one they'd armed up as a gunship, and it was coming after the cutter. Which seemed to me like an extraordinarily bad idea, but then, they didn't really know what they were dealing with. I worried for a moment that the gunship would notice us dropping, would deviate from its course and wipe all three of us out with a sweep of its proton cannons, but it had a singular focus, rocketing off toward the cutter's last position.

I wondered about that all the way to the ground, debating whether they'd missed us and we could slip in unnoticed. It was a nice fantasy. It comforted me as the three of us touched down in the tall corn, towering over it instead of being hidden in its depths, plowing forward through it. Twenty steps, a gap of I didn't know how any seconds, but it was instinctive, something I'd done enough that I didn't even have to count them.

"On the jump!" I said after I was sure the jets had cooled down enough to avoid blowing up on us if we used them again.

We passed over hills whose shape I hadn't had a true sense of until now, seeing them from above in the mapping display. They reminded me of the hills on Dak Shepherd's ranch on Brigantia, and I wondered if the ways this planet had brought to mind that colony had influenced my decision to choose it over the others in what Dave used to call the Forbidden Zone. I was ready to mentally chastise myself for letting my thoughts wander, but then a smile slowly spread across my face as I realized that I *didn't* have to concentrate on troop positions, fire support, a complex operations order or any of the dozen other things demanding my attention back in the day when I'd been a platoon leader or, worse, a company commander.

The smile faded as I realized how much more time that would leave for me to worry about getting killed, or getting Vicky killed. Or getting the civilians killed. There was a hell of a lot that could go wrong with this. Lucky for me, it was only a few seconds before I had something else to occupy my thoughts. There they were, the tops of the buildings, visible over the crest of the hills as we rose up again on streams of superheated air. Nothing apocalyptic to be seen, no fires set to kill the hostages in the night, no smoke rising from explosions. Just the barracks, the storage building, and the farmhouse glowing with the same harsh, yellow lighting I'd seen the last time I'd been here.

That was the good news. The bad news were the thermal signatures glowing on my threat display, eight of them, each surrounded by a red enemy designation as the suit's Identification Friend or Foe system recognized them as Tahni High Guard troopers.

"I guess that means they know we're here." Wade was trying to sound cool and calm, but there was a noticeable waver in his voice.

"They're not holding anything back this time," Vicky noted. She didn't have to *try* to sound cool. It came naturally.

We touched down in a triangular formation without anyone having to tell us, thirty meters apart, pounding the dirt into hard-pack beneath our feet, legs flashing in a long, loping gait. The Tahni troops didn't stay in the air long, either, getting low below the horizon, still a kilometer out from us.

"What's the plan, Big Man?" Vicky asked Wade. There was a challenge in her tone, a callback to a time when we'd all been enlisted Marines together, but it was a good question. I had confidence in our ability, but there *were* eight of them and quantity had a quality all its own.

"They're probably gonna form a...a double-wedge on line," Wade stuttered. "Right?"

We were eating up four meters of ground with every step and the swell of the rise ahead was looming. When we topped it, there'd be no cover between us and the Tahni, nowhere to hide.

"We've got ten seconds until they're in firing range," I told him in gentle reproof. "Split up and each take a team or point the spear at the heart of one team and force them to come to us?"

Silence. Five seconds.

"What should we do?" he asked me. I wanted to be angry with him, wanted to blow up and call him out for insisting he be the one in charge, but he sounded so helpless, it would have been like child abuse.

I'd been trying to remember what this whole situation reminded me of, and it came to me just as we topped the crest of the hill, brushing through the last rows of corn, past the clusters of cottonwoods separating the crops from the gravel road and the dirt lot on the other side of it. This was just like one of the simulation runs I'd gone through at Armor School, a generic pastoral scene, rolling hills, trees, crops. It was where we'd assumed we'd fight the war. And we had, to some extent, though it had never been as simple as the simulations. There'd never been just a line of enemy coming out to meet us like this was some 18th Century European battlefield, because the Tahni hadn't been there to do battle, they'd been there to make the war unwinnable for us, to make the price too high for us to keep taking back worlds one at a time.

The only way we'd managed to do it was to become as hard and vicious as they were, which hadn't been too difficult for us. If studying military history had taught me anything, it was that humans had in their day, made the Tahni seem like the Little Sisters of the Poor. It was there in our DNA, genetically and historically, and it had only taken a little prompting to bring it back out.

These Tahni were no different to the ones I'd fought in the

war, and they wouldn't be any more hesitant to use our innocents against us. It came to me in a blinding flash of the obvious. They weren't coming out to meet us, they were trying to bring us to their chosen battleground, just like they had in the war. It was the only reason they would have kept the civilians alive and I should have known that already. It had been too long since I'd dealt with Tahni and I think I'd wanted to forget how they'd been, how they'd made us be. What they'd turned us into.

"Stay tight on me." The words tumbled out as if some ancient god of war was speaking through me, the decisions made on a level below conscious thought. "They'll be keeping close to the hostages, trying to use them as cover, so what we'll do is flank the warehouse and then come at them over the roof of the barracks. We'll hit together at their center mass, force them to maneuver around us instead of the other way around. And whatever we do, we stay between them and the civilians. Because *they* are the mission. Am I clear?"

"Yes, sir." My eyes narrowed, searching for any sign of sarcasm in Wade's reply but not detecting any.

The buildings rushed at us all at once, and the situation came into focus along with the readings of a dozen sensors, feeding through my suit display and the interface cables like my own senses. The Tahni High Guard troopers were waiting, deployed around the barracks building, hugging it close, four on the west side facing the farmhouse, the others on the south, facing the landing field. They were guarding the entrances on those sides, their weapons outward, ready to fire the second they saw us.

Eight electromagnetic slug shooters swung toward us, hosing gouts of hypersonic metal death.

[24]

"Jump!" I blurted, but the action preceded the word and the others copied me faster than they could have processed the command, as if their suits were slaved to mine.

I couldn't see the streams of tantalum darts ripping through the space where we'd been only a heartbeat before, but the puffs of dirt and the exploding trunks of cottonwoods told the story of their passage, shifting to their right, our left to follow our course and disappearing into the night, bound for a termination in the rocks kilometers away where gravity would ultimately pull them down.

Our termination was much closer and, I hoped, not as final. I'd given the jump-jets a burst of two seconds, just enough to take us out of their arc of fire, give us a boost forward a hundred meters. I landed in the lee of the warehouse, and a metal hail tried to follow me, slicing into the sheet aluminum there like butter, only the actual cargo stored inside stopping the determined gout of penetrator rounds from piercing all the way through the building and into us.

A spray of sparks flared from Vicky's shoulder and I knew one of the darts had threaded the needle of dense cargo and spalled off her armor. Concern twisted my guts but I couldn't afford to give into it. I let training, instinct, and experience guide me, as if the suit was controlling itself and I was just along for the ride.

One more burst of the jets combined with the muscle of the hip actuators propelling the Vigilante into a lunge forward, a move so fluid and acrobatic that it wouldn't have been possible if not for the interface running between the suit controls and my brain. The lunge and the short puff of superheated air sent me flying almost parallel to the ground, straight at the east side of the barracks building, low enough that their weapons couldn't follow me, or Vicky and Wade, if they did the right thing and stayed on my six.

I put myself into the head of the Tahni squad leader. It wouldn't be Zan-Thint. The Colonel had never been High Guard and wouldn't put himself in harm's way now. If the starship was gone, he was on it, either fleeing the area or, more likely, awaiting the events on the ground, deciding if things were safe enough for him to return. This guy would be a low-level officer or a high-ranking NCO, though the concepts didn't translate directly into the Tahni military. He'd be someone with combat experience but not command experience. He'd know the hows but not the whys, as Captain Covington had liked to say. And his reaction to my action would be, I thought, to move his forces, assuming I was going to break through the wall on the unguarded side of the barracks and free our people that way.

Which would have been a stupid thing to do since our goal was to save their lives, but would have seemed entirely reasonable to a Tahni who only thought of the civilians as assets to be taken off the board, and would assume we thought of them the same way.

Instead of going through, I went up and Vicky and Wade were so close behind me that my jets must have been scouring the finish off their armor. I skimmed the roof of the barracks, the spiked soles of my armored boots scraping over the sheet metal with a shrieking vibration I could feel right through the BiPhase Carbide, and when I dropped down on the other side, it was right on top of an enemy battlesuit.

I couldn't have described what I did next except in hindsight, and even then, it was hazy, one of those situations where you know how you wound up but couldn't imagine the path that had led you there. It was a combination of a twist in mid-air and a microsecond burst of the jump-jets, turning what would have been a collision of metal-clad legs on metal shoulders that would have left me off-balance and unable to press my advantage into a graceful touchdown only a meter behind the enemy suit.

My instincts were based on the way I'd fought in the war, and they screamed at me to fire a plasma gun I didn't have into the back of his head. I could have done that with the Gatling laser and maybe had a similar chance of burning through the armor at this range, but the weapon was longer and more awkward than the plasma gun had been and I knew if tried to use it this close, I would wind up damaging it. And it was pretty much all I had.

Except that heavy Gauss rifle. Normally, it wouldn't have scratched the finish on armor as thick as the High Guard suit, but I was within contact distance and I knew from hours and hours of studying and drills, getting and giving them, every weak spot in Tahni High Guard armor. Like the power lead running across the shoulder into the gun mount.

Every other actuator, every other cable, every other coupling was internal, covered by the armor, except that one. It was a short length of power coupling, exposed only out of the necessity for flexibility at the joint of the arm and shoulder, one of those design flaws that was never recognized during the war because how the hell would the enemy know about it and if they did, how would they exploit it? They'd have to be basically hanging over your shoulder at almost contact distance, and *that* just never happened....

I shoved the muzzle of the heavy Gauss rifle against the power cable and fired three rounds in the space of a second and a half. The recoil must have been fierce, but I barely felt the vibration through the shoulder of the Vigilante, couldn't hear the impact of the tungsten slugs because everything else was drowned out by the orb of witchfire that exploded out of the ruptured power feed. Static electricity crackled between us, lighting up the haze of white smoke that poured off the ruptured coupling, and he twisted around, swinging his suit's arm like a club, knocking aside the Gauss rifle.

I hadn't disabled his armor, but I'd left him without a weapon and limited him to only two workable options. He could jump out and hope I was too busy to shoot him on the fly, or he could grapple, try to keep me too close to shoot. I would have fought. He ran. Oh, it wasn't a bad decision. They outnumbered us and every second I spent on him was one I couldn't spend on the others. But I wasn't calculating things in a logical, risk-benefit-ratio sort of way and I shot him.

I might have been able to see the actual laser pulses with the infrared filters in my helmet optics, but the faint glow of coherent light was swallowed up in the eye-searing flash of air turned to plasma by the raw energy. The burning gas of the ionized corridor of air merged with the burning gas of the High Guard suit's jump jets and the sudden, disastrous whole was greater than the sum of its parts. I wasn't sure how many rounds I fired. The weapons connection was jury-rigged, the ammo feeding umbilical bolted on and not hooked up to the helmet computer, and the only way I'd know I was out of ammo was when the gun stopped working, but the lightning-strike crackle connected us for nearly a second and I estimated it had to be nearly fifty rounds.

I'd always considered the Gatling lasers to be less effective than the plasma guns we'd used in the war, but it was a false impression because the laser could fire off thirty or forty rounds in the time it took the plasma gun to recycle, and the cumulative effect of forty high-energy laser pulses was pretty damned fearsome. In this case, it penetrated right up through the turbines of the High Guard jump jets. I'd seen it happen before, and usually, the turbines simply flared out, still contained by the shielding of the isotope reactor behind them.

This time, it was a lucky shot for me, not so much for him. Either the laser penetrated his reactor shielding or the explosion of the turbines was powerful enough and at just the right spot to burn through it because the battlesuit was ripped apart from the inside, splitting at its joints and seams to spew out gouts of plasma. The suit had only made it four or five meters off the ground, and when it crashed back to Earth, it smashed through the front windows of the barracks. The tiny fraction of my concentration that could be spared for such matters nagged at the back of my mind with worry that it might have injured the hostages inside, but I didn't have the luxury of checking on them. The engagement with the enemy suit had taken seconds, but seconds were an eternity in combat.

All three of us had landed within ten meters of each other on the east side of the building, each engaging a High Guard trooper immediately, the theory being that the one left over would hesitate, trying to decide who to support and giving one of us time to dispose of our opponent and engage him. Unfortunately, it hadn't worked out that way. Vicky and Wade were spinning and shifting, blowing up clouds of dust and steam as they hovered a meter or two off the ground with their jets, trying to stay mobile, Gatling lasers spewing long bursts, but that last son of a bitch, fourth out of the four, came straight at me.

Tantalum darts chewed off bits of the wall just to my right, splintering wood and twisting off chunks of metal support beams on their way toward me. I jumped without thought and it still wasn't quick enough to avoid the stream. Sledgehammers pounded into my hip and spun me around in mid-air, throwing me back through the hole the first Tahni had made in the wall.

I landed only meters from the biggest chunks of his suit, whatever flesh and blood had resided inside burned to ash by plasma as hot as the heart of a star, leaving behind the metal, as if that was all he'd ever been. I was surrounded by fire. The remains of the suit had been white hot, and the barracks had been built from local wood and metal scraps because anything else would have been too expensive and attracted too much attention to what Hellnick and Eld were doing. On Earth, or one of the major colonies, it would have been illegal, a dozen safety violations, because it was flammable as hell.

I was in some kind of entrance hallway, not one of the bunkrooms, and there was a single body lying flat on its back where the suit had come through. I didn't have time to stay and give it a close-up look, but I didn't have to. It was wearing body armor and a KE rifle was lying next to its outstretched hand. It was a Tahni, one of the guards, but the relief I felt was short-lived.

The hostages. There were people inside here, and it was on fire.

And there was nothing I could do for them if we were dead. I punched backwards with both arms in a way that would surely have dislocated my shoulders if I'd tried to do without the suit, pushing the two tons of bulk far enough off the ground to safely hit the jets. The Vigilante spat out backwards through the opposite wall of the building and I barely registered the doorway as I smashed through it, scrambling to get my legs beneath me. Sparks sprayed off the pavement as the spiked soles of my boots scraped against it and I tried to ignore the yellow damage warnings blinking in the corner of my HUD, telling me that the armor over my left hip actuator had been stripped away and the artificial byomer muscle inside it had been compromised.

Yes, thanks, I know.

I had more important things to think about...like the fact that I'd popped out the other side of the building into the middle of the other team of Tahni battlesuits. They were poised in mid-motion, as if I'd interrupted them as they were about to head out for a late coffee, but I guessed they'd just heard the fight on the other side of the building and were about to hit the jets. Until I arrived and crashed the party.

I hadn't expected them and they hadn't expected me, but I had one advantage: I'd already been in contact, already been under fire. There was an edge it gave you, already having the adrenaline rush, a sharpness to your perceptions, just a fraction of a second's advantage, and I used it, taking a single step, a motion of two meters yet enough to bring two of them into line with each other, enough to take me out of the firing arc of the other two. The Gatling was quick on the draw, without the refresh lag of a plasma gun, and I played it like a fire hose between the two I'd lined up, two full seconds. It was as much time as I allowed myself and it was almost too much.

The pulses of ravening energy made me feel godlike, an avenging Zeus on the mountain top, throwing lightning bolts at the demons of Hades, but part of me knew there was a price to be paid for them. Molded HpE charges feeding through the hopper into the ignition chamber, consuming themselves in a multi-megajoule blast of heat energy, feeding it through the lasing rod and through the nano-crystal emitter, and once one was gone, it was never coming back and I couldn't reload. Fifty rounds, a hundred, a hundred and fifty maybe in the two seconds I held down the trigger and it was enough to burn straight through the thickest part of the breastplate of the suit only ten meters in front of me, the one who'd been stationed beside the doors.

Metal vaporized in eruptions as the armor cratered, then gave way as one round after another hit exactly the same place and the Tahni male inside was almost certainly dead before I shifted fire to the second. The others were moving, jerking away instinctively, the last one blasting off on his jets, the suit rising in slow motion to my sped-up perceptions. Tachypsychia. It didn't last long, but it was fascinating, like stepping into another dimension where time worked differently.

It was an illusion, of course. I wasn't thinking faster than normal, wasn't able to make decisions faster, or move faster. What was happening was that the unconscious part of my brain was making decisions faster than my conscious thought could follow, dragging the part of my brain that I thought of as "me" along after it, giving the false perception that I was seeing things move slower when, in fact, I was seeing them an instant after they'd already happened, the memory slowed down so I could make sense of it.

A trainer had explained it to me and I knew it was true, but I found it hard to accept. It meant that the decisions I was making were illusions, phantoms of logic and reason behind a reality rooted in the past. What I was doing was acting off practice, experience, ingrained habit. Nothing I did under this sort of pressure was the me who existed now, it was all the me who'd gone through Boot Camp and Armor School, the me who'd ditched on Brigantia in that lake, who'd watched helplessly as Maria Shepherd had died. It was the me who'd trained Henckel and led him into combat, and watched as he, too, had fallen. The me who'd seen Lt. Ackley and Scotty Hayes, and all those others die for the same cause, and yet kept fighting and pushing forward because there was just nowhere else to go that felt right.

It's who I am.

The me who'd been forged in battle took another step to the side, enough motion to keep the third Tahni in line from having a clean shot. He'd been moving to angle for one, with instincts he'd learned while losing a war, and when he couldn't get it, he shot anyway. I couldn't detect the hyper-velocity darts hitting the other side of the trooper I was shooting, but I felt the ones that didn't. They smashed armor plating off my left shoulder, down my left side, hitting hard enough to spall material off the inside of the suit. It stabbed into me, shrapnel traveling at a much slower pace than the tantalum bullets but blood washed over my side despite that and more warning lights told me what I already knew. I was in trouble.

I threw myself sideways, afraid to jump straight up, knowing the other one had gone that way, knowing he'd be taking aim even now, ready to add his own contribution to my eminent extinction. The only cover I could reach was a pair of dead Tahni, too stupid to fall over, and I used them, weaving a course between the two funereal statues and firing a long, reckless burst with my Gatling and a fusillade of single shots with the Gauss rifle. I couldn't aim both at once and I was unsure if I would hit anything, but I didn't want to die for lack of shooting back.

I took more hits but wasn't sure where. The hurt was generalized now, spread out and dulled, and I knew the suit was injecting me with painkillers, which only added to the urgency. In the short term, they would keep me from being overwhelmed by agony, but in the long run, they'd dull my thoughts and slow my reflexes. I had to end this fast. I wasn't sure how long I'd held the trigger down on the Gatling, but I let it go now, feeling like I was missing something.

I was. The Tahni was dead. He hadn't fallen because his suit wouldn't let him, but he was motionless, his weapon pointing at the spot I'd been two seconds before. Burn-throughs glowed white across his torso, and somewhere beneath the scored and charred armor, a Tahni High Guard soldier who'd survived the most violent and destructive war in the history of either of our civilizations had been ripped into pieces from the steam explosion of his own boiling blood.

The other one. Where was he? He'd gone up and I dashed forward back through the hole I'd put in the wall, the floor crunching under weight it hadn't been built to support. The roof wouldn't stop him from shooting at me, but maybe it would mask my thermal signature enough to keep him from hitting me. My conscience nagged at me that I was putting the hostages at risk going back into the building, but I shouted back at it that I was just going to go back through to the other side and it should shut the hell up and leave me alone, and I was fairly sure the painkillers were making me loopy.

My conscience won the argument when the roof collapsed on top of me halfway through the entrance hallway, and the last Tahni trooper came down with it. He didn't *quite* land on top of me, either by luck or design, but the shoulder of his suits slammed into my chest and sent me tumbling across the floor. I'd been hit by some big motherfuckers in my life, much bigger than me, but not one of them had hit me that hard, except maybe the mecha that had nearly killed me on Point Barber. I was rolling, wood splintering, concrete foundation cracking beneath me, and then I was inside a bunkroom and staring face to metal face into the eyes of Melina Pappas.

What the hell was she doing here? She was one of the refugees, not a vet. I had a second's glimpse of her, zip-tied into a crude, wooden chair, a strip of utility tape wrapped across her mouth. Her wife was beside her, a slender, sharp-featured woman with huge, brown eyes that were even bigger now than usual, her clothes hanging off of her like she was huddled inside a blanket fort.

I had a million questions and not a single second to ask them, so I rolled onto my side and hit the jets. It couldn't have been too comfortable for them, the hot blast of air, and I was fairly sure I saw both of their chairs turn over from the corner of my vision before I burst out of the room through the splintered wall. Splintered and burning. The building was burning. I had to get these people out, and I had to get back to Vicky and Wade and to do either one, I had to kill this asshole quickly.

He was shooting. Not hitting me, not yet, but tearing up the floorboards, the walls, penetrating to God knows who or where, reckless and profligate with his ammo and his aim because he didn't care who he killed. The tantalum darts didn't strike my armor, yet I felt every one of them as if they were piercing my heart. I had no time to shoot, not if I wanted to stop him. I smashed into him helmet to helmet, the back of my head bouncing off padding that couldn't protect my brain from the whiplash effect. We went to the ground and I tasted blood. He thrashed beneath me, trying to trap my arms, and the whine of his turbines spinning up was even louder than the ringing in my ears. He was trying to scoot out from beneath me with his jets.

The Gatling laser was useless. I didn't even know if I had any ammo left for it. I buried the muzzle of the Gauss rifle under his armpit and fired. The gun was semiautomatic by design, requiring a half a second for the capacitor to recharge, and I pulled the trigger over and over, the same control I would have used to launch missiles if my Vigilante had its wartime armament. Individually, the heavy, tungsten slugs wouldn't have been enough to penetrate the High Guard suit's armor, even at the joint of its underarm, but I fired at least four rounds before he began to slip out of my grasp, his jump-jets struggling with the weight of two battlesuits, over four tons.

One of them broke through. The armor jerked as if in sympathy with the dying Tahni within it and then fell still. I pushed off him, yanking the Gatling laser out of the death-grip of his suit's articulated left hand, lurching off-balance to my feet. I didn't know which rooms were occupied, but I knew Pappas was in the one behind me. She and Irena , her wife, were tipped over on their sides, looking dazed. I didn't trust the dexterity of my articulated left hand enough to try to remove Pappas' bonds, so I grabbed the seat of the chair instead and twisted.

The wood shattered and Pappas slumped, her bonds loosening as the wooden slats they were attached to disappeared. She ripped the tape off of her mouth, gasping for air.

"What are you doing here?" I asked, needing to know before I decided what to do next. "You were on their side." Her eyes went wide and I thought she recognized my voice.

"We...we made a deal with Eld," she explained, her voice rough and rasping, as if she was talking past a mouthful of sandpaper. "We were gonna get some money and no one was supposed to get hurt. But when the Tahni started rolling up everyone, a lot of us decided we couldn't handle that, and we got together in some trucks and tried to stop them."

"So, you're all in here with the vets?" It was ironic, and only the fact she'd come around and saw the light at the end kept me from laughing at her predicament.

"No," she said, eyes flaring with anger, maybe hatred. "They killed most of us. Most of the vets, too, the ones who tried to fight back. Mowed us down like cattle and took the ones who surrendered here."

A hard, cold knot twisted inside my gut and I was too drugged up to know if it was hatred or disgust, much less whether it was directed at the Tahni for being Tahni or at myself for not being there to stop them. I froze in the moment and only the harsh coughs that racked Pappas from the smoke drifting into the room jolted me back to reality. The fire.

"This building is coming down and I can't stop it," I told Pappas. "Get everyone out."

I turned and left her there, deciding I would have to trust her. There wasn't time for anything else. I hadn't been able to save the others, but Vicky and Wade were still out there, and I couldn't let them down.

[25]

Tahni soldiers were running from the building, two dozen of them streaming from the exits, abandoning their posts and their charges to the fire and their fate, almost ignoring me in their haste to escape. I wasn't prepared to allow that. I should have saved my ammo for the High Guard troops, in case any were left, but I didn't. I held the trigger down and swept the weapon back and forth like it was the grim reaper's scythe.

High-energy pulses that could penetrate battlesuit armor vaporized whole torsos, blew legs off, took down two or three of them at a time faster than they could realize what was happening. When the gun went dry, there were two left, sprinting away, heading for the warehouse. I took careful aim with the Gauss rifle and shot them down. Killing Eld's men had been foreign to me, something I'd never thought I would do. Killing Tahni troops was as natural as breathing.

They were down and everything was silent for a moment. Two High Guard suits were down, the one I'd killed and another that I thought was close to where Vicky had come down. That left two. But where the hell were Vicky and Wade?

I was about to break radio silence and risk calling them

when the display lit up with threat warnings from the direction of the warehouse. Thermal blooms lit up holes ripped in the sheet metal wall and the crack-crack-crack of weapons discharging echoed from somewhere inside.

Another threat warning flashed off to my right, the armor's sensors catching the thermal signature of one of the coil gun turrets powering up. They hadn't been able to depress far enough to shoot at us on foot, but a battlesuit was a bigger target and maybe one of the Tahni troops was a bright boy with innovative new uses for air defense artillery.

The turret was forty meters away, the emitters traversing toward me even as I broke into a run straight at the thing. My left hip actuator was sticking, giving the suit a limp, and I gave a puff of the jets with every second step to make up for it, keeping me upright, keeping up my speed, crossing the distance in under three seconds, just as the barrels of the turret began to depress.

The gunner's position was a covered seat hunched over a targeting screen, with steering controls reminiscent of the armored personnel carriers I'd seen Tahni ground troops use on their colonies. The trooper inside the turret control cage was yanking at them in desperate futility when I reached him. The protective cage had open sides and he tried to throw himself out of it but I grabbed at his leg and crushed it in the grasp of my Vigilante's hand. He screamed and I tossed him away with a negligent twist of the suit's torso, throwing him with enough force that I didn't bother to check if he was still alive.

Killing him wouldn't kill the turret though. A power cable ran up the right side of the turret from its base and the isotope reactor inside at a convenient height for me to smash it with a stomp of my footpad. Sparks flew from the free end and the barrels sagged forward from their own weight, no longer held taut by servos now lacking power.

The trooper in the next turret un-assed the control station

and ran, and this time I let him, concentrating on taking out the gun. In Boot, one of our trainers had told us there was no such thing as a dangerous weapon, only dangerous people, but for the Tahni to shoot down our cutter, they'd need the dangerous weapons, and I was going to deny them those. Speed was the key, now that I'd committed to this course of action and I didn't try anything fancy, just slammed my foot into the power coupling again.

Two to go. Unfortunately, the run was longer on the next one in line, and the gun was already turning, trying to depress far enough to take a shot at me, and firing anyway before finding out if it could. It was dark and the rounds had no thermal signature of their own for my sensors to detect, but the sonic shockwave they generated was enough to knock my Vigilante off balance and I thought for an instant that one of the huge rounds had actually hit me. I kept running because I knew if it had, I wouldn't have been around to think.

Then I was close enough that it couldn't have targeted me even if I'd been hovering thirty meters up and I fired off three rounds into the control compartment before crashing into the side of the turret, halfway out of control. The impact stole the breath from me, a brief stab of agony quickly suppressed by the drugs, just enough to remind me I was hurt just in case I'd managed to forget.

"Drop Trooper Two to Intercept One," I transmitted, trying not to gasp the words. "Do you copy?"

I sucked in a lungful of air, let it out slow and shattered the power feed to the turret with a kick.

"Five by five, Two." It was the crew chief, Ruthie whatever. "What's your situation?"

"We have a fire in the barracks and hostages trapped inside. Need your force on the ground immediately to aid in evacuation."

I lumbered toward the last of the anti-aircraft batteries, the suit's left leg dragging behind me, barely functional, but I didn't need speed this time. The Tahni who'd been crewing the gun had bailed out and was disappearing into the night, headed for the high corn, and I wasn't even sure I had a single round left to send after him, so I didn't try. The power cable split under my boot and I hissed out a sigh.

"Roger that, Two," Ruthie acknowledged. "We've disposed of their armed shuttle. Touching down in one minute."

One minute. That might have been a minute longer than those people had to live, but there was nothing else I could do for them short of dumping my armor and running into the burning building myself. And I wasn't that confident in my ability to walk without the armor at the moment. Even getting the fucking armor to walk was an iffy thing, so I hit the jets and flew at the warehouse.

What I would do when I arrived was an open question. I was Winchester on ammo, beat to hell, wounded and halfway out of my head on painkillers and I crashed through the sheet metal wall of the warehouse and collided with a stack of metal cargo cases, sending them and me tumbling to the floor with a cacophony of clattering metal. The sensor feed spun like a kaleidoscope and dragged my brain along with it, though my body felt disconnected from the whole thing. When I finally came upright, it was to a tableau of destruction.

The warehouse had been the biggest, baddest gun shop in the galaxy and now it looked as if it had been trashed by a rowdy group of anti-weapons activists. Crates and cargo containers had been splintered and broken open, and armor, KE rifles, ammunition, laser carbines, and proton cannons littered the floor. In the midst of it was a pair of battlesuits, one of theirs, and one of ours.

The Vigilante was smoking, charred, and scorched, but it

was moving, trying to drag itself forward by one arm, one of its legs ending abruptly at the ankle and the other limp and unpowered. The High Guard suit was dead. Inoperative would have been a more exact description, but it was hard not to think of the things as an extension of the man or Tahni inside, and that Tahni was clearly dead. His helmet, or what passed for one in the High Guard suits, more of a featureless grey dome, looked as if a huge, metal shank had taken a chunk out of it with giant steel teeth. It was an illusion caused by the overlapping circles of the laser burn-throughs starting at the left side and worked their way inward plenty far enough to have turned the head of the Tahni trooper to vapor.

The other two suits squared off with each other in the center of the open space caused by the fallen crates like fighters in an octagon, neither attempting a shot. They were both likely dry on ammo, I figured, though it was possible their weapons had been damaged. I had an instinct that the Vigilante was Vicky's. I couldn't have put the why of it into words, though it might have been my familiarity with the way she moved in a suit. Or maybe it was that I couldn't imagine Vicky letting her suit get as fucked up as the one crawling across the floor and I had to make myself believe that was Wade.

"Vicky," I transmitted, deciding to go with the assumption. "Keep him distracted. I'll hit him from behind and you go for his hip actuator."

"You killed all the rest of them yourself?" she asked, the question asked with an edge of what might have been outrage.

"Yeah, they're all dead," I confirmed. "Get ready, I'm going to launch into the back of his legs."

"No, you fucking aren't, Cameron Alvarez," she snapped. I could only see her face in my head, but I imagined the fire in her eyes, the set to her jaw. "This motherfucker is mine."

I stared at her, ready to argue, ready to hop in anyway, but she acted before I could, probably anticipating I would try to help. She threw herself forward and hit the jets, shooting at the Tahni's knees in a move that wouldn't have been out of place in the octagon I'd imagined, a move we'd learned in unarmed combat training on Inferno so many years ago. The Tahni might have had his own equivalent back on Tahn-Skyyiah, but it apparently didn't translate to fighting in a battlesuit. What he *should* have done was push down on the back of her Vigilante and boosted straight up with his own jets, but maybe I was being unfair. The back of his suit was almost solid black with laser burns and it was possible his jets didn't work. If that was so, he should have spread his legs wide and leaned forward into the push, keeping her weight beneath him, and trying to angle her own flight into the ground.

Instead, he went down flat on his back, arms flailing, beating at her with all the futility of a toddler wrestling with his older brother. But the beating Vicky gave him wasn't at all familial. Her Gatling laser was already shattered, nothing more than a club, and she used it as such, her arm moving like a piston, stabbing the jagged ends of the broken lasing rods into the same burn-through in the High Guard suit's torso over and over. Sparks showered her, though I couldn't be sure if it was from the rods scraping on the chest armor, or if she'd managed to penetrate to a power feed and slice through it.

The Tahni trooper finally did something intelligent and planted a foot against the floor, trying to push Vicky off him and gain the advantage, but she'd been expecting the move. She raised both arms and smashed them into his chest, slamming him back into the floor and raising her suit to its feet simultaneously, then hit her jets again, rising up through the gap in the retractable roof from which the High Guard suits had originally emerged, a good ten meters up...and then cutting her jets.

I gasped. I couldn't help it. The fall was survivable in the suit, but it wouldn't be pleasant and my guts turned at the thought of what could happen. What happened to the Tahni, though, was much worse. Vicky's suit came down feet first straight into the chest of the High Guard armor, two tons of BiPhase Carbide focused into one point of pressure, falling at...I tried to do the math in my head and failed. Falling pretty fast.

I winced at the chest-deep thump of the impact. A cloud of dust rose up from the floor, obscuring the combatants for long seconds, and nothing moved through it.

"Vicky?" The word came out as a rasp.

Then the dust cleared, the light from the few panels still functioning in the wrecked warehouse shining rays through it, lighting up the silhouette of a Vigilante. She stood with one foot atop the crushed chest of the High Guard suit like some painting of an ancient hunter celebrating his kill, and only an unsteady stumble forward spoiled the image.

"I'm okay," she said, though the words were strained. "I mean shit, I might have just broken my leg, but other than that, I'm okay."

Wade had stopped trying to crawl, rolling his suit onto its back, and cracking open its chest plastron. He crawled out, yanking free the interface plugs from his jacks, and limped through the debris littering the floor. He'd pulled his sidearm from its chest holster and held it down at his side, walking toward the center of the storage chamber, toward the tarp.

It had been partially ripped away, though I hadn't noticed it during the fight, my attention being commanded by Vicky and her opponent.

"What are you doing, Wade?" I asked, but he didn't respond.

I tried to take a step toward him, but my hip actuator had given up the ghost and the suit froze in mid-step, refusing to budge on general principles. I swore and popped open the chest hatch. I nearly forgot to unplug and the cables tugged at my temples, a subtle reminder of a life that wouldn't let me go. I was gentle with them, pulling them out carefully and letting them spool back into their receptacles. You never knew when you might need them again.

Crawling out of the suit overrode all the good work the drugs had done and I could suddenly, intensely feel every single abrasion, contusion, and spall penetration, and it seemed like the only part of my body that didn't hurt was the tiny patch on my neck where the painkillers had been applied. But pain was no stranger and I welcomed the confirmation that I was still alive. It hadn't seemed at all a sure thing.

Vicky had climbed out of her Vigilante as well, and if her leg was broken, it wasn't badly enough to keep her from limping along by my side. I chuckled at the sight of us, my clothes bloodied and torn, hers covered in soot.

"All we need now," I murmured, "are a couple guys with a fife and a drum."

"Huh?" she asked, frowning.

She obviously hadn't been paying attention in military history class. I shook my head and struggled to catch up to Wade.

He was still heading into the tarp with single-minded determination, but I found it hard to focus on him. Instead, I was staring open-mouthed at the thing inside. I thought of it as a "thing" because it defied description, and not just because I lacked the words for it. It was a shape that almost seemed to shed my eyes, something oblong and naturalistic and utterly, completely inhuman, in a way that nothing I'd ever seen on any of the Tahni worlds could compare.

It wasn't simply alien. The Tahni were alien, but they were our sort of alien, far too close to us for coincidence, Dave had thought. The things they built weren't what we were used to, had motivations and uses we couldn't always guess, but they made sense. This...

I couldn't say how I knew it was a construct, a machine, but I did. And yet it also seemed to be something that had been grown, that had life. It vibrated with it, stronger now than when I'd felt it before, maybe because the sound and sensation was magnified by its presence, looming over me. I struggled to compare it to anything I'd ever seen and finally came up with an image of a seed pod from one of the trees on our property crossed with the egg sac of a spider. Neither bit of imagery made me feel at all comfortable.

"What the hell *is* this thing, Cunningham?" Vicky demanded, obviously more in command of her voice than I was, because I was still speechless.

Wade didn't answer, didn't seem to be listening. He was looking for something, though how he could pay attention to anything else when the *thing* was sitting right out in the open like that, I wasn't sure.

"I know you're in there," he called out, raising his sidearm to shoulder level. "The Tahni are dead. Eld's crew is dead. This place is going to be crawling with Corporate Security Force troops pretty soon, so you may as well come out now."

I wondered who the hell he was talking to, and had the thought it might be a stray Tahni trooper. I took a step back and patted at my chest holster, reaching for my own handgun, but then relaxed as Klaus Hellnick stepped out from behind the gigantic seed pod, his hands in the air.

He didn't seem nearly as cocky and arrogant as he had the last time I'd seen him, at the meeting. His hair was matted with sweat, his clothes stained, charred, and torn, his face bone white, and he was shaking so hard he could barely walk. It only got worse when he noticed Vicky and me, and I thought he was going to fall to his knees.

"Please," he said, hands still over his head, but the palms turned upward as if beseeching God. "I didn't know anyone would get hurt! Eld swore to me that no one would get hurt!"

I hadn't noticed Vicky moving, so I was shocked when she stepped into a punch that took the man across the cheek, snapping his head around, sending him stumbling backwards. He didn't go down, which was probably a testament to the thirty or forty kilos he had on her, but it stunned him and his eyes glazed over.

"But people *did* get hurt, you son of a bitch," Vicky growled, rubbing at her knuckles. She knew as well as I did that it was always a bad idea to hit someone in the face with your bare fist, but sometimes there's just nothing else satisfying enough. "People are *dead*."

"You saw all the soldiers they had!" Hellnick whined, rubbing his bruised cheek, cringing away from Vicky as if she scared him more than Wade's handgun. "What could I have done? They wanted this thing." He waved at the massive alien structure. "They were going to take it no matter what I did! Going along, I had the chance of surviving, getting paid, getting off this shithole and finding a home on one of the core colonies!"

He was spitting by the end, though not from anger, I thought. It was desperation, lack of control. I wouldn't have been surprised if he wet himself.

I don't remember hearing the footsteps on a conscious level, but my gun was in my hand and I was aiming it at the cargo entrance to the warehouse before I realized the black-armored figure striding through it was one of the CSF mercenaries. His pulse carbine twitched in his grasp, but he left it slung across his chest when he saw me lowering my weapon.

He swept up the visor of his helmet, revealing a face far younger than I would have thought.

"Sir," he said to Wade, "I tried to radio you, but you didn't respond."

"There's no reception in here," Wade told the man, nodding toward the alien structure. "That thing gives off some sort of electromagnetic interference."

"We've got the civilians out of the barracks," the CSF merc reported, ignoring Wade's explanation just as he somehow, inexplicably was able to ignore the massive seed pod thing. "Most of them. A few were dead before we could get in, maybe six or seven we think." The wind went out of me as if I'd been punched in the gut, but I said nothing. I'd known they wouldn't all get out, but there'd been nothing else I could do. "Some of them were already outside when we arrived. Some of the hostages had gotten loose and were trying to break the others out when we arrived." He jerked a thumb behind him out the door. "We brought some med kits along and we're treating the injured, but there's a lot of people. At least three, maybe four hundred out there. I'd like to send the cutter back for some more medical support."

"Do it. And once you clear the interference, tell the pilot to send a message to Chief Inspector Dukanovic." Wade scowled, as if the words caused him pain to utter. "Tell her that Zan-Thint is gone, but we got the artifact. We're going to need an extraction team."

"And take this one with you," Vicky told the CSF trooper before he could turn to leave.

She grabbed Hellnick by the shoulder and pushed him toward the mercenary. The younger man stopped Hellnick's stumble with the emitter of his laser against the colonist's chest, glancing between him and Vicky, confused.

"And do what with him?" he wondered.

"I don't care," she snapped, looking away. "Just get him out of my sight."

[26]

I waited until Hellnick and the trooper were out of earshot before I turned back to Wade.

"Okay, it's done. We're here." I jabbed a finger at the...artifact, he'd called it, which sounded as good as anything. "What the fuck is that? And how did you know it was here?"

"You're pretty beat up," Wade said, looking us both up and down. "Why don't we get you both looked at by the medics and we can talk later?"

He was obviously deflecting and I waved the suggestion away, impatience barging its way into my tone, my scowl.

"Fuck that. Neither one of us is hurt so bad it can't wait. Tell us what the hell all these people died for."

Wade glanced around with a furtive paranoia, as if he was afraid someone had snuck in and was intent not on killing us but rather ratting him out to his superiors.

"All right." He took a step closer to the thing, reaching out a hand to touch it but stopping a centimeter away, curling his fingers into a fist. "These things are the reason the Tahni never settled the worlds in what your friend called the Forbidden Zone." He shrugged. "We think."

"Things?" I repeated, catching the phrasing despite the distraction of exhaustion and pain. "There's more of them?"

"We've found three, so far. And we think Zan-Thint may have located two more, but we're not sure."

"You're not sure?" Vicky blurted. "He was just here with all his people! Couldn't you go look for them?"

Wade snorted a humorless laugh.

"All his people? Sandoval, this was a *fraction* of his forces. Why do you think we didn't charge in here with hundreds of troops the second we got your call? We knew he would bolt the second he thought we were coming in force. He's been doing this for months now, almost from the moment the war ended." Wade sagged, looking as tired as I felt. "He has thousands of troops, dozens of ships. He's in command of the remains of an entire Tahni combined arms task force. They were deployed in reserve, ready to hop in and pull the Emperor out at his orders, but the orders never came because their Emperor was an idiot who thought he was a god and that gods didn't need rescuing. That's why some straight-leg Force Recon shmuck shot him dead inside his own palace."

"Hold on a second," Vicky interjected. She tried to take a step toward him and stumbled, wincing and favoring her left leg. I caught her and let her lean against me, despite the fact I was pretty close to falling over myself. "If we know there's a rogue Tahni officer out there commanding a whole fucking task force, why the hell isn't the military after him?"

Wade regarded her with the sort of expression I'd seen on countless Drill Instructors' faces during Boot Camp when a recruit had asked a stupid question.

"Why aren't you two still in the Marines?" he asked. "Why am I not still in? Both of you wanted out and you got it, no questions. *I* wanted to stay in, but they let me go anyway. Wanna take a guess?" He rubbed his thumb and forefinger together demonstratively. "Money. The Commonwealth has been spending a shitload of money on the military for almost ten years now and no one wants to do it anymore. What's left of the Fleet and the Marine Corps is tied up in the occupation of the Tahni colonies, and we won't be pulling out of them any time soon."

"Even with these things out there, up for grabs?" I waved at the artifact.

Wade's gaze shifted and he didn't answer immediately. Which was answer enough.

"Oh, my God," I murmured. "The government doesn't *know* about the artifacts, does it?"

He shook his head, still not willing to meet my eyes.

"The Corporate Council is keeping the information compartmentalized."

I barked a laugh.

"Oh, that is *just* such a corporate way to describe it, Wade. Of course, there's more honest words you could use. Like fucking *treason*."

"You still haven't answered our question," Vicky said, cutting through all the other bullshit with a clarity and focus I admired about her. "What *is* this thing? What the hell does it do? Who made it?"

"We don't know." Wade sighed, closing his eyes for a moment. "Or, at least, if anyone *does* know, they're not telling me. But we didn't make them, and the Tahni didn't make them... and everywhere they've been dug up, the strata they're buried in is at least ten thousand years old."

"The Predecessors." I laughed softly at the absurdity of it. "You think the Predecessors made them."

"That's what our researchers think. I don't know what they've done with the other two we recovered, but I gotta believe they're experimenting on them somewhere. Carefully, I hope. But the important thing is, no matter what we believe, Zan-Thint is sure that they're Predecessor tech...and he's sure it's what he needs to take back what's his and wipe out the ones he blames for destroying his way of life. Us. And somehow, I doubt he's being nearly as careful with the ones he's found as we are."

"You shouldn't be telling us this," I said, alarms going off in my brain that I should have listened to before, and would have if I wasn't so damned tired.

"Well, no," he agreed. "But you deserved to know, and...."

"Bullshit. You *wouldn't* be telling us this unless you had a damned good reason."

Vicky straightened, pushing away from me, and squaring off with Wade as if she'd just figured out what I was implying.

"Yeah, okay." Wade ran a hand over his shaved scalp, rubbing against the stubble in what I thought was a nervous tic, though not one I'd seen when we'd served together. "I've been authorized to offer both of you a position in the task force."

"To do what?" Vicky asked. "Try to find more of these artifacts for the Corporate Council? Because you can stick that shit up your ass. The Corporate Council is about the only organization I trust less than the federal government."

"No, not to find them," Wade assured her. "They have research teams for that. The Task Force was set up to hunt down Zan-Thint. We have to get back the artifacts he stole before he figures out how to use them. Because he believes they're weapons, and some of our researchers think he might be right. And if he figures out how to use them, these last two wars we fought against the Tahni, well...they'll look like fucking border skirmishes."

Vicky said nothing. Her expression was guarded, unreadable.

"You want us to work for you?" I asked him. "Be on your team?"

"With me, not for me. You guys had more combat experience and more rank than I did, and not only do I know it, Dukanovic knows it, too. If anything, the impression I get is that once you get your feet underneath you, you'd be running the whole search operation and I'd be along to operate a strike force under your command."

"We'd have to work together," Vicky said. I stared at her, eyes widening. "I mean, we could separate when we absolutely had to, but Cam and I work together or we don't work at all."

"You want to do this?" I blurted, shaking my head. "You really want to work for the Corporate Council?"

"Wade," she said, putting a hand on the man's arm and steering him toward the door. "Give us a moment to ourselves, would you?"

Wade nodded, limping off

"Tell me how you feel," she said. I blinked at the non-sequitur, not just of the words themselves, but the gentle tone in which she'd spoken them.

"What?"

"You're exhausted," she expounded. "You're bleeding, burned, you've just seen innocent people die, you've had to kill God knows how many Tahni...you should be a wreck. But how do you *feel*? Tell me the truth."

I started to reply that I felt like shit and wanted nothing more than to get drunk and forget this all had ever happened... but I couldn't. Because I couldn't lie to Vicky.

"Alive," I admitted, both to her and myself. "Useful. And it sounds funny, but I feel at peace with myself for the first time in a year. It's not you," I added quickly. "I love living with you. I just don't love this place, the feeling I'm just constantly treading water and never accomplishing anything."

She nodded, grabbing my hand, and squeezing I thought for a moment she was about to tell me she was leaving me. Instead, she smiled.

"I've felt the same way. And I didn't want to say anything because this was all my stupid idea."

"It wasn't a stupid idea!" I objected. "It was what we both thought we wanted. We wanted to try something different."

"And we tried it. And all I can think, every single day, is that we should have stayed in the Marines. That it was the last time I felt like I was doing something important."

"This isn't the Marines," I warned her. "We'd be working for the Corporate Council, and no matter what Cunningham says, I have a hard time buying that their motives are pure and selfless. A lot of people think it was the Corporate Council who kept the military from going in and taking out the Tahni after the first war, just so they could keep selling the Commonwealth ships and weapons for the next twenty-five years. If they want these artifacts, it's because they want to have a monopoly on Predecessor technology, just like they have a monopoly on everything else in our economy."

"And maybe that'll become a problem," Vicky admitted. "But right now, that's the secondary threat. Whatever shit the Corporates intend to pull with this tech, it's going to be something to give them more control. If Zan-Thint manages to figure out what these things do...." She cast a sidelong glance at the artifact, drawing my eyes to it as well. I could have sworn the thing was pulsing, like it was the egg sac I'd imagined when I first saw it and was about to burst open. "...I get the feeling the threat is going to be a bit more existential."

"Are you sure about this?" It was a stupid question, yet one I had to ask. Not to ask would have meant taking the chance that I was forcing her into this. "This could get us both killed."

She barked a laugh.

"Yeah, because farming has been so safe and restful." She pulled at my hand, tugging me after her. "Come on, let's go tell Cunningham we're taking his job."

The night smelled like death.

The fire was raging out of control now, some prehistoric monster roaring its defiance to the foolish mortals gathered in the shadow of its flames. The wind had picked up and it was taking the smoke away, billowing clouds of it blotting out the moon overhead, but it refused to carry away the stench.

There's nothing in all creation that smells like a burned body, and eight of them were laid out on a tarp one of the CSF troopers had salvaged from somewhere. I didn't recognize any of them, but then, I didn't look that hard. Instead, I stared at the faces of the survivors. There were dozens, hundreds, some wandering around aimlessly, others huddled together, crying, shivering.

Their faces were numb, etched with shock, and I realized that I'd seen those faces before. I'd seen them on every world the Tahni had conquered, after we'd come in and taken them back. The ones who weren't in shock were angry, some yelling at the very CSF troopers who'd worked to save them, others reserving their ire for each other, the civilian refugees blaming the vets and the vets blaming them right back. I tried to let the angry invective slide off me, not wanting to hear it, but some penetrated just the same.

None of them seemed to be cursing the Tahni or Eld's smuggler crew, most likely because they weren't alive to shoulder that burden and traumatized people need something tangible to blame for their problems.

We'd set out looking for Wade, but he was deep in conversation with one of the other CSF mercenaries, so when I saw Grace Kim and her family sitting cross-legged on the remains of a green blanket, I crouched down beside them. The kids were silent, staring at nothing, not even acknowledging each other, but they would, at least, have the chance to recover from it. Harold had his arm around the youngest and was whispering something into his ear. He didn't even look up at my approach.

Grace Kim could have just stepped out from under the maintenance hood of a harvester for all that the experience had rattled her.

"I hear you two went to bat for us," she said, nodding towards Vicky and me.

"I wish we could have done more," I told her. I didn't try to count the numbers of the survivors, but there didn't seem to be near enough. "How many...?"

"Some got away," she assured me. "A lot of families got warnings from the first the Tahni raided and they went out into the wilderness in rovers or on four-wheelers and hid away." Pain dragged at the corners of her eyes, her mouth. "But Melanie told me that dozens of the refugee settlers were killed when they tried to help us, tried to stop the Tahni." She wiped at something in her eye, but I couldn't believe it was a tear. Not Grace Kim. "Nothing's going to be the same here, Cam. Ever."

Somewhere, someone was moaning softly. The wounded, mostly with burns or smoke inhalation, were clustered in a group, being seen to by the mercs with whatever supplies they had, and apparently there'd been enough to keep the really bad cases quiet. But the ones who'd been triaged as stable had been left to rock back and forth or huddle in a loved one's arms, trying to live with their pain until the cutter returned with more medics, more drugs, more help.

"I thought this would be our home."

That was Harold. I hadn't expected him to speak, and once

he'd said the words, he fell silent again, looking vaguely ashamed at having complained.

Vicky said something that sounded comforting and reassuring, but I was already making a bead for Wade. He was still talking to the same Security Force trooper who'd come to find us in the warehouse, but he looked up at our approach, weariness sliding away at the sight of us, replaced by anticipation.

"Well?" he asked. "What do you say?"

The smells and sounds of war pressed in around me. I'd tried to outrun it, tried to put it behind me, but I should have known better. I might have been done with war, but war was certainly not done with me. What *could* I say? What was left to say?

"Get us the hell out of here."

[27]

I tugged at the hem of the shirt. It felt tight, though maybe the poor fit was more mental than anything to do with the accuracy of the measurements. The uniform was all black, unfamiliar, maybe a little pretentious. The cut was flattering, the mirror assured me in a stream of letters across the bottom of the image, and I was glad I had turned off the voice feature. Nothing creeped me out quite as much as a talking mirror. I knew it was a common appliance in middle-class homes on Earth and the core colonies, but I'd never seen one before outside a ViR-drama on the net.

I guess I'd better get used to a lot of unfamiliar things.

"You look fine," Vicky assured me. She managed to turn her own version of the Corporate Security Force duty uniform look very good indeed and I grinned despite my concerns and reservations. "It's not the Marines," she allowed, checking her own look in the smart mirror from behind me. "But I suppose it'll do for now."

She was right about that. I'd never seen a bedroom this big on any Marine base. The compartment we'd been assigned was insanely roomy for a space station, and I wondered if they were trying to impress us. The bedroom was as big as a platoon bay on Inferno, and the attached suite was lavishly appointed, right down to the artwork on the wall. It was a guest room, of course. We wouldn't be living here. I wasn't sure if we'd be living anywhere in particular, and the thought didn't bother me. I'd spent my whole life without a home, and maybe I just wasn't ready to have one, yet.

A chime filled the compartment and it took me a moment to remember that it meant someone was at the door. I looked around helplessly, trying to find the control to answer the chime, and Vicky chuckled, shaking her head.

"Come in," she called, apparently confident that the room's automatic systems would interpret the welcome correctly.

She was right, of course, and Wade Cunningham stepped through the door as it slid aside to admit him.

"You guys ready?" he wondered. "Chief Inspector Dukanovic wanted you there for the interrogation."

"Chief Inspector," Vicky repeated as we followed him out into the corridor. "What the hell does she inspect, anyway? She's not a cop."

"She sort of is," he told her, squirming just a bit, like he didn't feel comfortable talking about the woman behind her back. "The CSF is the only law enforcement in a lot of places like Hausos."

Workers and functionaries moved past us, giving us plenty of space and furtive glances that made me wonder just what sort of reputation the CSF had among the other Council employees. When we reached the lift, the four other people waiting for it stood aside and let us have the next car to arrive, though whether it was out of respect or fear, I couldn't say.

Wade worked the control panel to choose our destination and I didn't bother to watch, but I could tell we were heading inward, toward the hub, by the way my weight seemed to decrease. By the time the car stopped, the three of us grabbing at safety straps affixed to what had been the ceiling of the car at the start of our little journey and my inner ear was doing backflips.

"Why are they questioning Hellnick way up at the hub?" I asked Wade, pushing out of the car into a rounded corridor with no real sense of up or down. We weren't quite at the actual hub, but close enough that the perceived gravity was negligible and people propelled themselves along using a series of railings affixed at intervals along the passage.

"Because that's where the holding cells are."

Dukanovic was waiting for us there, anchored to what I designated the floor by the sticky plates in the soles of her ship boots, which were very handy for mooring yourself to a spot temporarily but much more awkward for trying to walk in microgravity than the magnetic boots I'd used in the Marines. I guess the magnetic soles were far too bulky to be fashionable, and Dukanovic was definitely fashionable, or at least fashionable as the secret police could be.

"I thought you military types were always fifteen minutes early for everything," she said, sniffing a laugh.

"It's hard to be early," I shot back, "when I have no concept of what time it is here."

I wasn't even sure how long we'd been on the station, since Vicky and I had both spent somewhere between a few hours and a full day in auto-docs on arrival. The upside of that was that I was no longer exhausted, didn't hurt all over and didn't look as if I'd been worked over with a cheese grater. The downside was, my circadian rhythms had taken a gut punch and I wasn't sure when they'd recover.

"It's time for this gentleman to do some talking," she told me, nodding to the thick transplas barrier separating us from the holding cell.

On the other side of the glass, Klaus Hellnick floated at the center of an empty chamber three or four meters on a side, dressed in a bulky, white pressure suit, the helmet a clear bubble, his only lifeline a narrow umbilical leading into a receptacle in the wall. The cell was in a vacuum and that single line fed him all the air he was going to get.

If I thought Hellnick had looked nervous back on Hausos, by now, he seemed close to a breakdown. A monitor set in the wall beside the entrance showed a closeup of his face, and it was so pale and sallow, I could almost believe he'd already passed away and it was his corpse floating in the cell.

"Mr. Hellnick," Dukanovic said, speaking in a normal volume. I assume she'd already arranged for what was said in the interrogation room to transmit through the captive's helmet, because his eyes snapped toward us at her words. "Do you understand your situation?"

"I'm floating in a cage." The man's voice was clear, if wavering a bit with obvious fright. "All I've had for the last two days is water, and I'm wearing diapers."

"Quite. But I was referring to your *legal* situation." He didn't respond, so Dukanovic went on. "You were apprehended during the commission of offenses which could get you thrown into a Commonwealth punitive hibernation center for a century. *If* there were any Patrol ships or officers in the system to arrest you. But this system is bound under Corporate Security Force protection by treaty and agreement, which means that a Corporate Council Chief Inspector has the authority to decide your disposition without the requirements for a speedy trial or a jury of your peers. And since I *am* a Chief Inspector for the CSF, that means I get to decide whether you live or die."

"You may as well kill me," Hellnick said. He was trying to sound tough and fatalistic, but only managing terrifying and unconvincing. "I have nothing to go back to. If you send me back to Hausos, the people there will rip me to pieces."

"Killing you is certainly on the table," Dukanovic admitted. "But it's not my only recourse. It's within my power to settle you on another colony. *If* you cooperate."

Images of burned bodies pulled out of the wreckage of the barracks swam across my vision like the afterimage of looking into the sun. They were going to let Hellnick go? Let him set up on some other colony? After he got so many innocent people killed?

"And if I don't?" Hellnick wanted to know. "If I was just a pawn and they never told me anything significant?"

I think he wanted that to sound challenging, defiant, but it came across more as pleading, desperate.

"You know," Dukanovic said, her tone cheerful, conversational, "someone in your position is likely most worried about suffocation, about your captors cutting your air supply. But that's really the most pleasant of the many, many fatal possibilities facing you right now. One of those that you might not be considering is that while you may have heard the old myth that space is cold, you're not, strictly speaking in space. You're in a vacuum, insulated from the outside, and heated quite effectively by your own body. And if we cut the flow of fresh air to your suit, you won't suffocate immediately. But you'll wish you had because you'll ever so slowly begin to overheat. And we can help with that since we control your suit temperature. The heat will do terrible things to your brain, but we won't let it kill you. Not until you're babbling incoherently and begging us to let you tell us everything."

I looked a question at Wade and he shrugged. I'd been wondering if she was telling the truth about overheating, but I realized he might be conveying his own ignorance of whether it was something she would go through with. Looking at the woman, I had no doubt she *would* do it, and might enjoy it.

Vicky was staring at Hellnick, her lips slightly parted as if she'd taken Dukanovic's threat seriously and was anticipating watching the show. Hellnick didn't seem to be looking forward to it quite as much.

"All right, I'll tell you what I know. It's not much, I swear! I mean, they didn't try to *not* talk in front of me or anything...it was more like they thought it was their house and forgot I was even there unless I said something." He was drifting into bitter recriminations and Dukanovic cleared her throat as if to remind him to stay on topic. "They came here looking for that thing they dug up. I didn't know at first how they had figured out it was on my property, but one of Eld's people let it slip a few weeks later that the Tahni, Zan-Thint had some way of tracking the things. I guess there are more of them somewhere, or at least they made it sound like this wasn't the first."

We already knew that much, but Dukanovic didn't stop him. I suppose from her point of view, it didn't hurt to have the intelligence they'd uncovered confirmed by another source. Very military of her.

"I need to know," she finally asked him, "where Zan-Thint would go from here. Did you hear anyone talking about any other bases or hideouts? Anywhere they would have taken the other artifacts for research and experimentation?"

"They didn't tell me nothing about that," Hellnick insisted, shaking his head. It wasn't a smart thing to do in free fall because it made him bob back and forth like a cork in the water. "None of them talked about shit like that, unless maybe Eld talked to Zan-Thint about it in private. The two of them used to talk alone a lot, not let anyone around."

"Think carefully," Dukanovic cautioned him. "Your memory of anything that might be useful may be the only thing keeping you from an untimely and unpleasant death." She shrugged. "I mean, to be perfectly honest, I might consider death before settling on a backward-ass colony world, but your priorities could be different."

"I don't know!" he stuttered, tripping over the words. "I swear to God! The only thing they talked about in front of me was how much they missed Thunderhead or Bathala..."

"Wait." The Chief Inspector frowned. "What was that?"

"Bathala. I guess it's one of the Pirate Worlds. Captain Eld used to talk about it all the time. He said he was part of a cartel he called the Kuratong. Used to go on and on about how he couldn't wait until the job on Hausos was over so he could go back to this one whorehouse he liked. He was disappointed at the choice of females on Hausos, I guess, but then, who isn't? Anyone who's halfway decent is already taken and the transients who come in on the freighters are all rode hard and put away wet...." Hellnick was bitching again, drifting off into some old rant he must have used to justify his treason to himself.

"Shut up, Mr, Hellnick."

She turned away from him, touching a control on her 'link, as if in emphasis of her order, and Hellnick's gabbling ceased as the connection to his helmet was cut off. Dukanovic's eyes were clouded in deep, dark thought and no one dared to interrupt it until she decided she'd ruminated on the ideas long enough to put them into words.

"Lt. Alvarez," she said, "I need your assurance that I can depend on you."

"Is there anything in my record," I asked her, trying to keep the current of anger riding just below the surface of my mind from breaking free and getting us both fired, "or in my actions on Hausos that would make you think I'm undependable?"

"Port Harcourt," she said without missing a beat. "You risked court-martial to save Tahni civilians from being massacred by a fellow officer, despite the fact that civilians in the same group had just committed a terrorist attack on your fellow Marines."

"You think that was a mistake?"

"Under the circumstances, it was the morally correct position. But according to the intelligence we've just acquired from Mr. Hellnick, you will be heading to a place where there may be little distinction between innocent civilians and hardened cartel killers...if there's any at all." She didn't move, yet it seemed as if she was closer, only centimeters from my face. "If I send you out with a platoon or two of my CSF troops, I need to know you'll do what you have to do in order to keep them alive and complete the mission."

"Complete the mission and *then* keep them alive," I corrected her automatically. She raised an eyebrow in an unspoken question and I expanded. "The mission, the men and you is how it's been taught for centuries to officers. The mission comes first."

She smiled thinly.

"The Kuratong are a criminal cartel based on Bathala in the Pirate Worlds. They're notorious for working deals with the Tahni back in the interwar period, particularly after the Pirate Wars. If this Captain Eld was Kuratong, then I'd be willing to bet that Zan-Thint has the two artifacts there. And if he doesn't, the Kuratong will know where to find them." She made a dismissive gesture. "Go. I want the artifacts or proof they've been destroyed." Her eyes were as hard as a naked lump of plutonium. "And I want Zan-Thint dead."

WHAT'S NEXT IN THE SERIES?

CONTACT FRONT
KINETIC STRIKE
DANGER CLOSE
DIRECT FIRE
HOME FRONT
FIRE BASE

ALSO BY RICK PARTLOW

If you enjoyed Drop Trooper, you will love Wholesale Slaughter!

Start a new adventure today!

FROM THE PUBLISHER

Thank you for reading *Home Front,* book five in Drop Trooper.

We hope you enjoyed it as much as we enjoyed bringing it to you. We just wanted to take a moment to encourage you to review the book on Amazon and Goodreads. Every review helps further the author's reach and, ultimately, helps them continue writing fantastic books for us all to enjoy.

If you liked this book, check out the rest of our catalogue at www.aethonbooks.com. To sign up to receive a FREE collection from some of our best authors as well as updates regarding all new releases, visit www.aethonbooks.com/sign-up.

JOIN THE STREET TEAM! Get advanced copies of all our books, plus other free stuff and help us put out hit after hit.

SEARCH ON FACEBOOK:
AETHON STREET TEAM

ABOUT RICK PARTLOW

RICK PARTLOW is that rarest of species, a native Floridian. Born in Tampa, he attended Florida Southern College and graduated with a degree in History and a commission in the US Army as an Infantry officer.

His lifelong love of science fiction began with Have Space Suit---Will Travel and the other Heinlein juveniles and traveled through Clifford Simak, Asimov, Clarke and on to William Gibson, Walter Jon Williams and Peter F Hamilton. And somewhere, submerged in the worlds of others, Rick began to create his own worlds.

He has written a ton of books in many different series, and his short stories have been included in seven different anthologies.

He currently lives in central Florida with his wife, two children and a willful mutt of a dog. Besides writing and reading science fiction and fantasy, he enjoys outdoor photography, hiking and camping.

www.rickpartlow.com

Printed in Dunstable, United Kingdom

74904195R00180